War's End:
A Brave New World

Christine D. Shuck

Table of Contents

Part One

"So tonight you better stop and rebuild all your ruins, because peace and trust can win the day despite all your losing." –
Led Zeppelin

A Café on Main Street

"*We overstayed our welcome. We bullied, we pushed, we invaded…and when we were done, when the world had felt our presence in every corner of it, felt our hand on their backs, shoving our way into every aspect of their lives, faiths, even their very existence…we were hated. God, were we hated. In retrospect I can feel no real surprise for what happened next. Our time had come. For our hypocrisy, for our crimes, we each paid such a terribly high price. The world we had known, the nation that our parents had been told to be proud of, a place of fast food and 'freedom fries', home of the consumer, center of capitalism, world leader, it all ceased to exist. It was a slow, painful end, an extended death rattle, as we slowly tore ourselves apart, and then allowed others to finish off what*

"Drink it slow," an unfamiliar face in the crowd swam into focus.

The woman's face was prematurely aged, her brown hair streaked liberally with gray. Her brown eyes crinkled at the edges as she smiled at Jess. Jess blinked and accepted the steaming mug offered. She was sitting in a café, at a battered little table right across the street from Banks Grocers. It had been the last place she had stood before being ripped from Warsend some seventeen months earlier. She couldn't see it right now; too many people were blocking the way, staring in through the window, staring at her. Some looked vaguely familiar, but most were strangers. The café, dimly lit, and packed full of the mayor, Mr. Banks, and far too many others, was charged with excitement. Jess's fingers nervously traced the cracked Formica top of the table and tried to will away the rising anxiety. She hadn't seen this many people in a long time. God, they were close, so close; she could barely breathe.

Tina had scrambled under a table and buried her

face in David's leg as he stood awkwardly. The little girl was shaking like a leaf. It had been a very long time since Tina had seen this many people in one place. David, his dark hair disheveled, a smudge of dirt on his cheek, wasn't doing much better. He kept attempting to move closer to Jess, seeking some amount of space between this overwhelming mass of strangers and him. Quincy stood at attention, glued to Jess's side, eyeing the crowd warily.

Another mug appeared before David, who sat down awkwardly, his sister wrapped around his leg, clinging to him with a tenacity that would rival that of a lamprey eel.

The same woman who had spoken to Jess lightly touched his shoulder, "Would the little girl like anything? I might have a packet of hot chocolate here somewhere."

David shook his head, "No thank you, ma'am. I'll just try and get her to drink out of my cup in a minute or two."

The woman nodded and smiled again before slipping back behind the counter, giving up the space to Todd Stevens, the militia leader, Mayor Farley, and old Mr. Banks, who had, after all, been the one to discover them in the first place.

Jacob mouthed a hard, dense biscuit.

Madge had shown Jess how to make them, pointing out their uses, saying, "They are good for traveling, since they never go bad, and when Mi'-da-in-ga begins teething, they will give him something to chew on." She had winked at Jess, "Believe me, Mi'-na, they are worth the trouble to make."

As with everything else she had taught them along the way, she had been right about this. The biscuits had provided countless boosts of energy, propelling Jess, David, and Tina down miles of road and kept Jacob from fussing. One tooth nub was finally poking through his little gums, with a second not far behind, and the edge of the sling was now dingy and encrusted with biscuit slime.

Mayor Farley and Mr. Banks had sat down in chairs around the small table. Jess thought that Mr. Banks looked much older than she remembered him. His hair was a shock of white and hadn't been cut in a while. The mayor, who had once been obese and shaped like a big round ball with skinny legs and possessing an overly large red nose, was now rather lanky, the extra skin hung in folds, but his nose was as red and large as ever. As she looked around the room, Jess couldn't see anyone who was overly large. The mayor spoke first.

"Now, you are, hmm, Angelica?"

Jess shook her head and Thurman Banks spoke up, "This here is Jessie, Michael and Julie's daughter." He said, correcting Mayor Farley's mistake, "You remember Julie baked bread, taught classes, and helped organize the farmer's market. Before the…" He looked distinctly uncomfortable, "Well…you know."

Jess could see by the slightly blank look on the

mayor's face, who she still thought of as the president of Congress Bank, where Mom and Dad had had all of their accounts, that he didn't remember her mother at all.

"Of course, Ang…err…Jessie," he smiled at her broadly, before turning his attention to David and Tina, "But who are these children? And this baby there?"

"This is my son, Jacob," Jess answered without any further explanation on that topic, "This is David and Tina Farnsworth. They are from Clinton."

"*Your son?*" The mayor blinked, looking scandalized. "And the father of the child?"

Jess felt a quiver of anger run through her, "He has none."

"I see." The mayor's voice definitely held a tone of disapproval now.

Mr. Banks, who understood far better than Mayor Farley put a hand on Jess's thin shoulder. He could feel her bones sticking sharply through the fabric and he suppressed a surge of fury at the mayor's lack of tact. Here was one of their lost children, who had gone through God knows what, returning to find only disappointment and misunderstanding.

"One of our own, everyone, Jessica and her family have traveled a long way to return home again." He said it loudly, so it would carry to the crowd outside, and he emphasized the words "family" and "home." He had long suspected the mayor was an officious, small-minded fool, and Farley was proving him right by leaps and bounds.

"What Jess and the kids need right now are food, a safe place to rest, and some time to settle in."

He ignored the mayor, who was trying to hush him and muttering something about the two younger kids not belonging.

He looked around at the crowd expectantly, "I think we can give them a good home-cooked meal while Todd goes and scouts out the Aaronson house to see what shape it's in."

Todd Stevens, who had been watching this whole exchange, nodded and stood up.

"I'll go and do that right now. What's the address?"

Jess found herself stumped at such a simple request. Her address? When was the last time someone had asked for that? She closed her eyes at the memory of those tents, the group of men sorting the prisoners.

Name? Family?

But even they hadn't asked for an address. It seemed so immensely mundane, so *normal,* that her mind just went blank for several long seconds before memory kicked in. She rattled it off to him and he nodded, gave her a small encouraging smile, and slipped away through the crowd.

They could hear Sarah, the woman who had given Jess and David the steaming mugs of tea, talking in the kitchen of the small café, issuing directions to a young woman a year or two younger than Jess. Wonderful, mouth-watering smells began to waft their way and the kids' stomachs began to rumble painfully. Jess was so grateful for old Mr. Banks's intercession that she could barely speak. And then, of course, she remembered Allen, and his visit to Tent Five, the first and last time she had ever seen him since she had left Warsend.

She turned to the old man, leaning close so that the others could not hear, and said, "About Allen, Mr. Banks."

He set a large, callused hand over hers and shook his grizzled head, "Not now, Jessie. Later. You tell me later, all right?"

He could see from the look on her face that it was unlikely his grandson would ever return home. Despite wanting to know, even if the details hurt, he couldn't bear it in front of such a large crowd. Better to keep his grief close and to care for the living. The girl had obviously been through terrible trauma. And from the wary look on the boy's face, he and his sister had as well.

"Right now we need to get you all fed and a place set up to sleep for the night. I'm assuming you all want to stay together?" Jess and David nodded.

"Okay, I'll see what I can do."

Farley, who had been quiet far too long, felt the need to intercede.

"Now Ang…I mean Jessica, where exactly have you been all this time? In Clinton?"

"No sir, Clinton is in ruins, although there continues to be a lot of fighting and different troops moving through there," Jess answered. "I was held by the Western Front until a year ago. I escaped with Erin McGowen, discovered David and Tina in Clinton, where Jacob was born, and we over-wintered in a cave near Truman Lake before heading back through Clinton and up Highway 71."

"A *cave*? You lived in a *cave*?" The mayor looked incredulous.

He would have said more, but at that moment the food arrived. Two large plates were set in front of Jess and David. There were eggs, thick slices of homemade bread with butter and a dollop of homemade jam, and slices of bacon still sizzling.

Jess winced as her empty stomach rolled ominously, reminding her of how she had just been sick not an hour before, and also that she hadn't had such rich food in a long while. Sarah Turner stood near her, her brown eyes soft and kind.

"Is the food too much for you, dear? Do you need something simpler?" David had already inhaled nearly half of the plate before remembering to offer a slice of bacon to his sister, who had folded herself neatly under his chair.

"I, um," Jess didn't want to be rude, but she felt exhausted. From hunger, from stress, and from the fear that her stomach would not be able to hold down anything she put into it right now.

Sarah patted Jess on the shoulder, "Don't you

worry, honey. I'll scrounge up some oatmeal for you that should settle your stomach."

She bustled off and Jess slid her plate toward David and Tina. The offer of a slice of bacon had been enough to lure the little girl from under her brother's chair and a grubby set of fingers snatched at a piece of the toast while David eagerly cut into the eggs. Quincy whined once, licking Jess's fingers, and she offered the dog a piece of her bacon.

Quincy pulled it gently from her fingers and gratefully swallowed the delectable meat, staring at her mistress with a hopeful look, hoping for more. She wasn't disappointed. David slipped a triangle of toast under the table to the hungry hound.

Farley looked even more disapproving. Jess was surprised this was even possible.

"Dogs use up limited resources."

Her spine straightened and Jess stared the mayor square in the eye and said, "Quincy hunts for her own meals. Squirrels, rodents, sometimes a bird." She broke a piece of bacon in half and handed it to her dog, "She's helped feed us and she's protected us too."

Mr. Banks interceded again; he was sitting nearest to the dog, "Sounds like a fine hound, well worth keeping."

The corners of Mayor Farley's mouth turned down, but he said nothing.

After all, he thought, *if the girl was fool enough to get herself knocked up, and take on more mouths to feed along her journey home, there really wasn't much point in talking sense to her. Was there?*

A bowl of oatmeal was set down in front of Jess and Mr. Banks introduced Sarah to Jess.

"Jessie, this here is Sarah Turner, one of our newest residents. She hails from back east, here with her two young 'uns for goin' on a year now. They were caught in a tussle between the Western Front and the Washington Guard; barely made it out of St. Louis. And Sarah makes the best lemon meringue pie I've had since my wife passed on. God rest her soul."

Sarah beamed with pride. "Not that we see many lemons these days, but I do manage to make a few each time we see a trader come from the Southern routes." She turned her warm brown eyes on Jess, who had managed a bite of the oatmeal. "Is that better, dear?"

Jess swallowed, her stomach settling some and said, "Yes ma'am, thank you."

"Call me Sarah." She reached out and petted the top of Jacob's head and then turned to look at David and Tina, both of whom had finished the food before them and were now running fingers along the plate to catch the last of the egg. Not a crumb had gone to waste.

"I would give you more, but that's a lot of food to eat after not eating much for so long. You take it easy, now." David nodded and thanked her.

Between bites of oatmeal, several in the crowd

asked Jess questions about missing friends and loved ones. She shook her head no too many times to count. No, there was no one else she remembered seeing. Only Allen and Erin, but Erin and her family were dead, and she wasn't going to speak of Allen publicly. That would wait for a private moment with Mr. Banks. He deserved to know what little she knew—but in private, away from all of these eyes and questions. Jess found herself wondering if coming here was a good idea. No Mom, no Dad, no Chris. And the way that stuffed shirt, that bank president turned mayor, Jonathan Farley kept eyeing Jacob—it made her angry. As if she had *asked* to have a baby. As if she could have stopped it.

Jacob began to fuss then, turning and nuzzling her shirt, picking up on her emotions and wanting reassurance, wanting food. He was just a baby, innocent and sweet. As her body responded to his need, the milk rushing into her breasts, she was filled with love for him. Never mind how he had been conceived, or the dark thoughts she had had about him while pregnant, walking those long miles with Erin. He was hers, and she loved him deeply. And wasn't that as it should be?

Jacob pulled at her shirt, more insistent now, and Jess looked for an exit. She wasn't going to breastfeed here, near this officious stuffed shirt and dozens of prying eyes. Her eyes met those of Sarah, who had seen the baby nuzzle at Jess's shirt. Sarah slipped out from behind the counter and made a beeline for her.

"I think that Jess needs to rest a little, away from everyone," she said diplomatically, "after such a difficult morning. There is a couch in the back, dear, why don't you and the baby go in there and relax for a few minutes?"

Jess nodded gratefully, stood up, and let Sarah lead the way, the crowd opening for them.

Mayor Farley looked decidedly out of sorts. He had been in the middle of pressing for details on Erin and wasn't satisfied with Jess's short answer that she had died outside of Clinton. Jess suppressed a wave of anger; he hadn't even remembered Erin either, only Erin's brother Toby, who had been an Eagle Scout and the valedictorian of his graduating class. The mayor looked as if he wanted to follow Jess out of the room. He was the type who wasn't used to being told "no"—and his recent elevation to mayor had made him even more pigheaded than normal. Sarah Turner had quelled him with a stern look as he began to stand up and follow and Farley had suppressed a desire to physically push her out of the way. She wasn't even *from* Warsend. But at that moment one of the townspeople had tugged on his sleeve and suggested he update the crowd outside. The mayor's attention was successfully diverted to one of his favorite tasks: speaking authoritatively to crowds.

The back room was quite obviously where Sarah and her family lived. There was a large living and sleeping area and a candle gave them a dim light. Jacob was fussing, pulling at Jess's shirt, insisting on being fed, *now*. Jess sat down on the couch, eased her shirt up and allowed the hungry infant to latch on. He made satisfied little grunts as he greedily sucked.

"Thank you, Sarah," Jess said. "How did you know?"

Sarah just smiled, moving a small box with the letters SAP carved into it, and put it out of view.

"How did I know the crowd was too much, or that you needed to nurse? Women's intuition, I guess." She busied herself clearing a chair free of books before adding, "That Mayor Farley is a real butthead. Don't you worry one second about what he thinks. He treated me the same when I showed up with two kids and 'no man to care for me,' is how he put it." She rolled her eyes, "As I hear it, they let him be mayor just to shut him up. He was carrying on so about how we needed 'structure and organization in this time of chaos.'" She grimaced. "I think it was because he just wanted to be able to tell others what to do." She winked at Jess, "*And* get out of serving on regular patrol in the town militia, like the rest of us have to do. They even look to me to participate in the patrols, now that I've been here long enough to be trusted."

Jess smiled in return, and relaxed for the first time since returning to her hometown. Warsend was the same cozy little town she remembered, yet different. But then again, wasn't everything?

Everything had changed. Jess wondered if her home still stood, and whether they could go there, right away, because she wasn't used to this, the people, the questions, the judgment. Not from everyone, obviously. Sarah was nice, and so was Mr. Banks. The militia leader, Todd Stevens, was young, maybe in his mid-20s, and he had seemed okay. Warsend was organized, well-defended now, which was more than she could say for any of the other towns she had traveled near since this whole conflict began. Jess sighed. Perhaps, just perhaps, they were truly home and safe.

She closed her eyes and melted back into the couch, switched Jacob to the other breast, and barely cracked an eyelid open when Sarah led David and Tina in. They had been walking since daybreak, in the cold, with nothing but the hard biscuits to eat. But that wasn't what pushed Jess into an exhausted sleep. It was all of the people, the questions, and the prying looks. There was that and the black disappointment—after all this, all the running, all the struggles—her dream of returning to her family, to her Mom, Dad, and Chris—to learn they had never returned was overwhelming. If they weren't here, if they hadn't made it back by now, then they really were all gone. That was the last thought she had as she succumbed to sleep, and it would be the first thought she had when she woke up two hours later.

CHAPTER TWO

WHAT HAPPENS NOW?

"Sitting there, with so many people surrounding me. Knowing Mom, Dad, and Chris weren't there. That after all this time, they must be dead and that I was alone now—just Jacob, David, and Tina. I wanted to stand up and walk away from it all. Start down another road, to search for a place that the war hadn't touched and where no one would look at me with suspicious eyes, or pity, or disgust. But I sat there, I ignored their stares, and I kept telling myself, 'Here is where I belong. Here is where I need to be.' It didn't get any easier, not for a long while, but, eventually, I think I accepted it, and was accepted, by those who counted most." – Jess's Journal

"Hey Jess," a hand shook her shoulder lightly, rousing her. Sarah's warm brown eyes were smiling down into hers. "Todd is back from checking out your house. He says it needs work, but you can stay in it tonight if you would like. Or we can find you lodgings at some of the nearby houses if you would prefer."

A soft dog tongue licked her fingers and she could feel Quincy's soft, warm weight against one leg. Jess shook off the fog of sleep. "How long was I asleep?"

"A couple of hours," the reply came from David. He was standing nearby, his arms full of a large box filled with cans of food and a large bag of oatmeal. "It's mid-afternoon, and they rounded up a cart and horse to take us over there. How far is it, anyway?"

Jess sat up, Jacob squirming in his wrap against her, also waking up. "Oh, about a 25-minute walk. By horse? Something less; I'm not totally sure." She changed Jacob's diaper, which was a cloth diaper lined with moss and sweet grass. She gingerly pulled a sodden wad out of the diaper, then added more of the dry mix before pinning it on the wiggling, and now fully awake, baby.

Sarah watched her, one eyebrow raised. Jess smiled at Sarah's dubious expression, "It helps absorb, and means I need to wash the diaper itself less often." Sarah just shrugged and looked thoughtful. She knew of several families who might try this out; one of the women had been complaining non-stop that there were no disposables left in the town stores. Of course, she also deemed cloth diapers 'disgusting' so Sarah wondered how bad she would react to the moss and sweet grass. Not well at all, to be sure. Others might be amenable though. She made a mental note to ask Jess more about it later.

They headed out of the tiny little apartment behind the café and into the crowd. The faces were different, but it was just as packed and just as curious. Jess saw several familiar faces and nodded to them. One of them had been her teacher at Kentucky Trails Elementary when she was a kid. Jess could see how much was changed in Warsend. Many of the buildings were gone, especially those that bordered along Highway 71, which ran through the middle of the town, the 'old' side to the west and the 'new' side of town on the east of the highway. The town had never been large by city standards. There were three sets of exit ramps and overpasses, another to the south, halfway to Peculiar, and all of them were now blown up and gone.

Todd explained this to them as they followed Y under one of the ruined overpasses and the horses plodded on through a maze of concrete rubble and twisted rebar. "What the troops didn't destroy, we did. And then we put up rows of concrete barriers at the borders—on 155th and Highway 58 exits. Any single vehicles can usually make it at a crawl, but a big unit would be stopped in their tracks. Well, at least, that's what we hope will happen." He changed the subject quickly, not wanting to get into the long and steady arguments in the militia headquarters of why that was such a bad idea, considering they didn't have the sheer numbers of militia fighters they would need to defend against another major incursion. "Looks like the herd's been moved over toward your neck of the woods."

A large herd of cattle, some 100 strong by the looks of it, were lounging on each side of 163rd Street. Two of the town militia members were standing near a tall fence that stretched in each direction, north and south, until the ends disappeared into the trees. The militia wasn't just in charge of town security, but also the cow herd, Todd said with a grin, "Which means we handle the distribution rights when it's butchering time." He went on to explain that the herd had ambled in from Raymore one day, walking just as nice as you please down Highway 58. They had investigated the tags, driven through Raymore and south to just outside Peculiar, and found devastation wherever they looked. "If anyone had survived the massacre they were long gone," Todd explained.

The cattle herd, along with about two hundred goats and literally thousands of chickens, had been the only things untouched by the rampage. "They killed the farmer and took what they could scavenge," Todd told them, "but the fools missed the huge corral and chicken house behind a stand of trees. We had gotten hit hard here in Warsend. Raymore had pretty much been wiped off the map. We would have starved that winter if it hadn't been for all of those animals."

They approached the fence and one of the militia men approached, nodding at Todd, and casting a long, curious glance at Jess and the kids, before noticing Sarah and her kids and nodding again. He undid the chain and opened a section of the fence for them to pass through. The horse and cart proceeded through and Jess heard the gate close behind her. It made her a bit nervous. They were being locked in?

Todd noticed her discomfort, "It's only for the cattle, you understand. We have several sets of gates and fencing systems in the area. And you and the others can come and go as you wish with no restrictions." Jess just nodded, feeling the fears rise up. *This wasn't Tent Five*, she reminded herself, *I have nothing to worry about here. This is my home.*

The landscape around them was both recognizable and not. She saw ruin where houses used to be. Some were still standing and showed signs of fire, along with broken windows. Others were water-filled pits, the houses gone and only the rain-filled basements remained. The devastation was widespread.

"It wasn't just the troops," Todd said quietly, "There was also a bad storm last year. Straight-line winds; some even reported seeing a small funnel cloud. But the lightning was what did several of these houses in. And it was summer, as well, and it had been dry for weeks. The lightning started fires, which spread to several of the houses and, before we knew it, a good part of the neighborhood was on fire. Your street had some damage, but your house is fine."

And with that pronouncement, they turned the corner and she was on her street. Most of the houses were gutted and empty. After a year on the road, she could usually tell in a glance which was occupied and which wasn't. It was as if they had a certain presence, one that declared that they existed for a purpose, that of sheltering a family within. Seeing the devastation around her left her full of dread and Jess stared in dismay at the state of her family's home.

Todd had been kind enough to do a quick fix on the front door.

"It had been hanging by a thread, mostly off its hinges," he told her. "The fix won't last forever, but it means you can at least open and shut the door for now. Maybe we can find a new one for you; there's plenty of abandoned houses on the west side of town to choose from."

She thanked him and walked into the house. It felt like a familiar stranger—someone she had known well and then lost touch with. Most of the nice touches, her mother's touches, the things that had made the house feel like a home, were gone.

What wasn't gone was covered in cobwebs. No wonder Sarah had insisted on bringing a broom.

Jess and the kids began by knocking down all of the spider webs and sweeping what they could of the floor in the living room, kitchen, and front entry. Several of the townsfolk, including Todd Stevens, Mr. Banks, and Sarah helped clear the house enough for Jess and the kids to sleep in the living room and had promised more help in the morning. Jess and the kids had met Sarah's two children, Cody and Laura. Cody was two years younger than Jess and Laura was four years younger, just one year older than David. She was delighted with the baby and insisted on holding Jacob while Jess helped clear out trash and broken glass from the kitchen. The clearing of the living room and kitchen was a good start, and the rest would wait until morning.

Night had fallen and the house was chilly. Unbelievably, the pot-bellied stove in the living room was still in place, although it looked as though scavengers had tried their best to move it. Deep grooves were cut into the wood floor where the stove had been dragged. One leg had actually broken through the floor and the scavengers and simply given up at this point. It took all of Mr. Banks's, Todd's, Sarah's, and Jess's strength combined to return it to its original position and then re-attach the vent. David and Jess had then built a fire in it and lit two candles.

The back sliding glass door in the kitchen was boarded up and, along with the newly fixed front door, provided safety from any larger marauding vermin. The windows of the house were intact for the most part, with only one window in the master bedroom shattered.

The others had left and Jess and her little family were now huddled together on the floor of the living room, which had been swept clear of broken glass, dirt, and blown-in leaves. Outside the moon had risen in the sky. Just a crescent sliver, with a vast array of stars surrounding it—identical to the moon she remembered, and the home she had grown up in. They had eaten a small dinner—two cans of green beans and one of Vienna sausage—straight out of the cans, too tired to bother trying to heat them up.

Sarah had instructed them to just come and eat at her café in the morning and Mayor Farley had grudgingly offered some of the community food stores to get them started. Other families had offered them a rotation of daily meals. No one had much, but many were willing to share what they could.

The house had been ransacked, and not just by the invading Western Front troops. Every canned good was gone, and so was most of the furniture, clothing, and what little jewelry Jess's mother Julie had owned. Jess didn't blame the townsfolk; after all, she had done the same while on the road. For that matter, so had David and Tina—you did what you had to do to survive.

Surprisingly, nearly all of the books were still there. Jess's mom had collected books the way some women collect shoes. The classics, science fiction and fantasy, some biographies, and stacks of antique books she had scouted from antique stores or inherited from her grandparents. Considering that most people had used books as kindling in the hard times, Jess was amazed to see most of the books right where they had been left, undamaged and untouched.

Mice had definitely moved in, along with spiders, and what appeared to be a nest of birds. The floors and walls were filthy and Jess suspected that, if she had been able to better see the extent of the damage and filth her family's home had suffered in the gloom, she would have been unwilling to stay the night inside. Only Jacob was able to sleep. The rest were huddled close together, jumping at every creak and groan, straining to listen for the telltale scurry of vermin, and uneasy at the thought of one of the large spiders invading their bedding.

"What happens now?" David's voice asked, just as Jess had begun to slip into an uneasy sleep. She jumped, and Jacob whined quietly and sucked on his fist.

Jess didn't answer at first and they both could hear the subtle scratching and scuttle of a mouse nearby. No doubt it was distressed to find so many large predators within its comfortable and quiet home.

"We get some furniture, plant the garden, and…" Jess paused, stunned with the realization that her parents' home and extensive gardens were now hers and, more importantly, her responsibility to care for. "We…survive, I guess. And…make this place our home—a place for all of us."

A few moments passed, and Jess listened to Jacob's and Tina's steady, rhythmic breathing. David spoke again, his voice thick with exhaustion, "It's… nice, Jess. I'm glad me and Tina came with you. It feels…safe." And with that, his breathing deepened and Jess lay there for a few minutes before also succumbing to the oblivion of sleep. It had been a very long day.

CHAPTER THREE

I CAN'T FORGET

"Two persons love in one another the future good which they aid one another to unfold." – Margaret Fuller

Jeremy Deeds levered his body to a standing position, biting down on a scream. The bones in both legs had been put back together as best as possible with their limited resources and the knowledge of a sixteen-year-old girl. And the left one was almost as good as new, some three months after the crash. The right leg, however, had been in worse shape, broken in three different places. Liza Perdue had done what she could, but it seemed that the leg was never going to be what it was. He would never run again, never serve on the town militia, and probably never marry. What good was he? He could barely get around.

He wasn't sorry he had done it. Liza Perdue was alive and unharmed and they had stopped the murdering bastards and saved another little girl from an unspeakable fate. But there were moments when he wondered how in the world he could ever be any good for anyone anymore.

When he had been able to get up and move around, albeit painfully, he hadn't left the parsonage. The Methodist church was now home to a long-term care facility of sorts. Two elderly citizens of Tiptonville were there, along with Jeremy, mainly because none of them had family to care for them. There were also the orphans, just a handful of them, but the kids sought him out regularly. And of course there was Reverend Thomas, who was growing more forgetful by the day.

Jeremy had never been much of a religious man, although his parents had been regular attendees of the Church of Christ nearby at 515 Church Street. That tiny church's ruined, fire-blackened bricks still stood, but not much else. Something appealed to him about the Methodist church, however, especially after something that Reverend Thomas had said to him early on in Jeremy's recovery.

The ward Jeremy was in currently held eight hospital beds, but only three of them were filled. Mr. Keenan silently rocked back and forth. The most recent stroke had robbed him of his speech. His wife, their only child, and all three grandchildren had died in the invasion by the Western Front nearly eighteen months before.

Mr. Asner, lost to dementia, was convinced that Jeremy was his old college buddy Jake, who had apparently died during Operation Speedy Express in Vietnam. At times, Mr. Asner seemed to think it was the end of their training at boot camp, other times it was after Jake's funeral, and most of the time he seemed stuck right in the middle of a firefight. It was a rare night when he didn't scream at least once, "Get down in the foxhole, Jake! Them goddamn dinks have got us surrounded!"

Reverend Thomas had come into the main sleeping area the third week after Jeremy arrived. By then the pain was bearable, at least when he lay still in the bed and didn't shift the wrong way. He had asked the small group whether they had a preference on what part of the Bible he read from. Jeremy, in a fit of pique and self-pity, had said, "None, there isn't any point to religion anymore."

Reverend Thomas had just eyed Jeremy for a moment, then smiled, "Let me share something about *religion*, as you call it. You might appreciate this." He winked and then said, "The Catholics say, 'the Virgin Mary says…', and the Baptists say, 'the Bible says…', and the Methodists say, 'Well, it seems to me…'"

He paused for a moment, and said, "It *seems to* me

that we should believe in others because God is within all of us. There are plenty of people left in this town that are worth believing in. So, perhaps, Mr. Deeds, *that* in and of itself may be the point of it all."

Jeremy had been surprised by the reverend's calm answer. No threats of hellfire and damnation or of "cavorting with the devil"—and later that week they had engaged in a long discussion on the merits of Elvis Presley and other late rock legends.

They saw each other daily, and soon Jeremy was seeking out the Reverend, or vice versa, for an animated discussion on history, religion, or philosophy. He was surprised to learn that Reverend Thomas had served in the Korean War, not as a man of the cloth, but as a soldier. Looking at the white-haired man in front of him, Jeremy had difficulty imagining Reverend Thomas at war, with a gun in his hand. That is, until the old man's face lit up with grim excitement as he described the fierce fighting during Operation Killer in late February 1951. It gave Jeremy a new respect for this man, who had seen war and yet turned to far more peaceful pursuits in the years since.

When he looked back on those days of painful recuperation in the church's infirmary, Jeremy was unable to explain how or why he decided to become a minister. Perhaps it was his way of paying back the reverend's kindness and patience with him, or perhaps he just didn't like to leave stories unfinished. A month into Jeremy's convalescence, he had been listening to a familiar story, one of his mother's favorites, the Book of Esther. Reverend Thomas had just gotten to the part where Mordecai learns of the impending slaughter of all Jews in the land when the reverend's face went slack. Not wanting the reverend to feel embarrassed or to lose the thread of the story, he quickly spoke up, recounting how Mordecai gave a copy to Esther of the king's decree dooming the Jews. A few minutes later, the reverend snapped out of it and picked up the tale when Haman was being warned by his wife and friends to stop pursuing the death of Mordecai. Later, Reverend Thomas thanked Jeremy for his timeliness.

"I was diagnosed back in 2014 with it, and it has slowly been getting worse. Especially since there's been no medication to be had these last few years," the old man explained. They struck an unspoken deal of sorts: the reverend would share his sermons with Jeremy and, if he faltered, Jeremy would intercede, first with the kids' Bible lessons and the stories the reverend shared with the men, and eventually with the weekly sermons. He learned to recognize other signs of the disease, which included confusion and mood swings, as the Alzheimer's began to increasingly affect the reverend's daily life.

Before the year was out, Jeremy was helping Reverend Thomas with all other factions of his work —coordinating weekly church meals, writing sermons, caring for the orphans and new patients in the infirmary, and visiting parishioners. It was this last duty that brought him back in contact with Grace Wilkes, who had withdrawn after her father's death and the attack on the Wilkes farm. A visit to her mother from Jeremy and Reverend Thomas had revealed her mother's concern.

"She won't go much farther than the back porch there," Karen Wilkes said, gesturing to the back of the house. Jeremy and the reverend could see Grace huddled on the bottom step, close to where they had buried her dog Danny. The devoted old Border collie had died defending her against the raiders. "And she won't say nuthin' but maybe a whisper in response to a direct question if she can't find a way out of saying nothing at all." Karen's face twisted in pain, "I don't know if she thinks Danny and her Daddy dying was her fault or what, but she just won't talk at all nowadays. Barely eats; I just don't know what to do, Reverend."

Jeremy stared at the girl. She was small for her age, just thirteen and looked eleven at the most. What she had escaped, he shook his head, remembering what Chris had told him about the man who had tried to take her and Liza. She was just a kid. He turned back to the reverend and Karen Wilkes, "Ma'am, we could use some help with the orphans, if you could spare Grace. We could come and get her a few days a week, get her out of the house and around others. The kids are all small, she'd be of use, and," he paused, staring back at her silent unmoving form on the steps, "maybe it would help her snap out of it."

Karen Wilkes had been leery at first, but as the weeks wore on and Grace continued with her silence and sadness, she had quietly arranged for her stepson Tommy to bring Grace with him on his way to serve militia duty. Tommy had come by the church, Grace following a distance behind, and handed a note to Jeremy. "Mom said to bring Grace here and give you this." Tommy had been eight when his mother died and barely nine when Anthony had remarried and Karen moved in, giving birth a year later to Grace and then Victor just three years after that. Tommy was quiet, but his face bore the strain of filling his father's shoes as he struggled to keep the Wilkes farm going with a grieving stepmother, and two young half-siblings to care for.

The note was difficult to read, and Jeremy had been surprised it was given to him, although this would become a growing trend in the months to come as the residents of Tiptonville increasingly turned to Jeremy for the things they would normally have gone to Reverend Thomas for. The note from Karen, full of misspelling and obviously written with difficulty, asked Jeremy to please help Grace "wit her leters" and noted that Grace was very kind and "thoughtful" and would be good with the children. Essentially, it appeared that Karen wanted to send Grace into town every Monday, have her stay at the church with the orphans and then have Tommy pick her back up on Friday to spend the weekend at home.

Jeremy smiled at the girl, and handed the note to Reverend Thomas. The reverend read it with difficulty, squinting at the scribbled words, then nodded and said, "Grace, there is a cot in the girls' dorm where you can stay during the week. Why don't you have the girls show you where it is at?" Once she had gone, the old man turned back to Jeremy, "They don't have much in the way of food right now, and Mrs. Wilkes is terrified that Cooper will come back while Tommy is out in the fields or off on militia duty. She would feel safer if we could watch over the girl during the week while Tommy is away."

"How did you get all that from that note?" Jeremy asked.

The old man smiled, "I didn't. I just took a good look around when we were there visiting last month. They don't have much in the way of livestock, and Anthony never was particularly successful at farming. Figure in the bad soil, and not enough crop rotation..."

The old man's eyes had a faraway look and his mouth turned down as he added, "And from the amount of locks on the inside of their front door— I'd say Karen Wilkes is terrified, morning and night. She's doing the right thing sending the girl away during the week. Fear like that is a poison."

Tommy would prove to be a far better farmer than his father, and eventually the Wilkes farm would help subsidize the church's infirmary and orphanage through bushels of produce. Grace's schedule never changed though, and as the months passed she would stay with Jeremy, Reverend Thomas, and whoever was gracing the infirmary or occupying the orphanage. She slowly began to speak again, shot up three inches during the space of a few months, filled out, and Jeremy thought she looked quite pretty.

One day, shortly after Reverend Thomas's Alzheimer's had taken a turn for the worse, she and Jeremy were working in the kitchen. He sat on a chair at a low table chopping vegetables. His legs ached constantly and sitting was somehow easier. Grace was stirring a huge stock pot of vegetable soup which would serve for two of the three meals they would be eating the next day.

They worked so often in silence that Jeremy was startled by Grace's voice in the gloom of the large commercial kitchen, "I can't forget."

"Forget what?"

"What happened that day—the day Daddy and my dog Danny died." She continued to stir the soup, took the remaining vegetables he had finished chopping, dumped them into the soup, and then turned the heat down to the lowest setting. The blue flames sputtered for a moment and then settled, lightly flickering. Grace peered at him through a mass of brown curls. "You saved me. I heard what that man would have done to me if you and Mr.

Perkins and Chris hadn't come and stopped him."

"We did what was right, Grace. No one deserves that. I wish we had known sooner. I wish we could have saved the Austins, saved your daddy, and your dog." Jeremy closed his eyes, wincing at the memory of Karen Wilkes cradling her husband, soaked in his blood and screaming.

Grace stared at his legs; the right one was still twisted and Liza had tried to convince him to let her re-break it and set it straighter. But Jeremy had had quite enough of being bed-bound and in pain and told her no. "You can't walk right anymore 'cause of me."

Jeremy shrugged, "It wasn't you that caused the accident."

Grace nodded, "Well, I'm gonna do what's right too. When I'm old enough, I'll marry you and take care of you. Mr. Perkins is way too old and Chris is already married. And besides," she said, as Jeremy gaped at her, "I think you are plenty good-looking." And, having spoken more than she normally would in an entire week, she pulled her apron off, walked over to where Jeremy was sitting, and pecked him a goodnight kiss on the cheek. Then she left the room.

Jeremy sat there in the room for long minutes, in shock, turning over in his head what she had said. *She's fourteen,* he reasoned, *just a kid. She'll grow out of this.* And with that thought a reassurance to him, a man of thirty years, nearly old enough to be her father and terrified of being labeled some pedophile child rapist, he felt better. After all, *he* was way too old for her. Jeremy hobbled off to bed.

CHAPTER FOUR

THERE'S NO PLACE LIKE HOME

"I took the news hard. David said I didn't talk much for days and that when I did, a huge piece of me was simply 'not there.' But in the weeks that followed, well, I didn't have time for self-pity. There were repairs to be made, seeds to be planted, and skills to be bartered. I guess the sorrow played itself out and was drowned in the sheer amount of work to be done. I survived. Somehow I even survived understanding that there would be no answers, no bodies to lie to rest. But it hurt so bad. It still does; their loss haunts me to this day. I guess it will forever." – Jess's Journal

It was a beautiful warm spring day. It had rained last night, a big booming thunderstorm with wild winds and strong rain. By the time the sun rose in the morning, the clouds reduced to wisps, drifting high in the clear blue sky. There was no wind now, not even a real breeze, and the earth was already warming. Spring had come early again this year and summer was close on its heels. Already finished with their blooming, the jonquils and tulips were now making way for the iris. The grass was green and lush where it had been left to grow wild, and already rows of lettuce and other greens were ready for harvest. A few feet away, Tina was quietly picking strawberries. From the looks of it, more of them were ending up in her belly than in the basket.

Jess pushed into the rich, loamy soil with her bare hands, setting in the last of the bush beans she had been given and pulling at the opportunistic weeds. Beneath all of the neglect, there was richness waiting. This soil was dark and loose in her hands and the weeds came out easily when pulled. So many years of love and attention would trump the year and a half of abandonment.

She thought of her mother, Julie, hair piled up on top of her head, streaks of gray flying in wisps, and a halo of stray hairs around her head. Her hands had dug deep in the dirt, just as Jess's hands did now. Those memories of her mother struck so often. Julie Aaronson lived on in this garden and it gave her daughter bittersweet memories of her each day. Here in the yard, shaping, digging, planting, and weeding —Julie had poured her heart and soul into the rich loam. She had done her best to make this tiny patch of suburbia into a green paradise, despite her lawn-loving neighbors.

Jess remembered as a child that their neighbors would look at the family's trellises, fruit and nut trees, and raised beds and shake their heads. They would mow their perfectly green, dandelion-free lawns, and talk among themselves, convinced that the Aaronson's were just a little on the odd side.

That had all changed after Black Monday. When times had gotten tough, they had changed their tune and the rest of the neighborhood had transformed. "Victory gardens" had once again become vogue and sprung up in every yard, even the unoccupied ones. Julie Aaronson had taught class after class to their neighbors, and even to scores of city-dwellers from the surrounding metro, who were all eager to learn how to raise their own fruits and vegetables. She had readily passed on her knowledge of composting, companion planting, cooking with fresh herbs and more. Jess's dad, Michael, had even caught the teaching bug and enthusiastically educated scores on how to construct and install rain barrels, build raised beds, and even—Jess grinned at the memory of the students' faces—how to compost human feces in buckets of sawdust. That last one had been a real winner.

Jess's mom had even begun writing a book on gardening in Missouri. This had become difficult when the power started going out regularly. She had begun writing notes longhand, muttering over the order of the pages and asked Jess for help with sketching the different plants. That had all changed when the Western Front troops had marched through, cutting through the streets, ransacking, burning, and taking whatever and whoever they wanted.

It seemed that most of their neighbors had not made it. The yards and the pitiful remnants of their victory gardens were now full of weeds and lay untended. Half of the houses on their block had burned to the ground and most of the others were badly damaged. Jess's home was one of only two still standing. It was eerily quiet. Jess kept listening for the sound of a mower, but there was not a sound to be heard but the birds and a distant hammering, probably old Mr. Banks. He had said his shed needed a new roof.

She reviewed the list of projects in her head. *Fix the northeast corner of the roof, install more raised beds, repair chicken coop, till the south side of the house, and plant a crop of corn.* Each morning she and David sat at the table in the kitchen and discussed the priorities for the day. Tina was good at fetching and carrying small items. And she could watch Jacob in a pinch, but it was Jess and David who shouldered the burden of getting the mountain of tasks done.

The townspeople had helped them enormously. They had dipped into the community stores and brought them jars of food, most of it grown fresh and canned the year before. The town was in better shape than any others they had encountered along the way, as well as well-armed and organized. Jess and David were required to put in time with the local militia each week, patrolling the outskirts of the town for intruders, much as Thurman Banks had been doing the day they arrived. There was a schedule posted on Main Street and everyone adhered to it faithfully. Their survival, individually and as a community, depended on it.

Visitors to Warsend were rare, but a returning 'Ender was rarer still. The ones taken by the troops that bleak day now eighteen months past had not come back. If they had it had been soon after. Wounded, they had trickled in half-dead, starving. Most had died within days of their return. The town's inhabitants had kept themselves alive by retreating from the rest of the world. They let in the odd trader, watched them at all times and sent them on their way quickly. Any strange soldier was drawn down on and shot if he did not leave immediately.

It also helped that Warsend had nothing that anyone else might want…at least not visibly. Well hidden from sight, they had a plethora of cropland and seed, and several large herds of cattle. In this new world, they were well placed. This area of Missouri had a decent growing season and an excellent water supply, with fertile land and livestock. There was plenty to trade.

Part of the roof, damaged in a recent storm, was actively leaking. Farley, who had been a banker and was now mayor, told her that it would have to wait until the crops were in the ground before fixing it, "You can't depend on handouts," he admonished her, as if he were speaking to a child, "You will have to make sure and produce enough food for you and yours to eat."

Jess refrained from pointing out that they had been surviving on their own for well over a year, and rather well at that, without his patronizing advice. Still, she had to admit that he was right; the repairs to the house would have to wait until the means for survival were well in hand. Meanwhile, to minimize the damage any rainfall might do, they draped a tarp over the affected area and held it in place with landscaping stones.

Jess's dad, an avid homebrewer, had planted hop plants along the entire length of the south side of the house. Already they were beginning to emerge from the ground. By summer, they would wind their way up the trellis mounted to the walls of the house. The vines would reach all the way to the roof of the house and then, a few weeks later, the first of the hop flowers would emerge. Jess figured they would be a good item for trade to those interested in brewing beer. She would keep some, as according to Madge's notes the flowers could be used for stimulating appetite and also as a sedative.

The rest of the south side of the property they tilled and planted with corn. When the corn emerged and grew to half a foot, Jess would plant beans and squash at the base of each stalk—an ancient method of companion planting known as the 'three sisters.' Madge had spoken of this planting method and Jess wanted to try it and see how successful it was. By fall they should have a lot of canning to do.

The back yard of the house was fenced and Jess and the kids planted peas and beans along the entire perimeter, stapling chicken wire to the base of the fence for the plants to climb on. She realized, as she walked through the front yard, that many of the plants her mother had growing in it were actually herbs or beneficial wild edibles. Here was wild carrot, yarrow, and lemon balm. Madge had filled a handwritten journal and Jess's head with all kinds of details on how these plants could be used. Some were good for eating, others eased nausea, relieved menstrual cramps, and still others had antibiotic or healing properties.

Jess knelt on the ground, loosening the dirt around an emerging plant. This one was foxglove, also known as digitalis, a powerful heart stimulant. It was dangerous in just about any quantity. Madge had said that even nibbling the leaves could kill you. Jess debated on whether or not to keep it. Everything in the gardens and yard had to have a purpose. Mainly that purpose was to ensure the survival of her little family. She worried that Jacob would get into it. He would be walking in a few more months and she had to think of what would be safe, or not. As she debated, Tina walked over, hands caked with mud.

"Whatcha doin'?"

"Trying to decide what to do with this plant."

The little girl knelt beside her, "Grandmother showed me this one. It's called 'digee'…uhm, digee-tall-us…"

"Digitalis?" Jess asked.

"Yeah, digitalis." The girl didn't miss a beat, "For the heart, don't eat it." She recited, proud that she was able to remember. At four, the little girl's memory was unbelievable; she could remember hundreds of plants, their names, and their uses.

Jess smiled, "That's right, Teen, very good!" She gave the little girl a hug. "But we don't need something like that; maybe I should just dig it up and get rid of it. I wouldn't want Jacob getting his hands on it and eating it."

Tina shook her head. Her mouth was streaked with red juice and tiny black dots of the strawberries she had eaten. Despite this, the basket was heaping with strawberries. "We should keep it, Jess, so's we can be doctors and takes care of people when they're sick. Put a fence 'round it, a metal one likes you got on the big fence."

Jess looked at the girl with confusion for a moment until she realized Tina was referring to the chicken wire. Putting chicken wire around it made sense. She grabbed the rest of the roll and cut a piece that was big enough to prevent a short little baby hand from reaching the plant and placed it around the emerging plant.

"Good idea, sweetie." She looked over at the girl again and asked, "So, you want to be a doctor?"

Tina nodded solemnly, "I am gonna be a doctor. Then I can go and fix Mama and Daddy and Erin and Grandmother an' they can live with us again." Jess winced in pain. She thought of her own parents. Then she hugged Tina close to her again. If the kid wanted to be a doctor, so be it; it sounded good to her.

Jacob gave a small squawk beneath his blanket. She had laid him between two layers of blanket next to her on the ground while he slept, but now he was awake and kicking. Tina gave a small crow of happiness; she loved holding Jacob, which made Jess a little nervous since she was so small and he was a hefty fifteen pounds or so now. "Can I hold him? Can I hold him?" she danced up and down with excitement.

She deflated like a popped balloon when Jess shook her head. "You're all muddy, kiddo." The girl's sad expression was hard to take so Jess continued, "Later, sweetie, after you have washed up." She dusted off her hands, picked up her son and cooed at him. He grinned back at her, his wide smile showing the one lone tooth in his mouth, and then he shoved his entire fist in to his mouth.

"C'mon Jacob, you and me and Tina need to fix some lunch and figure out what to plant next." The baby gurgled happily in response.

The rest of the front yard was slated to become an orchard. Already they had three trees, two peach and one apple, and Mr. Banks had come by a week earlier to tell her he had several three-foot apricot and apple saplings ready to transplant. "They'll take a while, Jess," the old man warned her, "A few years at least before you have any to harvest." He came by regularly, bringing them extra items that would help make their lives easier, even volunteering to help with the roof later when it was time for repairs.

"Yes, I remember my dad planting the peach trees." She looked up at them, noted the blooms, and hoped they would get a lot of peaches. "I'll look forward to getting those and planting them, Mr. Banks. What can I give you in trade?" This was a phrase she had learned quickly. The jars of food, supplies of any kind, she had learned that these things came with a price. It was normal practice to ask what another would want in trade for such things. She had come to understand that even the food they had been given when they first arrived must be paid back. It made sense—for the community to survive they were given a helping hand—but they were expected to return the favor as soon as they were able.

Mr. Banks had looked uncomfortable when she asked the question. He'd looked at the ground with his big hands stuck in his overalls and shuffled his feet. After much hemming and hawing he had managed to explain that he was lonely. His wife Mary had died right before the invasion, his son Mark had died on the day of the invasion, his daughter-in-law, Allen's mother Annette, was gone in the fire that had leveled his son's home, and his only grandchild, Allen, was long missing and his whereabouts were unknown.

He had everything he needed to survive, extra even, and knew that Jess and her little family had a struggle ahead of them. They struck up an arrangement of sorts where he would bring by what he could spare, and she would fix him dinner and let him spend time with her and the kids. "Someday I'll be gone, Jess, and if Allen never returns, well…" He left the rest of it unfinished, but she understood him. All that was his would be hers if his grandson didn't come home. And as much as she appreciated his offer, Jess fervently prayed for the umpteenth time that Chris and Allen had made it out and were holed up somewhere or heading home even now.

As she walked to the north gate she glanced at the saplings, six in all, and smiled. In a few years they would help shade the east side of the house from the hot morning sun and begin to produce fruit. She was looking forward to making peach preserves and pie.

Through the north gate she ran into David. He had turned twelve three weeks ago and announced he was a man now. His reasoning was simple. Jess was "mom" and matriarch, so he had to step up to the plate and be the patriarch. He had actually used those very words. Jess maintained a straight face, restraining from laughing with some effort.

Later it hit her that the kid was right in some crazy sense of things. When other 'Enders came by, they spoke to either Jess or David with a level of equality they were unused to from adults. Mayor Farley was the only one who treated them like children or felt free to lecture them.

The brutal fact of the matter was that everyone was too damned busy struggling to survive. It didn't matter how young or old you were, merely that you were competent. It was what you did, how you carried yourself, and what responsibilities you took on that dictated how others perceived you. In the years that would follow, through acne and hormonal surges, David would earn that level of respect of his neighbors and the townsfolk through his hard work and courage.

He had his arms full of old tools and was struggling with the side door to the garage. "Whatcha doin'?" Tina asked her big brother as she opened the door for him.

"Organizing the tools and getting them oiled. Mr. Banks said they'd last longer that way."

"We have oil?" Jess asked.

"Yeah, the stuff that turned rancid from the heat, that big tub of peanut oil." He dumped the tools onto the open floor of the garage and said, "Might as well use it for something."

"It's gonna stink."

"I can handle it."

Jess grinned. She had watched him throw himself at projects around the house since they had arrived, always with that dogged determination to show no weakness. She wondered where it was coming from. Why did he feel the need to prove himself? Was it because he was worried that some part of her still thought of him as a kid? It wasn't particularly fair of her; four and a half years' difference wasn't a very long time. They were both still children when measured to the standards of 'before.' She reminded herself again to not slip up and call him 'kid' again like she had two days ago. He deserved better from her.

"I'm gonna fix some sandwiches, y' want one?" she asked.

"Sure."

"Wash the oil off before you come in."

"Okay."

There was no electricity in the house. Come winter, they would be dependent on the stove and the fireplace for heat. The rapidly approaching summer was of far more concern to Jess. No air conditioning during the hottest days meant stewing in muggy, 90 plus-degree heat. If the mild winter was any indication, the summer promised to be a scorcher.

Jess had mastered the art of nursing while in

motion. Jacob nursed contentedly against her in a wrap while she cut slices of cheese off of a block Tina fetched from the cool basement, laid them on thick slices of homemade bread and added a dollop of pickled vegetables that they had received from the community stores. David walked in, wiping his wet hands on his pants. He ladled a cup of lukewarm chicory from the pan on the stove into a cup. He sipped and screwed up his face, "Ehhh, wish we had some sugar."

"You'll have to suffer until this fall. Mr. Banks gave me some heirloom albino beet seed last week, and it's good for making sugar. So, you planted all of the seeds?"

"Almost. Got the okra, squash, cucumbers, and more lettuce in. Oh, the collards, carrots, and bush beans too. I didn't figure you wanted me messing with the herbs or the pumpkin or pole beans, but everything else is done. We'll want to keep at least 2-3 plants from each crop to use for seeds next year. Maybe more, 'cause Mayor Farley says they're gonna start asking for contributions to the community seed bank in late summer." Jess handed him a sandwich and he took a huge bite, then his next words were impossible to understand as he tried to talk around the food in his mouth.

Jess snapped, "Don't talk with your mouth full. Now…what did you just say?"

David rolled his eyes, chewed, and swallowed. "Geez, who died and appointed you Mom? I said that I want to go hunting. I'm hoping to get us a good-sized deer."

"Well, if you want good-sized, you're going to have to wait. They're all still skinny runts after winter. Besides, after planting we need to get started on some of these repairs. Aaannd," she said loudly as David began to object, "I need you to figure out how to fix the chicken coop and build a chicken tractor. Mr. Banks said he's going to bring us by some pullets so we can restart our own flock."

"Baby chickens?" Tina's interested was piqued. She set her sandwich down and Jess noticed her hands were still crusted with dried mud, "Can I take care of them?"

"Not if you can't even remember to wash your hands before you eat," was Jess's brisk reply, "Go wash those hands right *now*!" She finished the last word with a howl, as Jacob bit into her breast with his new tooth. The baby was so startled by her shriek that he let go and began to wail. As Jess swore and yelled, Tina and David exchanged looks and quickly disappeared outside, sandwiches in hand. Quincy trotted past them, heading for a shady spot in the yard. Even the dog knew when to make herself scarce.

They sat outside, near the small pond, and finished their lunch. Little of the sizable yard had grass in it. Instead there were planters rising from the ground, filled with small sprouts and dark, rich earth. All of the beds had been weeded now and the weeds piled in the far corner of the yard near the damaged chicken coop. This place felt good, well-defended, thanks to the town militia. For the first time since leaving the cave, David felt safe. It wasn't home yet, but it would be in time. The four of them would make this a home and defend it if necessary. As they sat, ate, rested, and daydreamed, the clouds began to gather in the west. Later that afternoon, a heavy, life-giving rain began to fall, wetting the newly turned soil and waking the seeds from their slumber.

That evening, miles to the south, the storm was fully engaged over the pitiful remains of a ghost town once known as Clinton. A mile outside of the ruined town, a woman screamed. Lightning flashed and rain dripped through the roof of a dilapidated house.

Serena screamed at the top of her lungs for anything that could stop the pain. As Brad held her hand, he could see the baby's head crown then disappear back up. Another push and scream and the head and shoulders appeared. He let go of Serena's hand and reached down to cradle the tiny head, holding the baby as it slid out and coughed. A sharp, thin wail issued from its mouth.

He looked past the umbilical cord, "It's a girl. Baby, we got ourselves a little girl!" He smiled through his disappointment. He'd wanted a boy, but a girl was fine. What bothered him most was the baby's jet black hair and ice-blue eyes.

He wiped her down, cut the cord, wrapped the

tiny baby in a clean blanket, and handed her to Serena, who looked both excited and exhausted. The lightning lit up the room and the baby squawked in fear at the loud thunderclap. Serena took in the baby's features and met Brad's steady gaze. He smiled again, reached out, and stroked Serena's cheek, "She's beautiful. What should we name our baby?

Relief washed over her. "My mother's name was Rebecca. We'll call her Becka for short."

"Becka it is."

Brad held Serena close and kissed her hair. Serena Kearney was a beautiful woman. Her blond hair was a mess and he could see she'd closed her beautiful blue eyes in exhaustion. It had been a long labor, and she'd been so frightened. Brad eased away from her, stood up, and lit a lantern. They were safe here, he was sure of it. Max and Annie were asleep in one of the upstairs rooms. He headed for the dark hallway and pitch-black bathroom, lighting the way with the lantern. His reflection gave him a start. They'd been on the road and away from mirrors so much that he'd grown used to not having one. He ran his hand through his light brown hair, peered in the mirror at his eyes, which burned and felt bloodshot. Damn, it had been a long birthing. He'd read up on it, so he wouldn't be a complete fool, but it had been hard for both of them.

He stretched, relieved himself in the dry, filthy toilet, and thought about the baby. Becka…huh.

He'd figured it wasn't his, but it hurt in some strange way seeing the truth. He'd paid at least some attention in science class back in high school. Serena was blond, his hair was light brown. His eyes were brown; Serena's were this gorgeous deep blue. You didn't make a black-haired, ice-blue eyed baby with that combination. For just those few moments he allowed his thoughts to turn dark.

That bastard. Raping women, always blond, always blue-eyed. Raping them over and over until he filled them full of his seed and then, when they showed, he killed them. What kind of monster does that? His hands curled into fists at the thought. He picked up the lantern and headed back to the living room where Serena and the baby lay sleeping.

For just a moment he thought of killing the child. Cooper was far away, too far away and too damned powerful to kill. But he could…Brad felt his fingers clenching into fists…a moment passed…then the thought of wrapping his hands around her and choking her to death made him shiver. What was he thinking? The tiny creature whined slightly in her sleep. Black hair and blue eyes, the child was beautiful, even freshly born and red and a little bit squashed-looking. Brad shook his head, cleared it of the dark thoughts and smiled. He imagined her smile, thought of how it would sound to hear her say "Daddy" and reached down and stroked her cheek. Her tiny head turned and rooted for his finger. He smiled.

"Hi Becka, I'm your Daddy." He could have sworn she smiled.

THE FACE OF EVIL

"There is no good and evil, there is only power ... and those too weak to seek it." – J.K. Rowling

Cooper's skin felt hot and stretched tight. He hadn't eaten in two days, and, as he stumbled and fell over the tripwire, his last conscious thought was that he really hated the thought of dying like this, in some goddamn trap he should have had the sense to avoid.

The tripwire malfunctioned, however, and instead of filling him full of agonizing holes and more shredded flesh from the homemade bomb the tripwire was *supposed* to detonate, he simply ripped open his festering wounds on the gravel path. His head bobbed back, covered in blood, mixed with greenish-yellow pus, the infection from Riley's bone shards and the crash trailing down his cheek to mix with the blood. His vision faded to black and he passed out cold. Not even the sharp kick of a booted foot in his ribs a few moments later revived him.

A slightly built, pale-faced teenager kicked again, harder this time, and earned a small groan in response. "Well, you ain't dead. Not yet at least." She raised a hand to her mouth and trilled a bird call. There was a distant shout in response. She shifted her rifle from her shoulder, sat down on a rock nearby, and watched the man on the ground.

A few minutes went by. "Whatcha whistle for Delwen?" A young man in his late teens, followed by two younger boys, came to an abrupt stop at the sight of an unconscious man within the AR's borders. "Oh shit, ya bagged one."

Delwen eyed him and pointed to the tripwire. "You rigged it wrong. It shoulda gone off, but it didn't."

The young man glared at her for a moment before turning back to Cooper, still lying on the ground, unmoving. "He stinks," he grinned at Delwen, "what, ya want him for your boyfriend or something? Setting your sights awful low, aren't ya?"

Delwen returned his needling with a withering look, "Oh, shut it, Heim, he's as good as dead. I got a look at his face 'fore he face planted. That blood isn't just from the gravel; he got messed up a while back, and it looks to have caught up with him." She stared at Cooper and thought for a minute, "Sul will want to talk to him, though. Look at his clothes… those are Western Front colors."

Heim chewed on this for a moment. "Think he's alone?"

"You *see* anyone else 'round here?" One of the younger boys sniggered at the sarcasm in her voice. Heim reached out and smacked him on the side of the head, and the boy yelped and slunk out of range.

"Right. Let's bag him and tag him, then." Delwen and the other younger boy fastened Cooper's hands behind his back with zip tie, and then bound his ankles as well. After they were sure he wasn't going to jump up and make a grab for their weapons or their throats, Delwen patted him down, removing a large knife, along with a Hi-Point nine millimeter. Heim barked in derision at the sight of the handgun. "What a piece of shit. Hell, he'd be better off shooting himself in the head with that damn thing."

"I afur nives," Cooper's voice was muffled and indistinct. His eyes had opened and the young boy jumped back, while Delwen jerked in surprise. The instant she did she felt a sting of embarrassment. This bloody mess at her feet couldn't hurt her. If Sul had seen, well, he was harder on her than the rest; it wasn't as easy as the other girls thought having the commander of Amerika Reborn for a father.

"Christ, Kerwin, stop being such a pansy. He's

tied up like some damn Christmas goose; he can't hurt you." She rolled Cooper over on his back, "Now, say that again?"

"I said I '*afur nives*," Cooper's mouth wouldn't stretch the right way. He could feel the crusted goo, and the grinding of the bones that obviously had not set right. Eating had been agony, and he hadn't had the need to talk to anyone in weeks…obviously, he needed practice.

"What the hell's he sayin?" Heim asked.

"He's saying he prefers knives," Delwen half-smiled at Scott, a bit of a thrill twisted through her. "My kind of guy, 'ceptin he's uglier than Camelia."

Camelia was their resident slave, as many of the Amerika Reborn members thought of her. She was Hispanic, one of the 'coloreds' they had picked out of a small group holed up miles from here. The rest they had shot or let burn to death in the fire the AR had set to the buildings during the fighting. Camelia had a jagged scar that cut across her face and down one arm. She couldn't walk right either. She had survived the Amtrak Train Bombings, but not without losing her looks in the process. Before the Collapse she had been a nurse. Medical knowledge, even packaged in the wrong-colored skin, was a benefit the AR couldn't afford to discard. So they had tied her up and dragged her out of that house of death well over a year ago now, and kept her busy cleaning wounds and patching everyone up ever since.

"Let's get him out of here and on back to Sul," Delwen said, "he's definitely gonna be interested in this guy."

Half an hour later, with Cooper fevered and close to collapse, the group of child-soldiers had dragged him into the main AR camp. As soon as they had come into the clearing, within sight of a small assembly of cottages and low, dark buildings, a crowd of at least twenty adults had gathered immediately, all of them armed. Many sported tattoos that curled from under their heavy shirtsleeves and collars to wrap around necks and hands. Swastikas, skulls, and SS bolts adorned several of the men's shirts and coats as well.

The colors of the Western Front started a flurry of angry muttering among the adults, and two burly men stepped forward to help drag Cooper to a building near the center of the clearing. It was much larger than the rest, and the area had obviously been a popular campground pre-Collapse. The buildings were arranged in straight lines with neatly laid gravel paths winding between them, expanding as they approached what had most likely been a communal kitchen and social area. There were other buildings, of newer construction, scattered about—as well as several yurts and large tents. Through another stand of trees there were several fenced areas, one filled with horses, another held sheep, and Cooper could make out a cultivated field beyond that.

This camp was obviously organized and well-established. A wonderful aroma of cooking food wafted out of the building and into the clearing. If Cooper had felt even half-human, and not consumed with fever and exhaustion, his stomach would have rumbled in response. As it was, he was having difficulty maintaining consciousness.

A few moments later, Cooper's eyes focused blearily on a tall, bearded man. Sulwyn Kingmaker had gray hair and piercing blue eyes. He looked to be in his late 50s and had the appearance of a kind father. At one time, Sulwyn had had a different name, a rather mundane one at that. But that was before the Collapse, before Amerika Reborn had risen like a phoenix from the ashes of the broken fragments of the American Nazi Party.

"A soldier? And from the Western Front, I see." Sulwyn's eyes narrowed as he took in Cooper's appearance, and turned to Delwen, "Any sign of others?"

"No, Pops…I mean … no sir. No one," Delwen stumbled over her words.

"Hmmm. Well, take him to Camelia and have her patch him up." He started to turn away, and then turned back and added, "And tell that colored woman I don't want her wasting any of the remaining antibiotics on him. I've yet to see if he is of any use to us. Might be some cowardly deserter. Enemy or not, we don't need deserters."

Cooper soon found himself in a dim room, hoisted onto a hard metal table, with a scarred

Hispanic woman bending over him, examining his face wounds in great detail.

"He's running a fever," she said out loud, mostly to herself.

"I can tell that, Spic," Delwen sneered, "anything else?"

Camelia didn't react to Delwen's insult; she was focused on her patient. "Yes. His jaw is badly infected and he needs it reset and wired shut so it can heal right. He will need a good dose of antibiotics."

There was a pause as Delwen turned and met Heim's eyes. She stared at him, never breaking the gaze as she said, "Sul said to get him patched up and give him whatever he needs." As Camelia opened a large metal cabinet and began selecting instruments and some of the last of the antibiotic packs, Delwen closed the distance between her and Heim, "I know what Sul said, but I got a feeling about this guy." She said it in a whisper, brushing her lips against the older boy's ear. "You…won't tell…will you?"

She felt Heim shudder a bit in response, and he shook his head silently. Heim had been following her around like a puppy dog ever since she had started to fill out, and she used this obsession with her to full advantage whenever possible, teasing him, and then pushing him away. Little Eric Brown, now known as Heimdall Stonekiller, was nothing better than a tool. But he was *her* tool, and she liked it that way.

The chain around Camelia's ankle clanked as she

moved back to Cooper, who had passed out by this point, and Delwen couldn't help but snicker. If the stupid Spic hadn't kept trying to escape, they would have left her unchained.

Sulwyn, Delwen's father and leader of Amerika Reborn, had explained to Delwen that some coloreds were worth keeping alive, although it was never acceptable to breed with them. "Their blood is full of disease, the muddy bastards. Never, ever allow a colored to touch you, Del," he had grasped her shoulder, bruising flesh and continued, "the only reason we keep that colored Spic around is for her stolen medical knowledge. We must keep looking for a better replacement so that we aren't exposed to her filthy diseases any longer than necessary."

Sulwyn had led the fight on the Spic compound over a year ago now. The Spics had been overwhelmed by the AR's superior firepower and guerrilla fighting tactics. Sul had ordered everyone killed. No point in keeping around some screaming brown babies, or helpless women. The Spic women weren't anything like the Amerika Reborn women— they were soft, helpless, and useless for anything except spreading their legs and giving the white man diseases, Sulwyn had explained to his group.

But when they had set it all on fire, they found Camelia in one of the back rooms, performing surgery on a mortally wounded boy. Sulwyn had recognized her abilities immediately and stopped one of the men from blowing her head off. They had dragged her away, fighting and kicking, screaming until one of the men had cuffed her hard, sending her head flying back, cracking the glass of the side window in the lead truck and knocking her unconscious.

When she had woken up, she had caught on pretty quick to keep her fool mouth shut, Delwen mused. She had focused her efforts on trying to get away until Sul had her chained and told her if she tried again he'd cut through the tendons in her ankles, laming her permanently. Delwen wasn't sure if it was the threat of never walking again, or the strength of the chain that had kept Camelia from trying again. But sure enough, she stayed put from then on.

It would take nearly a week before Cooper was able to stand unassisted. Camelia had managed to repair the half-healed wreck that was his jaw, but there was no hope he would ever be good-looking again. A large dimpled scar ran along his right jawline, jagged thick white scar tissue buckling and twisting the skin. It would be another month until he could eat any solid food.

As soon as he was fit to stand, however, Delwen dragged him back into the headquarters. Her father was sitting at a large, ornate desk, reviewing an almost illegible report from the man in charge of the barnyard animals. It looked as though they would need to raid if they wanted enough sheep and goats for breeding stock *and* plenty of meat. He paused, frustrated by the man's illiterate scrawl, and removed his reading glasses. Scott stood before him in the same stinking clothes he had been in when they found him, but he stood straight, and waited for Sulwyn to address him.

"Name?" he asked Scott.

"Cooper. Scott Cooper."

"So…deserter or spy?" he asked Cooper.

"Independent agent…sir." Cooper managed to delay on the 'sir' just a fraction longer than was respectful.

"I see, and how does one become an independent agent?"

"One does the best with what he's got, sir. The Western Front collapsed, due to an improper mixing of color, sir." Cooper wasn't stupid; he had listened carefully, and seen the tattoos. He figured it was the most expedient way to save his life, and possibly, just possibly, regain some of what he had lost in that raid.

"And I'm to believe that you share our values?" Sulwyn asked, raising an eyebrow in mock disbelief.

"Believe what you like, sir. I'm in need of a bath," Cooper said calmly, "That Spic medic you have, I wouldn't doubt that she has lice; more than likely scabies as well." Delwen sniggered quietly behind him.

Sulwyn Kingmaker, formerly John Stump, a former television repairman from Southie, smiled, "A bath then." He turned to Delwen, "Have Kerwin

take care of it and keep watch over him." He turned
back to the reports and slid on his reading glasses,
quite obviously dismissing him.

"My knives, sir."

Sulwyn glanced at Cooper, "You have not
proven yourself to me, Cooper. When you do, we
will discuss it further." He turned away, again
dismissing the young man in front of him.

Cooper turned, as if he were capitulating, and
then moved stunningly fast, his arms and legs a blur
as he ruthlessly attacked the large guard standing at
attention behind him. Within seconds the burly man
was dead on the floor and Scott Cooper stood there,
the guard's knife in his right hand, covered in gore.
Cooper slowly set the weapon on the floor next to
his victim.

Delwen had an AK-47 aimed at his belly and the
two other guards from outside the office were
pointing their weapons at Cooper as well. He stood
there, smiling. "Is that the proof you were looking
for, sir?" He didn't move any closer to the leader,
didn't move at all, which was for the best—he had
three people within a hair trigger of killing him.
Despite this, he was as calm and cool as ice.

Sulwyn spared a glance at the piece of dead meat
currently covering his office floor with a spreading
pool of blood and turned to Delwen, "Make sure he
gets his knives back." Then he turned back to
Cooper, "Stay within the boundaries of the clearing,
and out of the armory, or I'll have my men shoot

you on sight."

By the time he could eat solid food a few weeks later, Cooper had quietly carved out a comfortable niche for himself within the Amerika Reborn group. He refused to change his name, however, which had been a tradition among the AR since the Collapse. He quickly rose within the ranks, leading devastatingly brutal raids and bringing vast stores of food, ammunition, and other supplies, along with able-bodied men and women to swell the numbers of the neo-Nazi group.

Scott Cooper had found a new home.

CHAPTER SIX

FIRST SUMMER

"I figured I would eventually get used to it. And we make do, because really, what other choice do we have? But I miss air conditioning, I mean I really, really miss it. It's been, what, over ten years now? And when that crazy hot, muggy summer heat hits I just sit around like a limp noodle. Ugh. It's hard to believe that my grandparents grew up without it and all the generations before that. Of all the things I miss… having that ice-cold air conditioner is near the top of my list."
— Jess's Journal

Sweat trickled down Jess's face. The sun beat mercilessly down on her as she moved through the backyard. On the back porch, the solar oven had two loaves of bread inside and they had been baking for over two hours. The heavenly smell she kept getting whiffs of indicated it would soon be time to take them out. For now she ignored the smell of the bread, and the heat of the sun, and continued tying the tomato plants up. The heat had spiked a few weeks ago and invaded every corner of the house and the yard. The tomatoes seemed to be the only living thing that thrived.

Jess and the others had all moved down to the basement; the slightly cooler temperatures were a relief from the unending heat and they slept, windows open at night, desperate for a breeze.

Thankfully, the screens on the two tiny windows were intact. This prevented a majority of the voracious swarms of mosquitoes from feasting on them. Some still made it through, as the itchy red lumps on Jess's arms and legs could attest to.

The unrelenting heat was hardest on Jacob, since he was only a baby and unable to regulate his internal temperature as easily as Jess and David. Even Tina struggled with the heat, turning red quickly and losing her appetite. She got her wish to hold Jacob more, the two of them relegated to the basement while Jess and David handled what they could of the gardening and chores.

Jess was worn out from struggling to pull a cart loaded with water from the creek. The only nice part about this duty was the messiness of it. They would pull a handcart loaded with one or two large rain barrels to the creek, then use buckets to fill them, which meant she was soaked down the front of her shirt and pants within minutes. When the barrels were full, they would turn the cart around and slowly pull it the three blocks back home, taking care to navigate the chewed up blacktop and various obstacles—mainly bricks and wood from the collapsed and burnt houses—strewn about. It was hard work pulling the cart back, the slightest incline involved muscles she hadn't known she had.

Once back, they would hook up a short hose to the spigot near the bottom of the barrel, letting a barrel drain slowly into one or two of the raised beds. When the barrel was empty, they would switch to the other one and drain it as well. One trip in the early morning to water selected beds in the backyard and one trip in the evening, to water the backyard— thus avoiding direct sunlight. Until they could dig a well, it was their only option for keeping the plants alive. They had also decided to allow their new flock of chickens to run free of the confines of their protected chicken coop and yard during the day after two of the younger hens, who had just begun laying, died from overheating.

The odd little flock of nine laying hens and one rooster had been cobbled together from donations by townspeople. For a few weeks, after they had help from Thurman Banks repairing the chicken house and coop, which was intact except for one smashed window, Jess and David received a bird here and a bird there. A neighbor would show up at their door, squawking chicken in one hand, a packet of seeds or some bread in another. One or two of the hens looked a lot like the Ameraucana birds that Jess's mom, Julie, had owned. Jess later concluded that they must be Ameraucanas when they found a stash of medium-sized pale green eggs. Others were larger breeds that lay large brown eggs. With a rooster to fertilize the eggs, it was possible that they could enlarge their flock quickly if they continued to have broody hens.

"If we just lock them up at night, so the 'possums and 'coons don't get 'em, then let them out in the morning they can be free to find the coolest part of the yard," David had suggested. It had proven to be the perfect solution and the chickens could often be found resting under the shade of tomato plants in the cool dirt, or in a dark corner of the fence under the grapevines. It had its drawbacks, though; they tended to nibble on the tomatoes and had completely demolished the grapes before Jess and David devised a barrier with chicken wire.

A tiny warble at her elbow startled Jess. One of the hens was eyeing her curiously. She was one of the Ameraucana, one that looked distinctive enough from the rest to be named. Tina had decided to call her Little Miss Crankyfoot, or Cranky for short, but the young hen was anything but cranky. The rest would run from Jess and the others, but not Cranky. Jess figured Cranky's brain had to be just a tad bigger than the rest—she stayed close to Jess and David, watching as they dug into the earth, and was rewarded with tasty grubs, fat green tomato hornworms, and now, as the summer progressed, juicy grasshoppers. Jess spied one now and tossed it to Cranky, who devoured it quickly.

Work on the house was moving slowly now. Everything moved slowly in this oppressive heat. The rooms had slowly been cleaned out. Furniture, dishes, books, and more, some of it quite familiar, often appeared overnight on the front stoop. Old Mr. Banks had explained it kindly one evening when he showed up with a butchered goat for the family and then stayed for supper.

"Folks did what they had to survive, Jessie. Along the way, they maybe saw stuff that was nice, or made 'em smile, and they picked that up too. After all, someone who is gone, they don't need that stuff anymore, right? It wasn't stealing, per se, just filling a tiny desire. You understand, right, Jessie?" His eyes had pleaded with her to accept that what was taken would find its way back in due time. And Jess shrugged and nodded. Hadn't she done much the same thing in countless other places along the way? The day her mother's cameo, handed down through three generations of women before her, returned, still nestled in its worn, velvet-lined box, she sat down on the front stoop and cried. It made her miss her mom even more.

The remnants of the once-thriving town of over

20,000 souls was tattered and threadbare, a mere one in thirty had survived. Despite this, or perhaps because of the loss of so many, those left pulled together wherever and whenever possible. Jess could count on one hand the number of meals she and her family had missed since their arrival in March. It was hard for her, though, to ask for help.

Sarah Turner had given Jess a stern talking to a few weeks before when she learned that there was a gaping hole in the roof, which poured rain straight into the master bedroom. "Don't be a fool, Jessie," she had said to her as she surveyed the damage. The floor had buckled and part of the drywall had collapsed. Soon it would affect their nest down in the basement. "This isn't safe for the baby, or any of you; the rain will lead to mold, and then you will have some real problems on your hands. If we can't find someone to help you fix it you'll have to move into the dorms they've set up at Research. But that's been a hotbed for some bad strains of flu through the winter—I'd hate to see you or the kids get that."

Research had been the local medical center and part of it had been turned into a form of housing for orphans and the elderly after so many of the children lost their parents in a series of raids—first from the Western Front and later from bands of starving families holed up in the city. The old folks' home had been set on fire with most of the occupants inside, but the elderly who had lived on their own were now forced through need to live in the old hospital. In some ways being around so many of the kids had saved many of the senior citizens from fading away to nothing. The kids needed them, after all.

The last two winters had been hard ones—food shortages in the first winter immediately following the first invasion had taken their toll. With lack of food had come higher susceptibility to illness. The last onslaught of flu had killed all but a handful of the senior citizens and put a serious dent in the younger population as well. Jess had heard the stories and Sarah's admonition to get the house in order was taken seriously.

A week later the ripped tarp was pulled away and a handful of the younger men from the militia were hard at work, with a former owner of a local construction company supervising their progress. Two days after that the hole had been completely repaired, including the rotting drywall, patched from intact drywall salvaged from a home a few blocks away that had partially burned in the invasion. Jess had cleaned the room and, after a full-size mattress and box springs mysteriously appeared on their doorstep the next day, she had moved the bed and her meager belongings into the master bedroom. The heat had kept her downstairs, but she knew it wouldn't always be this hot. Eventually the nights would cool and she would actually have a room to herself, mostly, considering that Jacob would be sharing it with her. It felt strange to take this room that had been her parents'. Looking around it she could see the ghostly shapes of where each piece of furniture had stood, and the shadows of their presence still lingered in outlines on the floor.

One of the bedroom windows was broken. The former construction company owner, Mr. Kinsey, had offered to find a replacement window but Jess had shook her head and just asked that it be boarded over. She was relieved Sarah wasn't there to lecture her, or to go above her head and insist that Mr. Kinsey find a window for her. Having the roof intact was good enough and she knew that she was already owed enough for all of the help others had extended to her.

Jess had been lost in her thoughts for a while. Her back and knees were sore from crouching at the tomato vines and her fingers were rough and chapped from the twine she was using to tie the vines with. As she looked around, Jess found herself feeling almost…safe. Twice in the last month the militia had repelled invaders, killing the ones who were armed, and no one from Warsend had been hurt in the process. A small knot of cattle lowed peaceably nearby. The strong smell of them had become something of a comfort. All of her little family were filling out, the bones jutted less, and she had noticed her hair felt thicker and less brittle. Jess could also see the difference in Jacob's activity level as well as his size. He had begun crawling and gurgled happily, keeping all three of them busy taking turns watching him.

She had even heard Tina, so serious and quiet for her four years, laugh freely the other day. For that matter, David, too, seemed happier. They were adjusting. It had been nearly a year now, Jess realized suddenly, since she had first met David and Tina. Nearly a year since Jacob had been born in the middle of that storm.

What had happened to that soldier who had found them that night? She remembered him standing there, ready to fire, the rain soaking him, the wind lashing the trees in the background. He had looked so tired, so sad, when he saw Jacob, naked, covered in afterbirth, his umbilical cord still attached. His young face had been lined with grief at the memory of his own son. "I had a son once. His name was Jacob."

She hadn't thought of the soldier for a long time. Not much at all since that first night, the memory of him lost in the simple and basic struggle for survival in the days, weeks, and months that followed. For the first time she found herself pierced by a sharp curiosity—all the stories, all the lives cut short or forever altered by the events of the past two years. What was Sarah's story? Where did she and her kids come from? And Grandmother Madge…where were her children now? How could she tell them the story of their mother?

Jess looked down to find her left hand clenched around a thin long shred of mulch, clutching it as she would a pen. Before it had all come to such a terrible end, her life here in Warsend before the invasion had been filled with "scribbles," as her brother Chris had called them. "When you aren't reading, you're scribbling," he had teased her good-naturedly, "and sometimes it's both!" For nearly two years she hadn't written a thing. The journals were gone, and hadn't mysteriously returned on the stoop like so many other things.

Suddenly she felt that familiar longing, deep within her, an urge to write that was akin to a thirsty man begging for water. And not just write, but chronicle the stories of others, so that their words and thoughts and experiences would not be lost. *A record,* Jess decided, *of all of those who will speak, for themselves and for others who are gone. So that we will not forget.*

Jess stood up, brushed herself off and went to look for a pen and paper.

CHAPTER SEVEN

A HUNTING EXPEDITION

"If we deny love that is given to us, if we refuse to give love because we fear pain or loss, then our lives will be empty, our loss greater." – Author Unknown

Wes twisted his wedding ring on his finger. It was a simple band, yellow gold, almost a woman's ring it was so thin. There hadn't been much in the way of money, and with Cody on the way, there had been no time to save up for more. The mate to it, Sarah's, hung from his neck, next to Angie's ring, along with his dog tags. He toyed with taking all of them off, sticking them in a drawer and trying to forget.

He had done that once, when he started seeing Angie. She hadn't said anything, not a word of complaint, but one day he had realized he couldn't hang on to them and be with her, so he had slipped off his ring, and took Sarah's ring as well, and placed them in the back of his sock drawer in the box with the note from Sarah saying she was leaving him. They were memories of what could have been…if he had been the man he was supposed to be, a better husband, a better dad.

Cody would be, what, sixteen next week and Laura fourteen next spring. If they were still alive, that is. And in this crazy world he wondered…he wondered about that every day. Wes pushed his wedding ring back up his finger, until it nestled against his knuckle, a little loose; he had lost a bit of weight over the years, but the ring hung on, a part of his past that he couldn't let go, no matter that there would most likely never be answers, never be closure. He heard it clink against the metal of the rifle in front of him, currently in pieces, waiting to be cleaned.

It was nearly Thanksgiving, a time for hunting, and for Tiptonville, a time of terrible memories. Wes forced his mind away from it, focused on the rifle before him, cleaned and oiled it, then re-assembled it. As he did, Wes felt his thoughts turn to the outsider in their midst. Chris Aaronson was the one man in town that no one really knew. They certainly didn't know what Wes knew—that Chris had been a

conscript in the Western Front. They had swallowed
Fenton Perdue's story of Chris being a friend of the
family. They had swallowed it hook, line, and sinker,
especially after that raid and slaughter of the Austins
and Anthony Wilkes.

And honestly, if Wes were to think on it long
enough, he knew Chris had been telling the truth. He
had been a conscript, and he *had* escaped. But the
young man was the only one, the only witness to
escape the Western Front. It was time they talked,
time he learned more about the world outside of
Tiptonville, Tennessee.

Wes slung the rifle over his shoulder over his flak
vest. Strapped to his left thigh was his Bowie, the
flak vest held an arsenal of shells, blades, and a
Magnum .44 was in a right hip holster. He had
decided to bring the compound bow as well. As
usual, Wes was a walking arsenal. There had been a
time when he had not been, but he had paid for that
mistake with tears and blood a hundred times over.
He headed out of town, his F150 a dull roar as he
passed the patrols and headed toward the Perdue
farm.

The guarded look on Carrie's face when she
greeted him at the door had secretly amused Wes.
She ushered him into the house, looking pale and
wan, more than a trifle suspicious and sent little
Joseph off for Chris. Fenton had been friendlier, but
then again, Fenton seemed to have a knack for
knowing your intent long before you did yourself.

"Wes," Fenton clapped him on the shoulder, "you look ready for war, young man."

"Just going hunting for deer, sir; thought I'd ask Chris if he'd like to join me, bring back some venison for Thanksgiving and all."

Fenton nodded, "The boy needs a bit of fresh air, been inside too much recently, what with Carrie… er…feelin' poorly. I prefer y'all bring back a nice tender doe, if you don't mind." He winked at Wes, and Wes found his mouth curving in response. He didn't get the chance to smile much these days, and it felt strange and somewhat uncomfortable.

Wes was spared any further small talk as the front door opened and some of the chilly air blew in with Joseph and Chris. Joseph was bouncing about, begging to go hunting. After the raid, early in the year, the entire family had made a practice of going out monthly and doing some limited target practice. Mainly it revolved around making sure Joseph knew proper gun safety. The boy was now almost six years old, and had become a crack shot with a .22 caliber Beretta Bobcat. It was an elegant little piece, perfect for the boy's small hand. He had been attracted at once to the shine of the steel and the black grip. It had taken half of a hog in trade at the Trade Mart, but Chris had watched Carrie and Liza haggle over the deal for nearly an hour before the merchant, sick and tired of arguing, had thrown in two full boxes of ammo to go with it—a heck of a deal pre-war and a testament to the girls' bargaining skills.

Joseph had managed to net several squirrels and one skunk. Fenton had drawn the line at eating the skunk, but the rest had ended up in the stewpot with Fenton reminding everyone, "Y'all don't shoot what you ain't gonna eat."

Liza had rolled her eyes at that, "Sure Gramps, next time a raider comes by and we blow his brains out I'll bring him to you to dress and prepare for supper." Fenton had eyed her sternly and grumbled under his breath about little girls getting too big for their britches.

Joseph was bound and determined to go hunting with Wes and Chris, but Carrie deflated Joseph's excitement in one fell swoop when she shook her head and said, "You have lessons, Joseph; it's time we practiced reading."

"Awww! Carrie, but I wanna…"

Carrie eyed him sternly, "You get what you get…"

The boy pouted, "And you don't throw a fit. 'Sides I *never* throw a fit. I'm not a *girl!*"

Fenton suppressed a snort of laughter and received an irritable glare from Carrie, all too reminiscent of her mother, as she pointed silently at the den. Now that Chris and Carrie were married, they had moved into her room. The den had been left empty and Liza had pushed to have it turned into a classroom of sorts. Joseph slumped, contemplated rebellion for two short seconds and then slunk into the classroom muttering under his breath.

Fenton turned to Chris, "Now son, I want a nice pretty doe brought back. She will make a fine addition to our Thanksgiving feast. Think you can manage that?"

Chris looked at Wes, then back at Fenton. He felt out of his depth. Was this some sort of twisted male bonding experience? Was he supposed to spit and then shake hands? "Uh…sure, Gramps…one doe…I'll do my best."

That earned him a gruff, aborted bark of a laugh from Wes. The jerk actually looked amused. Chris wasn't sure what was happening here, but he wasn't sure he liked it. Half an hour later, as the truck bounced along the ruts of something that might have been considered a road one hundred years ago, Chris was more than sure he was out of his element. What did Wes want with him? They had gone through town and taken Highway 78, nodding to the sentries outside of town as they headed toward Wright, now abandoned, hit by raiders long before Chris found his way to Tiptonville. They angled around Reelfoot Lake. Chris wondered how long the dead trees would stand, upright, submerged in water, their leaves and beauty gone. It had been over two hundred years and it appeared that all or most of the trees still stood. It was as if they were waiting for something.

Wes followed Chris's gaze. "We cut 'em down every once in a while; more often these days since the Collapse. They make good firewood.”

Chris looked at the trees, then back at Wes. “What are we doing out here, Wes?”

“We’re going deer hunting, Aaronson.” The older man spared a glance at Chris and smiled slightly, which caused a large knot to form in Chris’s stomach. “You know, men go huntin’, provide for the family.”

“I provide for my family,” Chris said evenly, “I help run a farm, if you’ll remember.” He briefly considered opening the door and jumping from the fast-moving truck. An image of him running for his life with Wes armed to the teeth in hot pursuit flashed before his eyes. Wes had pretty much left him alone since the events of last March. Could he have changed his mind?

Chris turned back to see Wes eyeing him again, Wes barked out a laugh, “Damn, Aaronson, if I didn’t know better I’d think you were lookin’ to jump out of this here truck. What…d’ya think I’m plannin’ on huntin’ *you*?”

Chris glared at him, “Yeah, the thought crossed my mind.”

Wes did laugh then, long and hard, and the truck swerved and heaved over the rough road. “Relax, if I wanted to kill you I would’ve done it a long time ago.” He raised an eyebrow thoughtfully, “and I would’ve done it from the woods. Fenton ain’t the only one ’round here with experience in war, you know.”

Chris relaxed a bit. Not a lot; that was hard to do when you were being tossed about a truck cab like a rag doll, bouncing along what was now a tree-lined hill in the middle of nowhere. Wes seemed to be the old-fashioned type, so Chris figured if Wes did intend to kill him, he'd get some measure of warning. "I heard you were in the second Gulf War."

"Yeah, now that was a screwed up war, no winner, and it just dragged on and on. And it would've kept dragging on if the bottom hadn't fallen out of the war machine and every other damned thing here in the good ole United States." Wes's mood turned somber again, "It was just another messed up war, another excuse to kill good, honest folks who actually believed they were fighting for something more than sand and oil. What a crappie that turned out to be."

Chris felt a little more at ease; this guy wasn't the gung-ho, proud to be an American, gun-toting lunatic he had seemed to be at first, although Chris wasn't ready to rule out the gun-toting fanatic part of it. "Why are we out here, Wes?"

Wes eyed him, "You just get right to the point, dontcha, Aaronson?" When Chris didn't answer, he said, "Maybe I've got questions about the Western Front."

"After *eight months* you've got questions?"

Wes switched direction on the road with a spin of his steering wheel, and changed topics just as quickly, "Carrie looked peaked. She have another miscarriage?"

Chris's anger surged, "You leave Carrie out of this."

"Easy soldier, easy." Wes's eyes were glued to the road. That was good, because Chris sure as hell could not see any road at all. They hit a particularly large rut and Chris swore as his head hit the roof of the cab. "I ain't trying to rile you up, Aaronson."

"So you say, Wes. Then you go and call me a soldier again." Chris ground his teeth, "I'm not, and I never was."

"I believe you, Aaronson. Now relax; I've got no interest in fighting with you. I wanted someone to go hunting with and I knew you weren't on watch. Most everyone else is, you know, 'cause of the anniversary."

And of course, Chris knew exactly what he was talking about. They called it the Thanksgiving massacre. Just a couple of weeks after his hometown in Warsend, Missouri had been invaded, Tiptonville had seen action. A different faction of the Western Front had smashed through town, toppling the water tower, setting fire to several buildings, including a bank, and killing nearly half of the population, including both of the town doctors. This was the two-year anniversary of the event. The entire town came together and held a communal Thanksgiving dinner; at least, those who weren't on watch. Then they brought food out to the militia, posted on all of the roads that led into town, and took over the watch for them, standing in the night, armed, until the sun rose and the militia took back over the regular watch rounds again.

Chris had participated last year, on the first anniversary. The thought had occurred to him at the time that this was what true community and being an American was about. The United States was dead, but its citizens were not. He had been proud to be a part of the groups of townspeople watching out for the town. As an outsider, he hadn't been considered part of the militia and, until spring, had not been required to stand watch. After the raid by Cooper and his men that had changed dramatically. It was a few days until Thanksgiving, however. Was there some kind of ritual hunting to be done before the anniversary? Knowing little about Wes, he could only imagine what was going on in the older man's head.

"Where were you on that day?" Chris thought to ask. It was like asking his folks where they were on the day the Twin Towers fell or Ronald Reagan was shot. And his mind flashed on the memory of the Amtrak Train Bombings, when nearly sixteen hundred commuters and train personnel perished when terrorists detonated multiple bombs placed around New York's Penn Station. That one had become even more relevant when Carrie had told him that it was how their father Isaac had died, just a few months before Joseph was born. They had never found Isaac Perdue's body.

The truck shuddered to a stop, and Wes's face looked grim, "We're here, gotta walk the rest of the way to get to the high hide," he said, not answering Chris's question.

Wes slid out of the cab and grabbed a backpack from the truck bed. He didn't look back at Chris; he just set off in a southwestern direction, along a barely visible path. Chris stared for a moment at the man's retreating back and realized if he didn't follow quickly he would lose him entirely in the dense trees. Within minutes Chris was well and truly lost. He could wander in these woods for hours, hell, maybe days, and never find his way back home. His ankle, now twice-broken and still healing slowly, ached as he picked up the pace. The last thing he wanted to do was lose sight of Wes. He had no doubt the man knew exactly where he was in the dense forest, but Chris himself was disoriented. After walking through thick forest and undergrowth, they were faced with a meadow and high hide. In the middle of the meadow was a salt lick. Silently the two men climbed into the high hide.

Three hours later, as Chris shifted in the high hide, his left side numb from sitting still far too long, Wes finally answered his question.

"I was here," he said.

For a moment Chris didn't have a clue what Wes was talking about. But his silence, once broken, opened the floodgates.

"I was sitting here, in this high hide, waiting for a

deer when it all went down in town." Wes pulled his knife out of its sheath, and dug at the wood plank at his feet. "I heard it, of course. We're what, eight miles from town? Thought it was thunder at first. Wised up pretty quick, but I was too far out. By the time I got to town the water tower was down and the fighting was mostly over."

Two hundred yards away, Chris could see a deer step out of the woods into a clearing. He didn't know if he should let Wes finish his story, shoot the deer himself, or what.

He kept an eye on the beast and listened as Wes went on, "I guess you know a little about me. Liza and Carl always hanging together, and Abby and John comin' down for your weddin' and all."

Chris nodded, "I heard your wife took off with your two kids a few years back."

He hoped this was the politic thing to say, and he didn't elaborate on the details Abby Carter had given him. Chris didn't figure it was his place to mention the black eyes, the PTSD and abuse and alcohol. Wes knew the truth, and Chris didn't think it would be particularly conducive to his continued health to rub it in.

"That was over ten years ago now." Wes stabbed again at the wood, and still the deer stood in the clearing, calmly munching on the grass, occasionally raising his antlered head and looking around. Wes didn't seem to notice.

"I don't blame her."

Chris made some kind of strangled noise in his throat and Wes scowled at him.

"I know what Abby and half the town says. I was an asshole. I came back from that crazy, hotter 'n hell sand nigger-infested place and I was well and truly messed up. Too many missions gone bad, IEDs, blood in the desert. We didn't belong there, none of us did. The government sending us to hell. And for what? So they could jack up the price of oil and talk about democracy while good men died for absolutely nothing."

The deer had four, no, six points, and looked well fed. There was a movement in the trees behind him, and a gorgeous doe stepped out next, head up, watchful.

"I was messed up, and by the time I figured out how bad off I was, Sarah had taken off with Cody and little Laura. I looked for them, God knows I did. I stopped drinking, cleaned up, and kept looking." Wes stared at Chris and continued, "When it all came apart, when war broke out and they nuked Austin, I knew I'd never find them. It was my fault, and the government, for making me into that messed up piece of crap I had become."

Chris watched the doe step out further, ears flicking, then nose-down to the grass, tearing off a chunk, slowly chewing it. "Why are you telling me this, Wes?"

The fury that still lurked within Wes surged to the surface and he pulled the action back on his rifle, aimed, and took two shots in quick succession. The two deer that Chris had been eying for the past five minutes fell dead in the clearing, side by side. Chris gaped as Wes slid the rifle back over his shoulder and began to climb down from the high hide, "C'mon, we need to field dress them before nightfall."

Chris's work with Fenton on the farm had given him ample preparation for field-dressing the deer, but Wes was able to give him some pointers, "Don't push the knife in too far, or you'll rupture the stomach and intestines." The two deer were strung up by their necks, hanging side by side from a sturdy tree branch. The men stood shoulder-to-shoulder and Chris watched and then mimicked each move Wes made. "Take care with the bladder here," he said, pointing with his knife towards the spine, "pinch the urethra closed and carefully remove it."

They worked for a few minutes more in silence, blood and gore covering their hands as they carefully detached the hearts from the lungs and plunged them into a bucket of water Wes had brought with them. The kidneys and livers also followed.

"I know what it's like to lose someone," Wes said, unexpectedly after nearly half an hour of terse commands as they finished gutting and prepping the beasts to transport back to the truck. "I had found someone, someone who didn't give a damn about my wife leaving me. She didn't judge me for the person I had been, just the person I was when I was with her."

Chris waited for the older man to continue. Wes strode to a nearby stream, knelt down, and washed his hands and blades in the clear water. Chris did the same, whistling sharply at the chill of the water. It wasn't long before Wes continued.

"Her name was Angie. She had been staying with friends just outside of town when all The Collapse went down. No family. No roots. We met at a 4th of July picnic and things just…"

Wes settled back on his haunches next to the stream. He set the knives down to dry, picked up a rock and threw it hard into the trees on the opposite side. It hit the trunk high up and caused two birds to explode into flight from the remnants of greenery, chirping in alarm.

"She moved in a few weeks later and just two days before the Western Front blew through, she told me she was pregnant. I was off huntin' and she was left to die alone. She didn't make it out of the house more than a dozen steps before she was gunned down."

Although the circumstances were completely different, Chris couldn't help thinking of Carrie, her face pinched and sad, full of pain, crying softly where Chris found her hunched over in agony in the bathroom two weeks ago. This second pregnancy and miscarriage had taken Chris by surprise; he hadn't even known Carrie was pregnant when the miscarriage hit. The loss was still painful though, especially when he remembered how it felt to hold their first baby Amy Lynn, her tiny body so light, so impossibly feeble, for those few short moments she had lived.

Chris felt his throat catch on the words, "Carrie did have another miscarriage."

Wes nodded, "I figured as much."

They didn't say another word as both men rose and headed back to the two waiting carcasses. The sun was setting by the time they managed to haul the deer back to the waiting truck and load them up. As the truck bumped and jolted down the rough path, Chris said, "I'm sorry about Angie, Wes."

In the darkness, his face barely lit by the dashboard lights, Wes grimaced, "Yeah, me too."

Although Carrie asked, and Liza tried repeatedly to quiz him about that day in the woods, Chris never repeated what Wes had told him. Somehow, the relationship between the two men, despite the gap in years and the acrimonious way it had begun, changed that day. Slowly, over the years that would follow, Wes and Chris became regular hunting companions and Wes began showing up at both seeding and harvest time to provide much-needed assistance on the farm. Eventually he would become a fixture at the family Sunday dinner.

On this particular evening, though, Wes delivered Chris and a large doe to a very pleased Fenton, remarking as he left, "Maybe next time that fool grandson-in-law of yours will actually shoot one himself. I waited for him to take the shot for five minutes before I gave up and took matters into my own hands."

And with that parting shot, he strode back to his truck and drove away into the crisp fall night.

CHAPTER EIGHT

WOUNDED BIRD

"When my heart can beat no more, I hope I die for a principle, or a belief that I had lived for. I will die before my time, because I feel the shadows depth, so much I wanted to accomplish before I've reached my death." – Author Unknown

Quincy barked once in warning before they heard the stamp of boots and a knock on the door. It was mid-January, late afternoon, the sky was overcast and the house was gloomy and dim. Jess peeked out the peephole and saw it was one of the men who headed up the town militia. Her brain stumbled over his name, Ted…no, Todd Stevens.

Good God, we went out on two dates, why can't I remember his name?

He looked worried. Behind him, Jess could see his horse tied to the listing mailbox across the street.

"Who is it?" David's voice sounded at her ear and she flinched slightly.

Even after all this time she wasn't used to someone in her space, close to her, except maybe Jacob, who was walking now and clinging to her legs wherever she went.

"Todd Stevens here, I need to speak with Jess," Todd spoke through the door, his voice muffled by a scarf. He shivered slightly and bowed slightly at Jess as she opened the door, nodding gratefully when she invited him in.

He stomped the snow from his boots, unwrapped the scarf from his mouth and neck, and settled into an open seat at the kitchen table. Both Tina and Jacob were sleeping, curled together in a lump on the couch. They didn't wake.

"Something to warm you?" Jess asked, and Todd nodded gratefully, peeling his gloves off. His face was red where it had been exposed to the frigid air.

The cold snap had stopped everyone in their tracks, driving all occupants of Warsend inside. Even the plants in the greenhouse Jess and David had built died when the outside temperatures plummeted to the negative digits. It was one of the coldest winters in two decades.

Todd blew on his fingers and rubbed them

vigorously, wincing as the blood flow increased to the cold-stiffened digits, "We have a woman down at headquarters."

Headquarters was a small building off of Main Street that had housed a tiny museum and once been City Hall some eighty years ago.

"She's asking for you, Jess."

Jess stared at Todd blankly, "She's asking for me?"

"Yep." Todd accepted a steaming cup of chicory from David gratefully and rolled his eyes to the sky after the first sip. "Good sweet lord, that's good. Where in the world did you manage to find sugar, anyways?"

"Sugar beets. They make a fine substitute for sugar."

Jess smiled with pride; she had raised enough sugar beets to chop up and fill two gargantuan pots. She had then boiled them until they were soft. After removing the beets, she continued to boil the water, stirring it constantly, until it reached the consistency of honey. She had then set it aside to cool. Once cooled, the beet sugar had crystallized.

When they needed sugar they simply chiseled off a small hunk and drop it into a pot of chicory that they kept on the back burner. It was an especially nice treat now that the days were so frigidly cold.

Todd closed his eyes and smiled, "It sure hits the spot." His thoughts returned to business as he slurped down the last of the chicory.

"The woman's got a baby with her and she's been hurt, she's got a badly infected gunshot wound to one arm and she looks half-starved. Says she came here from Clinton?"

Jess gasped and she and David cried out at the same time, "Serena!"

Jess began pulling on her coat and gloves and a pair solid work boots. "There weren't any others with her? A man? A boy and a girl?"

Todd shook his head, "Nope, just her and the baby. She looks pretty bad off with that hurt wing of hers. The mayor told me to haul ass and come fetch you."

"I'll come too." David started to reach for his coat.

"We can't both go, David. Stay here, watch Jacob for me. I'll try not to be long."

Jess yanked on her two pairs of worn gloves. Each sported holes, but with two layers she ensured that most of her wouldn't end up being too exposed. David looked rebellious for a moment, but then nodded. He was feeling a bit stir-crazy these days. It was so cold and inhospitable outside that it was difficult to stay out for long. But inside the house, only the main living room and kitchen could be heated. There were days when it felt like all they did was trip and stumble over each other. But as much as he would like an escape, he couldn't leave Tina and Jacob alone in the house and it was bitterly cold out, too cold to expose either of them needlessly.

His shoulders slumped in resignation.

Jess smiled at him; she knew how he felt. "I'll make it up to you," she winked, "You can take my next watch shift."

With the movements of troops and scores of desperate, hungry people still out on the roads looking for something, anything that could be better than where they had come from, the militia had upped the watches. Jess and David were tapped regularly, along with the rest of the able-bodied population, and every few days one of them was sent to the town perimeter. There were miles of perimeter to watch, but in the two years since the invasion, the town had a rather effective system in place. Jess had seen towns that hadn't figured that out, and there wasn't much left of them.

"Gee, thanks." David replied sarcastically, while managing a half-hearted smile in return.

Jess finished pulling on her coat, three pairs of thick socks and some overly large rubber boots that had belonged to her dad. They weren't great at protecting from the cold but, for now, they were the best footwear available to her.

"Okay, I'm ready," she told Todd, who quickly downed the last of the chicory and smacked his lips in satisfaction.

He pulled on his gloves, wrapped his scarf back around his head and they left the house as quietly as possible.

"We can ride together," Todd suggested, and

then a slightly worried look crossed his face, "If you don't mind."

Jess steeled herself for the close contact. They hadn't spoken since the disastrous second date. It hadn't been his fault; Todd was a decent guy in his early 20s. He had been "nothing but a gentleman" as Jess's mother would have said, but she just wasn't ready for any kind of close contact with anyone of the opposite sex. The wounds were still there, the memories too fresh.

"It's fine," Jess said, forcing a smile. "Besides, we'll make better time."

He smiled down at her and held the horse still to make it easier for her to climb up. Then he swung into the saddle behind her. It was a close fit, but at least some parts of her would stay warm. Less than fifteen minutes later she struggled to slide off of the horse. Todd apologized even as he helped her safely down to the ground.

He's a good guy, she thought, *why can't I like him like that?*

The old post office on Main Street was now the town militia headquarters. Here is where they coordinated the watch duties of all of the town's able-bodied citizens. If you were old enough to hunt or work the land then you were old enough to defend your hometown. Some of the townsfolk had objected to the term 'able-bodied' and the ages, which were ten for firearms training and twelve for serving in the militia. But the concept of 'childhood' lasting until the artificial age of eighteen was as dead as the concept of an intact United States of America was.

Jess followed Todd into the building. It was warm at least, toasty warm. Every citizen of Warsend was required to serve the militia in some way, and not just on the active fighting side. There was wood to chop, bodies to feed, clothing to mend, and horses to care for. The low-slung building also contained several holding rooms for non-citizens and visitors, as well as a large barracks. Most of those who served with the militia did it in the same fashion as firefighters would have, on 24-hour shifts. Jess was exempted from this until Jacob was weaned, but she still had to serve lookout duty once per week.

They went directly to the front desk, where postal clerks had once stood, and a man that Jess couldn't remember the name of nodded at Todd.

"She's in the first room on the left. Doc's with her; she ain't doing well."

Jess could hear a baby wailing and the wail seemed to be coming closer. As Todd led the way through the access door to the main warehouse room, the wailing grew louder and closer. The massive room had once been used to sort incoming and outgoing mail, but now the racks were replaced with several large gun safes, barracks, and an industrial kitchen. The scents of breakfast still lingered in the air. Pancakes, judging by the sweet, rich smell of maple syrup.

Sarah walked toward them, a dark-haired baby wailing in her arms. Sarah's face was drawn with worry, "Hi Jess, how are you?" She jiggled the baby, made shushing noises at it. Jess just stared at the baby's face, horror mixing with recognition. The baby looked just like Jacob. "I have Laura fetching a cup of milk to feed this little one. She is absolutely starving and it looks like her mama might have dried up."

"Serena."

Sarah nodded, "You do know her, then. She says this little one's name is Rebecca, Becka for short."

Jess couldn't take her eyes off of the infant, "And the others?"

"There were no others, just Serena and the baby."

Jess's mind flashed to the two days spent outside of Clinton after they had left the cave. The man Brad, a very pregnant Serena, and the two kids, Max and…Annie? Yes, they had called the girl Annie. The baby continued to wail and Jess's breasts swelled in response, filling with milk, threatening to leak through her shirt.

"I'll take her," she said, and held her hands out to the baby. She was tiny, smaller than Jacob had been at that age, and she loosened her jacket and looked for a quiet corner. "I…uh…"

Sarah's eyes widened, "Oh, of course! Perhaps you should come into the other holding room. It's vacant, and there is a chair and a bed inside."

Jess nodded, "It won't take long. She's just hungry, that's all."

Sarah ushered her into the holding room while Todd stood back, looking uncomfortable. The door closed and Jess lay the baby down on the bed, slipped out of her coat and loosened her shirt. Little Becka did not hesitate and eagerly began to suck on a breast, drawing in the milk with a desperate hunger. How long had it been since this child had been fed? Jess could feel the baby's body relax; here was comfort, warmth, and food. It wasn't until that moment that it felt strange at all—nursing another woman's child—and Jess thought of how it must have been in ages past, before there was formula. Would a woman do this for another? They must have and it seemed like the right thing to do. Moments passed and Jess could hear the baby's rhythmic gulps as she took in the nourishment. Sarah had said that she thought Serena had lost her milk; how long had she been without it? How long had this baby been hungry?

It would be a solid thirty minutes before the baby stopped nursing and fell deeply asleep in Jess's arms.

YOUNG LOVE

"Love possesses not nor will it be possessed, for love is sufficient unto love." – Kahlil Gibran

The knock on the door came early; the sun was just beginning to peek over the horizon. Fenton, an early-riser out of decades of habit, muttered with no small level of concern as he limped over to the front door. He peered out of the window first; the kidnapping of Liza and murder of the Austin family the year before had left an indelible mark on everyone. Even young Joseph was armed with a small pistol when he ventured outside the house.

In the gloom Fenton recognized Carl Owens. His

black hair was tousled and he looked worried. He had just brought his hand up to knock again when Fenton opened the door.

He nodded at Fenton, "Morning, sir. I'm sorry to bother you so early, but I need to speak to Liza, if you please."

Fenton was perplexed. Carl was a nice young man, and certainly had his manners, except for the showing up at the crack of dawn part of things.

"Son, don't you think it's a tad early to come a'visitin'?"

Carl had become a regular visitor on the farm during the past summer. At first he had come with the excuse of helping out on the farm, something he had done in the past, but when he and Liza would scoot off together to go "work in the field" or "check for blueberries," Fenton had been sure it was more than helping out.

He hadn't been so keen on Carrie and Chris, and Liza was a full three years younger than her sister. The world might be different from when he was growing up, but some things didn't change that quickly so he had decided to keep a close eye on the two.

Carl blushed red, right to the tips of his ears, "No sir…I mean, yes sir, it's too early…I mean…" The boy took a deep breath and started again, "My mom's asked for her to come and see to Dad. He's not been feeling well. She said it's urgent, sir. She asked me to fetch Liza right away."

John Carter had been in Carl's life since he was a young boy. Fenton had always wondered why the man hadn't gone ahead and adopted Carl, especially since it was obvious how devoted he was to the boy and his mother. But for whatever reason, Carl's last name was different, and even after they had married and Tabitha had come along, that had not changed.

Chris had appeared at Fenton's elbow and Liza called from down the hall, "I'm coming! I'm coming! Just let me get my bag." Her voice still sounded heavy with sleep. There was still a congested wheeze to it. They were all recovering from the inevitable winter cold, with Joseph still in bed with a fever, coughing and whiny.

Chris nodded to Carl, "It'll take her a minute, Carl, why don't you come on in?"

Fenton looked embarrassed that he hadn't thought to ask the boy in out of the cold before Chris did. He shooed the boy inside, closing the door, and wished his knee didn't ache so during the winter. It made him more irritable than usual and he still felt bad for snapping at Joseph the night before after the little boy had whined about his congested nose.

If his wife Molly were still alive she would have gently reminded him that children were only small for a painfully short time, and to be patient, and not to snap. He sighed; how he wished Molly had lived to see their son Isaac's children…she would have loved being a grandmother.

But Molly had died when their son was still in high school. Isaac had grown up, gone off to college, and found the girl of his dreams in that bustling metropolis New York. Fenton had looked forward to each summer and winter visit when the kids were small. First it was just the three of them visiting, Isaac, Amy, and little baby Carrie. Before long they had added Liza, and then long after Liza, when Carrie was a teenager and Liza not far behind, Fenton had gotten the news.

"We're having one more, Dad." Fenton had heard Isaac's voice, excited and tinny over his cell phone, "Amy and I decided we would try just one more time. She's just entering her second trimester, so it's safe to tell everyone. The baby's due in mid-March and we just had the ultrasound done. She's having a boy! Amy and the girls are so excited! But hey, I gotta go, my train is here. I love you, Dad and we'll be heading down for Turkey Day, we'll see you then. Love you, Dad."

The phone had cut out before Fenton had a chance to tell his son he loved him too. It was the last conversation they would ever have. Hours later, in the deep of the night the phone rang again. He had answered it and heard the awful news. Isaac would never get the chance to meet his son. A series of terrorist bombings had taken the lives of over 1,600 innocent victims. Isaac's body, along with 83 others, was never found.

By Christmas, Fenton's home was full; Amy and

the girls had packed up their tiny New York apartment and moved to Tennessee. Amy's parents had both died years before and she had been an only child like Isaac. With a baby on the way, and Amy a stay-at-home mom since Liza was born, it made the most sense. They settled into the farm and the girls adjusted to small-town life and living on a farm.

After little Joseph was born two weeks early, Amy's will to live just seemed to vanish. Amy had slowly faded away, consumed by grief at the loss of Isaac in the Amtrak Train Bombings, and the undiagnosed cancer that the doctors found far too late. They had buried her in the family cemetery, with Joseph barely six months old.

"He's been vomiting for a while now, but there's nothing left, and he's complaining of pretty severe cramping. Mom's worried it might be his appendix."

Fenton's knee ached, creaking painfully as he shifted his stance, bringing him out of the past and firmly back to the present. Liza was questioning Carl about John as she pulled on her boots. There had been a recent snow and now the roads and paths around the farm were nothing but mud. Chris made a mental note to start collecting and hauling the smooth river rock near the cabin to pave the most heavily used paths. It would cut down on the mess, complaining, and cleaning that everyone seemed to be obsessed with by mid-winter.

"How long ago did he start vomiting?" Liza asked Carl. She was in her element, not fluttery or lovesick or making moon-eyes at her boyfriend. Instead she was focused, intense, and professional.

"I think it's been since last night. He did some fishin' down at Reelfoot, spent the day," Carl answered, running fingers through his tangled hair, suddenly fully aware of his appearance, even if Liza wasn't.

Liza nodded and pulled on her coat, reaching down for the medical bag. "Right, well, let's get going."

Carrie appeared at that moment, yawning, "What's going on?" Chris explained and Carrie just smothered another yawn and offered to make coffee. Liza shook her head and headed for the door, Carl trailing uncertainly behind.

Liza kissed Fenton on the cheek as she left, "Love you, Gramps." She turned and waved to the rest of them. "See you all later, please make sure and cover for me on chores, I'm not sure when I'll be back."

And with that, she was out the door, Carl close on her heels.

Fenton stared at the closed door, unsure of what to do. Liza was barely fifteen years old, and people were sending for her as if she were a full-fledged doctor. It boggled his mind. This was the first pre-dawn trip anyone had ever made to the Perdue farm asking for the girl, but from the looks of it, it wouldn't be the last. For a moment the old man was disconcerted and uneasy. *What was this world coming to, that others would look to a teenage girl for their doctoring?*

Chris put a hand on his shoulder, "We should all be proud of Liza, Gramps. She's taking on a lot, learning medicine like she is. She's taken care of you when you were hurt and I wouldn't be walking as well as I am if it hadn't been for her."

Chris was referring to the two separate ankle injuries that Liza had helped splint and heal for him. Fenton had managed to split his scalp open enough to need stitches more than a year ago. Recently the old man had figured out that Liza was adding some stuff to his coffee that thickened it up. He couldn't even pronounce the first word.

"Dia…diatom…"

"Diatomaceous earth, Gramps," Liza had told him patiently. "It helps with your blood pressure and cholesterol levels, and it helps a little with your knee pain and flexibility."

"There's nothin' wrong with my knee, young lady," he had told her, feeling old and weak and not liking the feeling of his own mortality at all that morning.

"Oh Gramps, just drink your coffee." She had watched him stand there, digging his heels into the rug at the base of his easy chair, the cup of untouched coffee in his hand. "Please, Gramps? It's good for you, I promise."

"Gramps?" Chris was still there, his hand on the old man's shoulder. Fenton came back to the present, with a soft sigh and shook his head.

Page | 113

"That doggone girl left without givin' me that diatom, that diatom…"

"Diatomaceous earth, Gramps?" Chris asked, a small smile on his face. He turned toward the kitchen, "She's told me how much to add; c'mon, I'll make you some." And Fenton followed, lost again in thoughts of how proud Molly would have been of her grandchildren.

Carl had not driven the Carter's van, which had been converted to biodiesel. They still had to go to a great deal of trouble to make the biodiesel, so a horse worked best for trips that didn't require hauling the entire family. One of the other families in town had started a small horse-breeding business. It was just enough to ensure that there were horses available for riding any time of day or night. They were housed in a communal stable near the Trade Mart and were guarded by the town watch at night.

A placid dappled mare was standing in the front of the Perdue house, reins lashed to the railing of the wrap-around porch. Carl held Liza's bag while she slid onto the horse and then climbed up behind her.

They hadn't been this close since the fall, when he had come out to help with picking the bushels of apples in the orchard. They had escaped to the woods, to the old cabin there, and made out for a few minutes, the most they could manage without Fenton's intervention. He had almost caught them kissing once and Liza had told Carl to stay away for a full month afterward. Liza's grandfather had not taken well to how Chris and Carrie had started their relationship, and he was even more watchful now as a result.

The mare started out at a good trot. It wasn't far to town. Carl was distracted by Liza's warmth and close proximity. He nuzzled her ear.

"So he's been vomiting for most of a day. Did he bring back any catch?" Liza said all business and not the least bit distracted or interested in his romantic advances.

Carl sat back, embarrassed; after all, his dad was sick, and he should be focusing on that, not trying to make moves on his girl. What was he thinking?

"Yeah, about six bass, maybe seven."

"Did he eat any out at the lake?"

"I dunno…maybe. Why?"

"Well, it could be that he undercooked the fish and has gotten some parasite, but that would be awful fast. Or possibly if he drank the water that could be a contributing factor."

She stared off in the distance and the horse trotted along, working at the problem, occasionally asking questions that Carl struggled to answer. It was a different side of her, one he had barely seen. He stared at her thinking she sounded so, so, *clinical*. Part of him, the young hormonal side, stung from the utter lack of response his advances had garnered. The other side of him was experiencing a dawning level of deep respect for Liza. She was focused and intense and dedicated. How often could you say that of a fifteen-year-old girl?

Carl thought about the hybrid bicycle he had been working on with Wes Perkins and Jim Dorian, who owned and ran the town's junkyard. Wes was his mom's cousin, and he had explained that Jim Dorian was autistic, but smart, "kind of like the guy in *Rain Man*," and then had to fill in the story since Carl had never seen the movie. Carl hung out with Wes far more than his mom knew or would approve of. Carl's mother Abby, a kind and down-to-earth woman, was uncharacteristically disapproving of her first cousin and sternly ordered Carl to stay away.

Carl had heard the talk and he could barely remember his cousins, a boy and a girl, he had played with when they were all very young. Their mother had disappeared with them years and years ago, taking them away from the angry, hard-drinking, abusive man that had returned from the Gulf War.

Mom didn't see it, but Carl did. Wes had changed. Slowly, but he had changed. Although, the man had practically become a walking arsenal after the attack a few years back by the Western Front. Wes's girlfriend, Angie, had died in the attack while Wes had been off hunting.

That had really shook Carl up; he had liked Angie. More than that, he had liked how Angie had settled Wes and made him not so hard around the edges. For a while after she had died, Wes had taken to spending long days on watch and riding the others to establish the town watch in a more formal manner than they had before. It had saved lives, and there wasn't much anyone could argue with his methodology after that.

After the raid and murder of the Austin family and kidnapping of Liza, Wes had changed again, in a good way, at least in Carl's estimation. Even Mom had noticed.

Abby had said drily, "I didn't think it was possible, but Wes isn't quite the bastard I'd thought him to be."

Carl had overheard her say it, with her not realizing he was close by. When Carl had the idea of creating a hybrid bicycle and cart, one that would work on human pedal power but also carry a light electric charge and make pulling heavy loads easy for one person to do, he had stopped by Wes's and then they had headed for Dorian's Junkyard.

Pretty soon they had found an ancient moped, one that actually included pedals along with its tiny motor. At present they were weighing the need for a bigger engine with the priority of keeping it as lightweight as possible, two conflicting goals. Every time he managed to escape from chores, or when he wasn't trying to see Liza, Carl had been at the junkyard, up to his elbows in grease and dirt as they worked to rebuild the ugly creation into a hybrid of lightweight efficiency and power. Like Liza, Carl was just as focused and intense. The realization struck him that it wasn't a bad thing, how clinical she was. Just as it wasn't a bad thing how involved he had become in the hybrid bike. It was the new normal.

They had passed the sentries, waved at the men in the towers and tried to ignore the ruined vehicles with the grisly blackened skeletons inside. Wes had explained what a deterrent the sight was to those infrequent visitors who came to town. They were usually traders, as Tiptonville didn't get many passersby since the town had never been on what would be described as a major thoroughfare, but Wes had told Carl and countless others that one never knew a man's intentions.

"They could be scouts, remnants of a renegade army, like those four men were, you never know. Those corpses on the side of the road will remind outsiders that we fight back, and win. It's a better show of force than the men in the towers will ever be."

Still, the sight of the grinning, blackened skeletons turned many people's stomachs. They understood the necessity, but in a way it seemed inhuman. Those men had been people, and many of the residents murmured that they deserved a decent Christian burial. Carl wasn't so sure about the Christian part, but he agreed it was hard to go through here without feeling a crawling sense of disquiet. If Wes could hear Carl's thoughts, he would have pointed out that that was exactly the point in having them there.

"I'm sorry," Liza's said abruptly.

"Huh? What for?" Carl asked, wondering if he

had missed something she said.

She turned back and kissed him. "I didn't mean to ignore you earlier. I was concentrating on the symptoms and all that."

Carl grinned and kissed her back. "Never feel sorry for being who you are, Liza." He pulled her close, "I think it's pretty cool that you are the town doc."

As the buildings on the outskirts of Tiptonville appeared, they pulled apart and Carl quickened the pace of the mare with a click and sharp rap of his heels in the horse's side. Within moments they had arrived at the small, nondescript house that John Carter had bought for his wife and stepson. Along with Tabitha, Carl's younger half-sister, they had lived there comfortably before The Collapse. Now the tiny yard sported a chicken coop, cold frames, and several projects at various stages of completion.

One of them was a windmill, inspired by the two that Chris had made at the Perdue farm. The first windmill that Chris had created powered the pump that brought water directly into the house from the well, just as was done in the days before city water. The water tower had been felled by the invasion of Western Front troops over two years ago and the citizens lacked the tools and materials to replace it. This meant that many wells had needed to be dug. Water became a precious commodity, hard to obtain, and nearly impossible to store.

The second had provided some electricity—not

enough to power the hot water heater that Chris had originally envisioned, but enough to allow them to extend the day somewhat with lights at night. It had helped immeasurably during the long winter months when the days were short on daylight but still long on tasks. When Carl had returned home from a visit to the Perdue farm, he had told John about it, which had prompted a visit to the Perdue's and then a trip to Dorian's Junkyard for parts.

Carl slipped off the horse and tethered it to the picket fence surrounding the small house. Then he reached up and helped Liza down. Not that she needed the help, but Carl had been taught well by his stepfather.

Normally John would be out by now, rummaging about in his project piles. The man rose with the sun, which was now lighting up the sky, a fiery ball in the east, and would putter about for hours outside. Today, though, he was in the house, vomiting and shivering violently. For a man so seldom sick, it was concerning for all of them to see him in such a state. It was a small wonder that Abby had sent her son to fetch Liza.

As they entered the house, the smell of sickness hit them like a cloud. Liza winced; this was definitely one of the areas of her new role that she wished she didn't have to endure. She had always had a sensitive nose and today was no exception. After leaving the cool, clean wood smoke-tinged air of the outside, the smell was an affront to her nasal passages.

Carl's mother Abby leaned out of the hall bathroom, peering through the gloom of the hallway, and called out, "Thank goodness you're here, Liza. He just keeps throwing up…and other things…I hope you can help."

Carl watched as Liza bustled down the hallway, doctor bag in hand, and on into the bathroom with Abby. Tabitha had woken to the sound of Carl and Liza arriving and stood in her bedroom doorway, rubbing sleepily at her eyes.

Carl smiled at his little sister, "Hey Tabby, mornin' kitty-cat."

Tabitha smiled at her brother, "Morning Carl." She looked confused then, "What's Liza doing here?"

"Just checking up on Dad, he's feeling kind of sick." He reached down and scooped her up, "Want some breakfast?"

He turned and headed toward the kitchen. He could hear Liza asking questions about John's fishing trip and whether he had eaten any fish there.

"Daddy's sick?" Tabitha asked, "Oh, poor Daddy!" She paused for a moment, "Carl?"

"Yeah, kiddo?"

"Is Liza your girlfriend? Joseph says you and Liza kiss each other when Grampa Fenton isn't looking."

Carl grinned, "Yeah, she's my girlfriend. But don't tell Grampa Fenton, okay?"

Tabitha grinned back, "It's a secret?" She was very into secrets recently and had finally figured out that secrets were something you didn't blab to everyone, otherwise they wouldn't be secrets.

"Yeah, sort of. So, let's cook up some eggs for everyone, okay kitty-cat?"

Tabitha giggled, "For Liza too, okay?" Carl nodded, and then the little girl asked, "Is Liza the town doctor now?"

"Yup, she sure is." Carl felt a curious thrill of pride. In the world that was, one that Carl barely remembered, he and Liza were merely children. But in the world of now, the one they all seemed rather stuck in, Liza was a doctor, and he was, well, what was he? Carl had yet to figure that out.

As Carl and Tabitha prepared breakfast, and Liza diagnosed John's illness as probably due to some undercooked fish, Carl thought about the future and what his place was in it. In the world that was, his thoughts would have been surprising and unusual for his age. But in the world of now, it seemed he was right on target. He had an attractive, brilliant girlfriend, two loving parents, and a sweet little sister.

But for the first time it struck Carl that he should be thinking about what he wanted to do. Did he want to putter with the bicycle hybrid that he and Wes and Jim Dorian had been working on? Did he want to become a farmer like Fenton Perdue and Chris? Was his future in hunting and fighting like Cousin Wes?

Later, as most of the family settled in for a hearty breakfast of eggs and greens from the cold frames,

Carl looked over at Liza, her blond hair a rumpled mess from her hurried departure this morning, and saw his future. He might be just a few months shy of sixteen, but he knew what he wanted.

He wanted *her*.

ANOTHER ORPHAN

"Seeing Serena, and holding Becka for the first time, it brought back all of those memories. I looked at Becka, took in that straight, dark hair and those pale-as-ice blue eyes, and it just shook me. Here was Jacob's half-sister, both of them, fathered by that monster. Life had emerged from such evil and pain and death. Others would have taken her, wanted to take her, but I told them 'no'. I told them Serena wanted me to take Becka, had begged me to, and that I could handle it. It was the least I could do for her. If only I had tried harder, if only I could have convinced her and Brad to come with us. In the end? Becka was family, she…fit. And I can't imagine life without her. – Jess's Journal

Anthony Ridley, the town doctor, was waiting by the closed door. He shook his head slightly at Jess as she approached the room where they were holding Serena.

"She's in and out of consciousness," he told her, "If I had been able to treat her sooner…but she's got blood poisoning, a high fever, and we don't have any antibiotics. I take it you know her?"

Jess nodded, "I met her on the way back here. We were on the outskirts of Clinton, her group was moving toward Clinton and we were leaving. From what I could see, there wasn't anything left for them to go back to. A lot of troop movements back and forth—different factions, and Clinton had practically been burned to the ground." Todd had rejoined her and was listening intently. "I asked her to come with us, but she had a man with her, a boy and a girl…" Her voice trailed off and both men looked grim.

"She was definitely on her own," Todd said, "One of the militia patrols found her on the edge of town, unconscious, in the trees. If it hadn't been for the baby crying, we would have never known she was there. But I know this; there wasn't anyone else with her."

"Can I see her now?"

The doctor nodded. Sarah offered to take the baby, who was sleeping peacefully in Jess's arms and Jess shook her head. If Serena was awake, she would want to see Becka. The room was dark, except for a small light in the corner, and it held a certain unexplainable smell. Serena was a tiny mound in the bed, barely breathing, her arm bandaged and hair matted with filth. Her skin was covered with a sheen of sweat and it looked mottled, red and white blotched, except for one eye which was swollen, and the eye socket looked fractured. She was painfully thin and Jess was sure this had affected her ability to produce any milk.

The baby, Becka, was deeply asleep in Jess's arms, her tiny belly swollen and full of milk. Serena's eyes fluttered when Jess said her name, but she didn't stir. Not once.

Hours passed, people came and went, and Jess sat in a small chair by Serena's cot. Waiting for Serena to wake up, worrying about the others and wondering if she should go ahead and send for David and the kids. In the end, a diaper change with Becka awake and fretful decided the matter. The baby kicked at Jess irritably, reaching for her mother, over and over. Serena finally roused, her eyes dull and confused. She turned her head and saw Jess.

"Jess?" she whispered, "They found you."

Jess smiled at the woman and took her cold hand in her warm ones. How could Serena be sweating and cold at the same time? Anthony Ridley had been in twice since Jess sat down to check on Serena. He had explained again, quietly, that there was nothing more that he could do for her. His knowledge was limited, after all. He was actually just a medical student and had been away in medical school before the Collapse. He had explained that the mottled skin, the difficulty breathing, all of these things pointed toward a steady decline and eventual death. The end was coming soon.

In some ways, it was harder to deal with. Here was a living, breathing human being. There would be no sudden death, only a slow journey into oblivion. Jess had seen plenty of violent, sudden death. This was new and uncharted territory.

She waited for Serena to say more, but she had slipped away into unconsciousness. Jess sat there, watching Serena and Becka. Becka had cuddled against her mother and fallen asleep again, her tiny body curled against her mother, reassured by her presence. Jess wondered for the hundredth time what had happened to Serena, Brad, and the two children. Her eyes became heavy and, just as she was about to slip into a doze, Serena spoke. Jess's eyes flew open. Serena was awake and looked…lucid.

"You were right, Jess, we never should have gone to Clinton." She whispered it, her voice weak and cracked. Jess leaned in close so that she wouldn't miss any words—words were precious now, numbered and limited. Serena continued, "They're all gone. Brad, Annie, and Max. All of them. I just… ran. I didn't know what else to do. I…took Becka… and I…ran." Her words came in short spurts; she sounded winded and exhausted.

Jess tried to shush her, to tell her they had time

to talk later, but somehow Serena sensed how little time they had left.

She touched her sleeping baby's face gently, "Dark hair, and those ice-blue eyes, Jess. She's Jacob's sister." Serena turned and smiled at Jess.

"You were right, about everything. It was okay at first, a struggle, and Brad loved her even though she wasn't his." She stopped, and Jess thought she had fallen back asleep.

"Please love her, Jess. Be her mother."

The last thing Jess needed was another baby to care for. They were struggling to survive as it was, and she closed her eyes so she couldn't see Serena's face begging her. She didn't *want* this baby. Jacob, with his dark hair, sometimes brought back nightmarish flashes of those dark months inside of Tent Five. But he was hers, and had her deep blue eyes.

Becka was what Cooper surely looked like as a baby. She was beautiful, no question, but it would be like having a reminder of that monster day in and day out in her own home. How could Serena ask this of her? She opened her eyes and saw Serena's gaze had not wavered.

"You'll be better soon."

"Don't lie to me, Jess. I'm dying and I know it. Please take Becka. Take her now and do this for me, please. I know I've no right to ask this, but I need your promise. I need to know that," again Serena paused and gathered the strength to continue to speak, "she will be with family who loves her."

Jess felt a huge surge of panic, "Serena, I don't know if I can love her like that. She looks so much like *him*. I…" She felt such a horrible dread in denying this dying woman her request, but the fear it evoked was overwhelming.

Serena smiled weakly, "Do you remember what you said to me when we met, Jess? You said that Becka was a part of me and that I would find the love inside me when she was born. You were right; she's *my child*. She's all things good, despite her beginnings." She took a deep breath, "So Jess, I'm asking you to love *my child* as your own. Please. *You*…no one else. Let me die knowing she is loved, because you have that in you, like no one else I know."

And after a long, painful moment Jess had said yes, the tears welling in her eyes. There had been no more words between them. Serena's plea had taken every last bit of life and strength that she had in her. Moments later, the woman fell into a restless sleep, her breathing hitching and rattling in her throat. Dr. Ridley assured her there was nothing more to be done and Jess asked Todd for a ride back home.

They bundled the baby up in a swath of blankets. The night was full of stars and frigid. Jess covered Becka's face lightly, trying to keep the baby as warm as possible. The horse's hooves rang out on the cement, echoing off of deserted buildings and past the lowing cattle. They rode back to Jess's little house in silence.

As they turned off of 163rd Street, Todd spoke, "She asked you to take the baby, didn't she?"

"Yeah."

"Are you going to be okay?" he asked, kindly.

"Sometimes I wonder if any of us will ever be okay again," Jess said softly.

"Jess, if anyone can make it, you will. You are stronger than you realize. That woman made the right choice." Todd's kind words warmed her in the bitter cold of the night.

Jess didn't trust herself to answer. The day had been overwhelming; the near future seemed just as daunting. She hugged the squirming baby close and then handed Becka to Todd to hold while she slid off of the horse.

"I'll make sure someone lets you know when she wakes up again," Todd said. But Jess knew that Serena probably wouldn't last the night. All of her dwindling energy had been put into making sure Becka was here, with Jess and Jacob.

"Come in for a cup of coffee?" she found herself asking, her voice cracking with the effort.

"No, I'm headed home." Todd reached down and touched her cold cheek with his gloved hand, "Get some food and rest, Jess."

In the months that followed, he visited often, bringing extra meat and provisions for Jess and her little family. So did others. The baby thrived and Jess's small family did as well. Before long, they couldn't imagine their world without Becka in it.

WHAT ARE THEY GOOD FOR?

The soul is healed by being with children." – Fyodor Dostoevsky

Camelia tried to ignore the growing agony; this was *not* the time. The lights flickered for the third time since she had begun surgery on a badly wounded Amerika Reborn soldier. He was young, maybe nineteen at most, and had tried to make a name for himself by rushing a small settlement a few miles to the east. Like the Amerika Reborn group, their target had chosen an old campground and was just a little more successful at farming than the AR. Small surprise there.

The only thing these idiots know how to do is shoot guns and run their mouths about "coloreds," Camelia thought to herself.

The raid had been a failure. Two men dead, this one on her table badly hurt, and no food to show for it. As much as she hated him, Camelia knew that if Sulwyn hadn't held Cooper back from the raid, it would have probably been successful. Alenoush had heard that the other settlement, in addition to the crime of sheltering a black "colored" family, had also had a small herd of goats. Meat was in short supply these days, and Camelia's mouth watered at the thought of it.

"I *need* those lights to stay on," she snapped. If she could just get the artery sutured closed he would have a chance. If he hadn't lost too much blood, that is. The lights flickered a fourth time and her belly rippled, agonizing pain shooting into her buttocks, up her back and down her legs. She didn't have much more time before…she bent over in agony, her sight temporarily blurring.

"What's *wrong* with you?" Alenoush hissed in panic. Blood still terrified her and despite a year of training she couldn't even handle a simple surgery without turning green at the gills.

Camelia would have laughed if it weren't for the agony she felt. *Sulwyn sure knew how to pick them.* Her belly twisted again and her sight blurred. It had been a hard pregnancy. She'd been sick for more than five months, barely able to keep food down, and then when it had finally subsided she had dealt with more difficulties.

She glared at the fool girl who had been sent to her to learn doctoring. Sulwyn had turned her over to Camelia only because Alenoush was completely hopeless at warfare, guns, or much of anything else. Months before, while handling a gun in weapons training, she had accidentally shot and killed her training partner. Sulwyn had been disgusted with her, but stuck her with Camelia as a last resort. Like the rest, she had taken on a white name. At eighteen, Alenoush Swiftblade wasn't very swift with any kind of blade and looked as if she were close to vomiting.

Camelia snapped at the girl, "I'm in labor, you fool. Now hold this clamp and don't move."

When her condition had become apparent, Sulwyn had summoned her, questioned her at length. And although she was tempted to tell him who the father was, she was far more frightened of what would happen to her if she did. Cooper had already firmly entrenched himself into the Amerika Reborn's leadership. He would find a way to hurt her, or the baby, who hadn't had a choice in any of this. Add to that severe leg swelling, back pain, and spiking blood pressure, Camelia would count herself lucky if she managed to keep this baby.

Sulwyn had not been pleased and he had looked positively enraged when she blithely replied, "Immaculate conception." If the Amerika Reborn group hadn't need her doctoring skills so badly he probably would have had her shot where she stood. As it was he had knocked her to the ground with a sharp crack of his open palm on the side of her head.

She gathered her strength as another massive contraction hit, breathed through it, and then focused on the man on the table. The lights flickered on and off twice more before she was finished. It looked as if the generator was going out, or that the AR had managed to steal a batch of bad gas on their last raid. Either was possible, and by the time she finished with the AR soldier on the table she was in too much pain to care.

Hours later, Alenoush washed and swaddled the tiny red-faced baby while Camelia cleaned herself up. The child was quiet; he had barely cried when he was born and was staring about in wide-eyed wonder at the new world he found himself in. This quiet demeanor would serve him well and allow him to survive the years to come.

Alenoush, known once upon a time as Trudy Denkins, smiled at the baby and cooed at him. She wasn't a complicated girl, rather simple-minded really, which made Sulwyn's choice to establish her as the next doctor so laughable in Camelia's eyes. She wasn't even as rabidly racist as most of them, and was delighted with the baby.

"He's beautiful, Camelia. And he's not so brown-skinned like you," the girl said smiling, truly unaware of unbelievably stupid she sounded, "He could pass for white."

"Could he now?" Camelia's response was dry.

"Oh yes!" the girl replied, then cooed again at the baby. Her admiration of the infant was interrupted by a voice at the doorway.

"So this is what has everyone in a dither," Scott Cooper said, leaning against the frame.

Camelia felt a line of fear run through her. "Is there something you need, Cooper?" she asked as evenly as possible.

She reached out and took the baby from Alenoush. He was so impossibly tiny in her arms, so perfect.

His eyes flickered over the child for a brief moment, taking in the dark hair and eyes, the pale skin. The boy was several shades more pale than Camelia's bronze skin. "What are they good for, anyway?"

Camelia wouldn't respond; she couldn't. This man had given her a baby, but it certainly wasn't out of love, or even kindness. He obviously cared nothing for children. He had told her as much, told her that there had been other women who showed, and that he had ended their lives.

The fact that she was the only doctor, and therefore under Sulwyn's protection, however limited that might be, meant that he hadn't killed her. But he had warned her that if she told, thereby endangering him and his progress inching up the racist neo-Nazi group ladder, that he would end her

Page | 137

life and the baby's.

Sulwyn had suspected that Cooper was the father of the baby. It wouldn't do for Sulwyn's new right-hand man to be coupling with a "disease-infested colored Spic"—especially since his precious daughter Delwen had professed an interest in pairing with him. It was why he had held Cooper back from the last two raids, which had had devastating results. Three men dead, one badly injured, and two horses lost to the group. The men had grown to depend on Cooper's tactical knowledge and fought well under him. Without him, they fell into a state of disorganization worse than they were before his arrival.

Cooper strode into the room and with one quick move pulled the baby from Camelia's arms. She screamed, "Wait!" she thought a moment and then blurted out, "I'm not telling you who the father is, but if you kill my baby, you can just forget about me doctoring another person, because I won't do it. That's my price. Let him live, let me care for him, and I'll keep doctoring." She felt a presence in the doorway, but ignored it, "I swear to you, I'll help no one if you hurt my baby. He's *mine*."

Sulwyn spoke from the doorway, "Give her back the little brat." He glared at her, "Threaten me again and I'll kill you and your half-breed runt. Caring for it had better not affect your doctoring or any other duties."

And he walked away, satisfied that Cooper

couldn't be the father—otherwise why would she have said to Cooper she wasn't going to tell him who the baby daddy was? For all he knew it could have been one of those idiots who had died on recent raids. Cooper was clean. It looked as if Delwen would get what she wanted after all.

Inside the room Cooper gave the tiny bundle back to Camelia, gave her a cold smile, and left the room. She released a breath she hadn't realized she had been holding until that moment. He was hers; she could keep him. She looked down into his warm brown eyes, his perfect face, and soft downy black hair. *Hers.*

Alenoush moved closer and touched the tiny patch of soft, downy hair on his tiny head. "What are you going to name him?"

Camelia's thoughts turned to a memory of a smiling Hispanic man, standing outside her car window, with soft black hair and warm, brown eyes. The rifle strapped to his back was unusual, but then again, the whole trip from New York had been surreal. Military everywhere, helicopters and unusual military aircraft filling the skies, checkpoints and questions about where she was heading, and long stares at her scars.

She had answered them all calmly, "I'm heading to Texas, and I've been offered a nursing position there."

The nursing home was filled with a mixture of elderly residents and a special wing for burn victims.

The perfect place for her, she had thought, a place she could fit in and not be stared at every day.

"Run out of gas?" he had asked her.

"Yes, it looks like it. I hoped I could make it to the next gas station. The ATMs were all down, and none of the bigger gas stations were willing to take my credit card," she had said to him. "I turned off the main roads, hoping to find a smaller place, but…" She tried not to feel nervous; after all, he didn't have the rifle in his *hands.*

"I'm Armando," he had said, reaching out a hand, "Armando Velasquez." She had taken his hand, shook it, and then he had said, "I'm really sorry I can't help with gas, there's been nothing but shortages in the area, but my house is just up the hill there."

He pointed and continued, "If you like, you could try calling someone to come pick you up."

"There's really no one to call." She realized as the words were coming out how bad that sounded. What if he were some crazy serial killer?

"I mean, I was headed to Texas, and…" She stopped when she saw the man shake his head and look sick. "What?"

"It's just that I heard over the emergency radio, well, there's been a nuke in Austin," Armando told her.

"What?! That's, that's…I mean, it's impossible. You can't be serious. What, who…" She stopped and took a breath, struggling to conceptualize of a nuke inside U.S. borders, "Why would someone do that?"

Armando shrugged, "I don't know. Things have been getting rather scary in the last few days. The military is putting up barricades, shutting down borders to the southern states. It looks as if…well, as if the United States is at war."

"With who?"

"With itself."

Camelia stood by the side of her car in shock. A thousand questions raced through her head.

Eventually, she let him help her move the car off of the road and bring her bags, and eventually her boxes of books and other necessities she couldn't live without, up to his large, sturdy home. There they would listen to the increasingly bizarre news reports on the emergency radio. Armando lived there alone. H was a widower, his wife having died in a car crash several years before. Slowly she told him the story of her scars, the remains of what extensive plastic surgery could not fix. She had survived the Amtrak Train Bombings, when so many others had perished. The scars, she said, were a testament to her will to survive.

He had touched them, ran long gentle fingers over the ridge of scars on her face, and told her she was beautiful, inside and out. She had stayed in his house, and they had fallen in love, quietly survived the chaos in the secluded mountain retreat. They had soon welcomed two more Hispanic families when the sentiments of the area had turned ugly and desperate.

A racist group, a leftover of the American Nazi Party, had been blaming the war and the nuke in Austin on Mexico. Between shortages of food, no power, and an intermittent water supply, the few Hispanic families in the area stuck out like sore thumbs. They had banded together, worked the land, traded with those who weren't spouting racist rhetoric, and kept to themselves. Camelia hated the memories of those last few moments, when the Amerika Reborn group had attacked them without provocation, seeking to rob them of what little food and supplies they had.

Armando had fought. All of them had. When Maria, the smiling, round-cheeked mother of two teenaged boys had fallen, though, Camelia had laid down her gun and got to doctoring. She had tried in vain to save the woman who had come to be her closest friend and confidante next to Armando. After that, the boys, Maria's husband, even Armando had fallen while she was busy trying to save Carlos, a young newlywed. As she worked, the southern wall was on fire, the fire set by the attackers.

The Amerika Reborn soldiers had grabbed supplies, ripped the medical supplies from the table next to her and even the needle and thread from her hand after Sulwyn stopping them from shooting her, seeing her medical expertise in action. She had been a fine ER nurse prior to the bombings, but scars like hers scared the patients too much. She had screamed and fought them, even as they pulled her from the burning building and past Armando's lifeless body. She had kicked them, bit at them, and tried to get away, until a hard punch had knocked her out and carried her away into the darkness, away from everyone she had come to love. And here she had been ever since, nothing better than a slave, nothing more than a tool to be used at the whim of Amerika Reborn.

Until now.

Tears came then, as she held the infant in her arms. How she and Armando had tried to have a baby, despite the troubles surrounding them. Armando had called it an act of faith, that the world would get better, that life would return to normal. But each month, there was such disappointment, no matter how often she prayed for "just one chance."

She stared at the baby's beautiful brown eyes and saw instead the eyes of the kindest man she had ever known reaching out to brush her hair from her face and tell her she was beautiful, telling her that the scars didn't matter to him. *You should have been his.*

She turned to Alenoush, "His name is Armando," she said.

CHAPTER TWELVE

NO SHOTGUN REQUIRED

"The first symptom of love in a young man is shyness; the first symptom in a woman, it is boldness." – Victor Hugo

Chris stopped in at the house for lunch, rinsing the dirt off his hands. It was April and planting season was in full swing. He felt an almost electrical current of stress in the air from the moment he walked in. Carrie and Liza were both in the kitchen and Liza looked tense. He gave his wife a quick kiss and tilted his head at Liza, "What's up, Liza?"

His sister-in-law was chewing nervously on a slender fingernail. She glanced toward the den. "Gramps is in the den with Carl."

"What for?" Chris began to ask and then thought of Carl and Liza's more outward signs of affection recently and groaned. "Oh boy." He had caught the two kissing and holding hands several times. It was just a matter of time before Fenton caught on, if he hadn't already. Carl had been a regular visitor on the farm for over two years now, and it wasn't as if the writing wasn't on the wall. The two had been an item for quite a while.

Liza was quick to defend herself. "I'm not pregnant!" Her face flushed at the thought. "We just…Carl and I…it's just time, that's all. He asked me and I said yes."

"Yes to sex? Or yes to getting married?" Chris asked a playful smile on his lips. Carrie slapped his arm, her mouth turned down disapprovingly, but her eyes crinkled at the corners, a sure sign of amusement.

Liza glared at him, "Oh yeah, Chris Aaronson, you're one to talk!"

She had a point. He and Carrie had "mixed up the natural order of things," as her grandfather had put it. That had been nearly three and a half years ago, and their marriage was a good one, despite the losses they had endured. Carrie's first pregnancy had ended in a premature birth, and there had been several heartbreaking miscarriages since. Fenton had come around, eventually, although the sight of the shotgun still gave Chris pause.

"If you must know, Mr. Smarty Pants, Carl asked

me to *marry* him. They've been in there for a few minutes." She bit off another fingernail and said, "I think it's going well. He hasn't started yelling yet."

That hopeful moment was shattered. "Where's my shotgun?" Fenton bellowed from the den.

Chris winced, "Oh yeah, Liza, that went really well." He then grinned at Carrie, remembering several moments of shotgun-induced terror that the old man had brought on for him. His wife rolled her eyes at him and walked toward the den to head the old man off.

Carl came out of the den first and made a beeline for Liza, who grabbed his arm and pulled him close. She wrapped a determined arm around his waist and whispered something in his ear, then kissed him. This earned another bellow from Fenton, who was limping down the hallway, Carrie slowing him down only the slightest bit.

"Are you pregnant, young lady?" Fenton was unusually brusque with his youngest granddaughter.

Liza stood her ground, holding Carl in his place and shushing him with a determined look. "Nope, Gramps, not yet." Her hazel eyes, snapped with mischief. "But if you give us a half hour, I'll see what I can do."

Fenton gaped at her. For that matter they all did. Carl looked terrified, "Uh, sir, I don't think she meant that."

"Oh yes, I did!" Liza said, her jaw firmly set. Chris looked bemused, Carrie stood wide-eyed, and

Page | 147

Carl's face had broken into a sheen of sweat.

"Gramps, I'm not a kid anymore."

"You are sixteen years old!" Fenton bellowed.

"I'm *seventeen* years old, Gramps, almost eighteen. And I know what I want," Liza countered.

Chris watched with admiration. The Perdue women were strong-willed, and Liza was probably the most strong-willed one of them all. Carrie held some of her mother's quiet calm, but Liza was fire and ice, especially when she felt strongly about something. She stood there, back straight, immovable, in the face of her grandfather's wrath.

Fenton faltered, ever so slightly, his wrath fading as he grasped at straws.

"What would your parents say to you getting married this young?"

His eyes began to redden and the old man looked exhausted. "You are barely more than children."

His gruff demeanor was nothing but a façade, and the vulnerability Fenton tried so hard to keep hidden came sliding into view. Above all things, he loved his three grandchildren, and his grandson-in-law. He loved them fiercely, deeply.

Liza's tone changed in response, "The world is different, Gramps. Carl and I," she pulled Carl closer and stepped forward toward her grandfather, "we've talked about this for a long time. And we love each other."

She stared into the old man's eyes, eyes that reminded her so much of her father, gone for nearly eight years now. Isaac would have liked Carl, just as Fenton did.

"We're getting married, Gramps." Her words were a statement, not a question. A moment passed and no one spoke. Then Liza continued, "So, will you give us your blessing?"

Fenton closed his eyes in exhaustion. He did not understand these young people, *so eager to hunt for blueberries and get married*. But he knew resolution when he saw it—and his granddaughter was full of it. Heck, the girl was overflowing with resolution. He thought about all of the smiles, the surreptitious hand-holding he had tried his best to ignore, and the way Carl fit into the farm, just as Chris had. *A good fit.*

Fenton opened his eyes and looked at Liza, standing there, Carl at her side. She looked so beautiful and so resolute. She had always known her own mind, and fearlessly faced her future. Just last fall she had successfully operated on one of the town boys who had come down with acute appendicitis. She had saved that nine-year-old's life and firmly established herself as the town's doctor.

Since then there had been a stream of steady visitors who would knock on the farmhouse door, day or night, with varying degrees of injuries and illness. At seventeen, Liza was accepted by Tiptonville residents as "the best at doctorin' in the area," as old Otis Liles had said to him at Christmas while Liza looked after a nasty cut the frail

Page | 149

centenarian had received after he fell in his cluttered parts shop.

It seemed that Fenton was the only one who still saw the wide-eyed child who had stood waiting with her mother and older sister at the airport. Her hair parted down the middle and fastened into two neat braids. All of them wearing black and still reeling from the loss of his son Isaac in the Amtrak Train Bombings. Amy, heavily pregnant, Carrie, her thin young face drawn with grief, and Liza, who had just looked up at him, opened her arms wide for him to pick her up, and said nothing. She had nestled her face in his neck and wrapped her small arms around him tightly. To him, she was still that little girl. But it was time he saw her for what she was: a young woman who knew her own mind.

Wearily he mustered a half-frown, *why oh why did they all have to grow up so quickly?* "Fine," he said, "you have my blessing." Then he pointed a gnarled finger at Carl who looked very relieved, "And you just wait on any fun stuff until *after* the weddin', you understand me, young man?"

"Yes sir," Carl nodded. And despite Liza's efforts to the contrary, he kept that promise.

They had a June wedding.

Their first child, Molly Ann Owens, was born on Valentine's Day the following year.

Chapter Thirteen

A Gift on Our Front Stoop

"I saw her huddled there on our front stoop, red curls matted with dried blood and piercing green eyes. She looked up at me, as if she knew *me. Like Erin had been reborn into her. She's not the Erin I knew, however. She's kinder, gentler, and almost magical. But in that first moment, when I saw her shivering there for the first time, it felt as if my friend had come home to me. How could I turn her away? In some way, it was as if I had a second chance. To make it right, to be there when she needed me. I know they are different, and that my friend is long gone, but still…"* – Jess's Journal

Jess and Becka were digging out the last of the potatoes, and David and Jacob were hard at work on the carrots. David's sister Tina was sitting cross-legged on the ground some distance away, oblivious to the cold, studying a new plant that had sprouted that year and comparing it carefully to a sketch in an old worn leather book. The skies were overcast and gray; there was a sharp bite to the wind. Any time now they'd see rain, maybe even a freezing drizzle. Winter had come late this year. But now it was clearly on its way. Some distance to the north there came rolling echoes of gunshots—one, two, and three—in quick succession. Quincy tensed, delicately sniffing the air, her hackles in the air.

Jess couldn't help wondering what the dog smelled. Quincy's reaction was far from comforting. A small whine sounded in her throat as she continued to stare in the direction of the gunshots, her ears pulled back against her head and her nose twitching.

"D'ya think Mr. Banks bagged himself a deer?" Jacob called out from the far side of the garden where he had been put in charge of digging up the garlic bulbs.

Jacob was lean, with tousled black hair, dark blue eyes, and a handsome face. He was seven now, and his last growth spurt had turned his pants into waders. His shirtsleeves ended well before his wrists. Jess made a note to ask at the community center for larger-sized clothes. Several of the kids over at Research were taller than Jacob; perhaps they would have some hand-me-downs to spare.

The boy looked hopeful, positively dreamy-eyed, at the thought of some fresh deer meat. They hadn't eaten venison in well over a month, and the old man would make them a fair trade in meat for some of the apples they had finished picking last month.

Jess had shown Becka and Jacob how to wrap the apples carefully in paper so they didn't touch skin to skin. There would be less rot that way. And there they would sit deep in the crawlspace of the basement where it was dark. The apples would stay fresh for months. Whatever did rot would be made into applesauce or fed to the chickens or put in the compost, depending on how bad off it was.

Jacob's mind filled with images of a nice juicy roast, or ribs, and resolved to beg his mother again to let him learn how to hunt.

Jess just shook her head and frowned, "Thurman never shoots like that. He fires once and waits; I just heard three in a row. That's a stranger or one of the town militia."

The town militia had changed drastically since Mayor Farley's son James had taken over. For that matter, the town had changed as well. Farley's influence was a powerful one. He was still the mayor and there had been no open elections held in over five years. As soon as James Farley had turned the 'respectable age' of twenty, Mayor Farley had pushed, pulled, and threatened a position for his son. Unbelievably to Jess and several others, he had finally dislodged Todd Stevens, who had been designated the head of the militia three years back, after saving the town from a devastating raid.

A group of well-armed men and women had tried to cut into the town from a little-used road on the northeast side, a weak area of defense, and steal the entire herd of cattle. The raiders had been occupying a series of caves to the north along the tattered remains of I-435, which had formerly been used for storage, for years. The problem with cave dwelling was lack of sunlight and space, both needed for raising livestock and crops. Pale and malnourished, they had still been savage in their attack. Several members of one family living on the outskirts had been murdered, and three of the town militia had also lost their lives before the attack had been repelled.

That had been a harsh but necessary lesson. The Western Front may have disintegrated, but there were still plenty of people on the edge, desperate to survive, and few left worth trusting. The waves of disease and malnutrition that had turned Kansas City and the surrounding metropolitan area into a tsunami of death long before the Western Front ever arrived on its doorstep were still pulsing through. The townships and their local militias were the only thing keeping most of them alive. Todd Stevens had understood this all too well.

Todd had been interested in Jess and actively courted her that first year after her return to Warsend. He was a good man, and she had thought highly of him, but having a man look at her with interest, any kind of interest, had been absolutely terrifying. She had quietly defined their relationship as being a friendship only. He had been disappointed, but accepted it. He had eventually turned his sights toward Laura, Sarah's daughter, courting her on a daily basis at the café on Main Street where Jess and her family had stayed their first day back in Warsend. They now had two small children.

After Mayor Farley had propelled his son into power, Todd and Laura had spent more time with Jess's small family. His parents were dead and he had talked to her, revealing a snapshot of the struggle from the inside of the higher echelons of the town militia, for power, for control. "I don't want to deal with the politics," he had said to her the summer before, "I just want to keep us safe. Why does it have to be like this?" A week later the announcement had come that James Farley was now in charge of the militia.

In a matter of a few months, the mayor's son had undone, if not destroyed, the seamless network of militia members. Those who had dedicated themselves to ensuring the town borders remained safe were pushed aside and the decisions and leadership positions farmed out to the untested and cronies of James Farley and his father.

Since he had assumed control, the borders had seen a dozen incursions. The last one had resulted in the death of an entire family. The raid before that had ended without any deaths of residents, but half of the old hospital—now an orphanage, old folks home, and college rolled into one—had burned to the ground. No one would be attending classes in the near future, several groups were struggling to find intact housing, and there was no lumber to fix what had been destroyed.

As a one, their heads turned toward the north, waiting for more noise, a shot, a yell, but there was only silence. After a moment of listening to the wind, and nothing else, Jess turned back to her chore.

The temperature was dropping, rain was coming, and they couldn't afford to lose these roots to an overnight frost. "C'mon you, let's get these out of the ground and into the basement." She nudged Becka, and then tossed a tiny potato at David, hitting him in the butt and giggling at his startled look.

He put on his sternest face, "You just better watch it, lady! You'll start something you can't finish! I'm armed with pointy carrots…hiya!"

He flourished the carrot in his hand like a deranged fencer, which set the younger kids to laughing. The bit of humor made short work of an otherwise long and tedious job. When they were finally done the sky had begun to spit fat drops at them, daring them to stay outside for any longer.

Tina had gathered up the old leather journal and her pencil, absently brushing at some plant matter that had attached itself to her patched and worn pants. Recently she had been adding to the book that Jess had inherited from Grandmother Madge, the old woman who had sheltered them over the winter in a cave east of Clinton. Tina was nearly eleven now, and she was a quiet girl who already showed an incredible knowledge of healing herbs. Her hair, once a muddy blond, had darkened to a golden brown. She kept the unruly curls cropped short and they seemed to be the most lighthearted part of her otherwise solemn demeanor. Her smiles, which were rare, were usually used exclusively for smaller children, like Jacob and Becka. Although she could not remember her parents, their abrupt loss, and the loss of Grandmother Madge less than a year later, these events had marked the child in a way that Jess or David seemed unable to change.

Despite this solemn demeanor, Tina was gentle and loving and cared deeply for her brother and the rest of their adopted family. It just seemed that she existed in a world of her own so much of the time. Few understood her. The town doctor, Anthony Ridley, was the exception to the rule. He had spent time with her one day while checking on Becka, still a baby at the time, and making sure everyone was surviving the winter without trouble. Todd Stevens, the militia leader, had urged him to drop in on them, worried that Jess was exhausting herself with so many children to look after. While looking over the entire little family, a strange mix of related and unrelated teenagers and children, Dr. Ridley had been surprised by an offering of some strange dried flowers and stems.

Tina had looked up solemnly at him, barely five years old, had handed the bundle to him, explaining that it was echinacea, "Missouri coneflower, it's good for keeping away colds."

He had looked intrigued and asked her to tell him more. "You can put the flower petals in a tea. Dry it first." He had asked her more questions and he had returned the next day to talk with her more and ask her for two other herbs she had pointed out, sitting next to her and gently holding the herbs she handed to him.

Over the years, through illnesses and injuries, he would always take an extra few minutes to discuss with Tina her latest miracle plants. After that first encounter, he had made an effort to learn more about herbs and, after a while, he began requesting that Jess and her family grow certain herbs or that Tina make certain poultices. He continued to encourage her to learn more and broaden her knowledge with the books that Jess and David collected for her. As time went by, more and more of Tina's infusions and decoctions helped heal the residents of Warsend.

Despite this, most of the residents remained blissfully ignorant that their medicines were supplied by a girl who wasn't even in her teens.

Inside the house, Becka staggered under the

weight of the potatoes she was carrying. Jess lifted the basket from her hands before the six-year-old could drop any of the precious cargo. Becka had jet-black hair that held long curls. Her eyes were still a hauntingly familiar ice-blue but that was where the resemblance to Scott Cooper ended.

Becka was soft-spoken and thoughtful. Jess was struck by the memory of Becka's biological mother, Serena, and the way she had spoken on the two times that she and Jess had met. Serena had been right; Becka was good and kind, just as Serena had been. The only reminder of her paternal heritage was in her features. Jess had spent hours studying the girl's face, seeing Scott Cooper in a completely different way. Had he ever been good and innocent? He must have been.

Jess wanted to believe that all children were, and she wondered what had changed. She had learned to love Becka, just as Serena had said she would. It wasn't hard; the child was sweet and loving, and it was obvious how well she fit in their family unit. Jess leaned down and kissed the little girl, who was protesting that she could carry the heavy load. Becka was also fiercely independent—a trait she shared with the rest of them.

For the first winter in years she could count on keeping most of this harvest and not losing it to marauding rodents—now that they had Lord Flea. Lord Flea, short for Lord of the Flea-Bitten, Bent-Eared, and Generally Ragged Felines, was a tattered-looking cat of indeterminate age. He was not friendly, and Jacob and Becka had learned to leave him alone after the first round of scratches and bites, but he did a bang-up job on the rodents. Nothing to complain about there!

And with the biggest harvest in three years, thanks to David's research into composting methods, they would have enough root vegetables to last them all winter with extra for trade, as well as seed for next year's crop. Thurman Banks, their nearest neighbor, would be happy to trade his meat for vegetables and for some of the herbs that Jess had painstakingly tied and dried in the heat of the summer.

Icy, stinging drops of rain on the edge of becoming sleet were falling by the time they finished with the last of the vegetables. Everyone was worn out and ready for a bath by the time they finished. "Rinse off as much of the dirt from your hands as you can in the pond and then help with carrying the buckets of water," Jess directed the younger children.

There were already four large pots of water on the stove, water boiling merrily away. If they conserved, the icy cold water from the well mixed with the boiling hot water wouldn't cool things down too bad and they could all get through their baths.

Bodies washed, stomachs full of fresh vegetable soup, the small family gathered in the living room around a few beeswax candles. Night had fallen soon after the rain began. Jacob snuggled up to Jess, his body transmitting warmth and comfort to her.

"Mom, will you read from the story tonight? The Harry story?" he asked her, sleepily.

He was very tired from the hard work of the day. David had found a set of books on a recent trip into the southern part of Warsend and brought them back for Jess to look over. She had smiled when she read the titles in his hands, and remembered reading the series when she was a child…Harry Potter…now there were a fine set of adventures! She had not noticed his flushed face when she had hugged him in thanks and excitement and he had scuttled away before she could see how her affection had affected him.

"Yes, sweetie, but just a few pages tonight," Jess stifled a yawn, "I'm all worn out."

She carefully opened the book to the marked page and began to read aloud. Barely a few paragraphs later she set the book down with a soft laugh and looked around. David, Becka, and Jacob were all fast asleep on the floor—softly snoring lumps buried under blankets and cradling pillows. She slowly stood and lifted Jacob up into her arms. He was lanky yet light, thin arms and legs, tall for his age, but she could still lift him easily in her arms. She carefully stepped over and around the others and quietly carried him to bed. The others would be fine sleeping the night out on the floor, but she was happy to burrow under the covers of her bed and listen to the tiny taps of ice-laden particles hitting the glass windows before she drifted off to sleep. For the moment, life was bearable and the winter could come—they were ready for it.

The light from the candle on her bedside table guttered and spit as she struggled to keep her eyes open and read over the latest narrative she had collected. For the past five years she had been slowly chronicling the histories of the local residents. It had started out with the question, "Where were you on November 4th? The day the Western Front invaded Warsend?"

Slowly the stories had changed, taken on different shapes and focus, and she was now chronicling Sarah Turner's life. Sarah Turner, who was actually Sarah Perkins, a woman who had run away from an abusive husband, changed her name and created a new life for herself, as well as for her children Cody and Laura.

She reviewed her notes, which she had taken two days ago while sitting in the café Sarah ran. She had asked Sarah what she wanted to contribute to the town's oral history and had been stunned by the life story that Sarah had shared.

The older woman's face looked haunted, "I did what I thought was best. To protect myself, to protect Cody and Laura. But I always wondered. If I had stayed…if I had managed to get him help for his PTSD…could we have made it?" She had smiled wanly, "In so many ways, I still love him, Jess. I never saw another man I wanted as much as I wanted him. I guess that either makes me a fool or…"

She had left the sentence unfinished. Jess's eyes fluttered closed, slipping into sleep as she thought about all the unknowns, all the lost loves in the world—her folks, Chris, Allen, and so many more. The papers slipped from her fingers. The candle guttered next to her in the growing pool of wax and then quietly extinguished.

To escape the nightmare, Jess woke up abruptly, surprised to see that it was already light out. The details of the dream were already fading quickly, but gunfire and the memory of a sobbing child were all that remained. She shook her head, as if to rid herself of the last vestiges of the nightmare. The nightmares came every night, but in different forms, and it was a relief to wake up and spend her days too busy to remember the night's horrors. Jess pulled her clothes on quickly and tried to peer out of an open crack in the wood planks covering one of the windows.

There wasn't much to see; the icy rain must have tapered off early in the night. Winter, it seemed, was delayed for just one more day. She pulled on tattered wool socks and her boots followed. A sweater completed her and she headed out the bedroom door and into the living room where the others were stirring. Jacob was already awake, sitting at the table and eating an apple.

"Hi there Sweetheart, you're up early." She smoothed his unruly hair with her fingers. The boy looked wide awake. He mumbled incoherently from his apple, eyes fixed on a picture book in front of him.

"Say that again?"

"I've been up 'cause of the cryin'," the boy repeated, "She just won't stop cryin' no matter how nice I am to her. She don't talk, and she won't look at me or nuthin'." The little boy looked disgruntled.

"Who won't talk, sweetie?"

"The girl on the front porch."

Jess considered this statement for a moment, "There's a girl on the front porch?"

Jacob rolled his eyes at his mother, "Uh, yeah, I *told* you she woke me up. But she don't talk or nuthin'; maybe she's 'tarded or somethin'."

Jess automatically corrected him, "Anything, *re*tarded, something, and that isn't nice, Jacob, calling someone retarded."

She headed for the front door as David struggled to a sitting position, still in the same place on the living room floor where he had fallen asleep, "Wha', who, what's goin' on?" she heard him mutter sleepily as she unbolted the heavy front door.

David received no answer as Jess simply stared at the small child huddled against her storm door, blocking it from opening.

Jacob walked up behind her, "You'll have to go

around; she won't move 'tall," he commented calmly and walked away down the hall.

The small, huddled child did not react, simply rocked back and forth, shaking in the cold. She was tiny, smaller by far than Jacob or Becka, maybe two or three years old. One thumb was firmly stuck in her mouth and her hair was a bright red, tangled, and full of burrs and leaves. Her face, what Jess could see of it, was filthy and tear-streaked. She was dressed in jeans or overalls, and a thick pink coat that had seen cleaner days. Her tiny sneakers were covered in mud.

"Oh my God," Jess jumped at David's voice in her ear, "What the hell?" He was rubbing the sleep from his eyes and looking as confused as she.

Jess said nothing, just turned and ran out of the living room and through the kitchen, the pantry, out through the garage which was now used as a small barn, and around the house to the front door. She skidded to a stop in front of the stoop, half expecting the tiny child to have vanished before she arrived. But the little girl hadn't moved, not an inch. She didn't even flinch when Jess reached down and gently picked her up in her arms. David held open the door for her then, now that the girl wasn't blocking it from opening.

By now, Becka and Jacob were both at the door behind David, Becka still bleary-eyed from sleep and Jacob curious enough not to be as annoyed with the girl now for not talking to him. Tina had not yet made an appearance.

The group of them moved like a school of fish toward the center of the kitchen where the light was brightest. Jess set the tiny girl on the floor and sat down cross-legged in front of her. Now she could see blood caked on her face, hands, and the front of her overalls. It was mixed in with dark black river mud and dissolved in tracks from the child's tears. She was shivering from fear and cold, and now she looked up at Jess with the most startling, piercing green eyes. "Erin," Jess whispered to herself, reminded painfully of the childhood friend she had lost. The child did not react, merely stared at her with tears welling up in her eyes, spilling down cheeks, and shivering.

The sight of tears was like an electric charge that sent Jess into action. Without taking her eyes from the child she began snapping orders.

"Becka, round up some towels and a washcloth. David, please draw some water and set it to boil; get more from the well in the other buckets. Jake honey, see if you have some old clothes that are too small for you in your closet or help Becka find some of hers. Someone get me a lamp lit and put it in the bathroom. Get the first aid kit from my bathroom!"

As the others rushed in various directions, she gently removed the dirty pink coat, pulled the child into her arms, and gently stood up. Above all, whatever had happened to the little girl in the past day or more, Jess was intent on helping her feel safe. She had to make sure that she wasn't hurt, get her clean and warm, and get some food in her.

David briefly laid a hand on her shoulder and said, "I'll take care of breakfast and the kids will help with chores; you take care of her." At seventeen he was every inch of a man in height and Jess was reminded suddenly of how mature and thoughtful he had always been. She could rely on him to take care of the details while she sorted out what injuries were under all of the blood and dirt on the little girl.

The next hour was a flurry of activity. Jess closed herself and the small girl inside of the hall bathroom and talked to her softly, speaking of the small family mostly, as she gently removed the girl's clothes and worked to remove some of the larger twigs and burrs from her fine hair.

"So Jacob is my son, and he's seven years old now. He really likes to have stories read to him. Right now we are reading a neat book called *Harry Potter and the Sorcerer's Stone.* Have you ever heard of it?" There was no response, but the tears and the rocking had stopped.

Jess just kept talking until there was a soft knock on the door, "Mom," came Jacob's low voice, "the bathwater is ready." In the background she could hear Tina's sleepy voice asking the others what was going on.

"Just leave it there Jacob, I'll get it in a minute," Jess replied encouragingly. She smiled at the little girl, who had jumped at the knock, and began rocking again. "I'm going to open the door and get the buckets for the bath, so you just sit right there."

She kept her movements slow and deliberate as she pulled the buckets of water in, alternately steaming or cold, and poured them one by one into the tub. No one appeared near the open door, and she silently thanked David for his help. Becka and Jacob were as curious as cats and would have been right there in the bathroom with her if he hadn't have warned them off or kept them busy with other tasks.

With the buckets left empty outside the door, and the bathroom once again closed with just the two of them inside, she gently held out her hands to help the little girl into the bathtub. "And then there is Becka, who was Serena's daughter, but she died so now Becka calls me Mom. She's a few years older than you; she's almost six years old now. She has five dolls, and maybe later on after we get you cleaned up she will show them to you. We've made very pretty dresses for them to wear."

She dipped the washcloth in the water and gently washed the little girl's face. Most of the caked-on blood did not appear to be hers, but there were a few scratches on her pale skin. She was a beautiful little child underneath the grime, and she stared at Jess with an intensity that Jess found both compelling and heart-wrenching. Again she was reminded of Erin, her best friend, and her heart contracted in pain. Whatever had happened, this child had seen something awful and, considering the amount of blood, whoever had been with her was either gravely wounded or irrevocably dead.

She put on her most encouraging smile, "I need to talk to David for a moment, sweetie; will you be all right for a minute or two?" She was surprised to get a small nod. "Okay, I'll be right back. Oh, wait," she turned around and began to rummage under the sink, pulling out two toy boats and a handful of battered plastic figurines. "Here, you could play with these if you liked." She plunked the toys into the water and slipped out of the door.

She was not surprised to see David standing outside, a plate of warm eggs and browned potatoes with the steam still rising from them. His face was knotted with concern as he asked, "How is she; is she hurt bad?"

She smiled a brief reassurance at him, "No, let's talk out in the kitchen." He followed her, still carrying the plate. "The blood on her face and clothes definitely isn't hers. But there's so much of it, David…whoever she was with, whatever happened to them," Jess closed her eyes and shook her head, "it doesn't look good. She's in shock and she hasn't said word one. I know she can hear and understand me, so I think she's just been horribly traumatized. Take the shotgun and head north, scout around and see if you can find anything…tracks, blood, anything. But be careful, for God's sake, and don't be out long or Jacob will want to follow along."

He nodded and looked over at the kids standing quietly in the pantry, trying not to be noticed.

Jacob looked sheepish for a moment, then rebellious, "But Mom, I…"

Jess quieted him with a glance, "Don't you 'But Mom' me. You stay here and help with the chores, Jacob; I need you here with Becka. She flashed a look at Tina, who was looking quite awake and alert now and said, "Tina is in charge and you had better listen to her or answer to me later for it. Now you and Becka go find me some clean clothes for the little girl."

And with that she took the plate of food from David, turned away, and headed back for the bathroom, ignoring the small mutter of complaint she heard issuing from her son.

When she slipped back into the bathroom the toys had floated to the far end of the bathtub, untouched. And tiny girl just sat there looking at her with those big green eyes.

Jess smiled brightly at her, "Hi, sweetie, I'm back to clean the rest of you. But would you like some food first?" She wrestled the fork around until she had a small bite of egg on it and held it out to the little girl.

The child opened her mouth like a hungry baby bird and ate the bite Jess deposited inside silently. The plate of food was nearly gone before she heard quiet scuffling outside of the door and Becka's quiet voice, "Mom, we brought some old clothes of mine."

"Just leave them there, hon, I'll get them." She heard the floorboards creak as the children departed. She had kept up a line of chatter all the time she was feeding little 'Erin.' But there had been no word from the child, just quiet chewing and that intense green-eyed stare. When Jess had asked her what her name was, the child had simply stared at her, and said nothing.

"Well, we have to call you something. Otherwise it will be 'Hey, you over there' or 'What do you know, little miss so and so!'" Jess looked the tiny child over, now out of the tub and a towel wrapped around her small body. "I had a friend once, and she was my best friend. We grew up together, played together, right here in this very house."

Her eyes blurred for a moment, her voice caught, "She saved my life, and no matter how bad things got, we always had each other. Her name was Erin. Perhaps, until you are ready to tell us your name, we can call you Erin. Would that be okay?" Little Erin stared up at her, eyes unblinking, and gave a small, almost imperceptible nod. Jess smiled in relief, "Well then, Erin it is. Now let me see what the kids found to dress you in."

The small pile of clothing outside was an insane mix of tiny clothing, worn out boots, and only one thing that looked like it might fit…pajamas. Well, that would work for now.

She grabbed the pajamas and pulled them inside,

Page | 171

closing the door behind her. When Erin was dressed in the pajamas, and Jess had made another trip out to find a pair of oversized socks to cover her feet, she was ready to meet the rest of the family.

Jess held Erin's tiny hand and led her out of the bathroom and into the kitchen and pulled up a chair for her to sit on at the table. She was so small her head barely peeked over the top of the table. There was a small pitcher of milk on the counter and Jacob had just finished rinsing the blood from his finger and wrapping it in a small rag. Tears of pain coursed down his cheeks.

Jess gave him a hug, "Oh Jake, I'm so sorry, sweetie."

The boy pulled himself up taller. "It's okay, Mom, Satan didn't hurt me too bad," his brave expression belied by the drying tears.

That damn goat was always trying to nip Jess or David, but today little Jacob had been the one to milk her and of course gotten bit for his trouble.

She turned to Becka, who was eyeing little Erin with barely contained curiosity, "Becka dear, get those old phone books out for her to sit on."

The door from the garage opened, and David walked in shedding his coat and wiping his boots. He shook his head, "I didn't find any tracks, Jess, nothing at all. And there's a big one blowing in from the West; looks like we'll get snow before nightfall." His eyes took in the small girl seated at the table and he smiled at her. "She looks better, clean at least."

Becka bustled up with the phone books and Jess lifted Erin up for the books to be slid underneath her, elevating her to a normal level, straightened up, and placed a hand on the child's shoulder. "Everyone, this pretty little gift that Jacob found on our front stoop is a bit shy and doesn't feel like talking right now. And since we don't know her name quite yet, I've told her we will call her Erin until she tells us different."

She smoothed Erin's damp hair with her fingers. "Now, she's heard all about you, and I know everyone here is very eager to make friends with you, Erin." She looked down into the girl's eyes and spoke softly to her, "Here you are safe, and you can stay with us and be part of our family until we find out where yours is." She felt the girl give a small shudder under her hand. "And no matter what, if we find your family or not, you can always stay here with us; we've plenty of room, food, and love to go around."

The rest of the group murmured affirmatives and Becka edged closer. She smiled at Erin excitedly, obviously overjoyed at the idea of having a playmate. "I have five dolls, Erin, but I'll let you have one of them for your very own. Her name is Stacey, but you could give her a different name if you liked. I'll go get her." And off she ran to retrieve the doll.

Jacob carefully picked up the pitcher of the goat milk and poured a glass full to the brim. "Here, drink this; it's real good when it's warm."

He set the glass down in front of her then ran to fetch a rag to mop up the slopped mess. David sat down at the table and watched her, taken aback by how pretty the tiny child was now that the grime and muck had been washed away. Erin reached forward and pulled the glass toward her slowly, taking sips, while never taking her eyes off of the other occupants.

Jess considered it all great progress when little Erin didn't pull away from Becka's reappearance next to her or the ragged doll that was suddenly thrust in her face. She just eyed Becka gravely, took the doll from her, and regarded the older child gravely. Jess sat down near her and ate the remaining eggs and potatoes that had cooled on the stove.

And the rest of the family slowly settled around the table in the kitchen, recognizing a need for calm and normalcy around the traumatized little girl.

It wasn't long before Erin's eyes began to glaze over, and her head began to droop. She didn't pull away when David stood, walked around to her side of the table, leaned over, and carefully picked her up in his arms, cradling her like a baby. He said nothing, simply walked to the bedroom that Becka and Tina shared and placed her gently on Becka's bed, covered her with blankets, quietly tiptoed out of the room, and shut the door silently behind him.

"Who knows how much sleep she might have gotten, or how long she was out in the cold," he said, shaking his head and sliding into a chair at the table. He scratched through his long hair looking frustrated, "I couldn't find any kind of tracks… maybe I should go out further."

Jess took his hand in hers, "There's no need. If she had family, which she must have had, all that blood belonged to someone else and there was plenty of it. Her clothes were absolutely *soaked* in blood. If she showed up on our front stoop it was because there wasn't anyone left to take care of her. Those shots we heard yesterday, it's all connected, David. You and I both know she's probably here for good." She missed the flush in his cheeks as he stared down at their entwined fingers and turned away seconds later as she disengaged her grip and busied herself with clearing the dishes from the table. "Kids…water from the well and dishes now, please."

The children obeyed without complaint, quiet, putting together for themselves what had probably happened to little Erin's family. No strangers to loss or death, it was sobering nonetheless, and all members of the little family were once again reminded of how easily ended life could be.

It seemed that the gift on their front stoop was here to stay.

WEDDING BELLS

"Let me not to the marriage of true minds admit impediments. Love is not love which alters when it alteration finds, or bends with the remover to remove." – William Shakespeare

"Reverend?" The woman's voice came from the doorway to the church office. Even now, after taking over all of Reverend Thomas's duties completely for the past two years, Jeremy still didn't associate the title of 'Reverend' with himself. He looked around for Reverend Thomas out of habit, but the old man had passed away in March, a withered, gibbering shadow of his former self. It was a hot day, the hottest yet this year, and Jeremy had just been wishing he was out under a tree, hanging out with the kids, watching them run and play. His head jerked back to the door and a large drop of sweat that had been collecting along his forehead dripped into his left eye, momentarily blinding him in one eye as he peered through his open right eye at Grace Wilkes's mother.

Crap.

Karen smiled tentatively at him as he wiped the sweat from his brow and cleared his left eye and motioned for her to come in. "Good morn… afternoon, Mrs. Wilkes," he stumbled a bit; the sermon he had been working on had been a difficult one and it had apparently taken him through the morning and into the early afternoon according to the antique clock in the corner of Jeremy's small office. The room was filled with Reverend Thomas's books and belongings. Jeremy kept looking at them and wondering if he should keep them or give them away. Reverend Thomas had never been married, never had children, and Jeremy was at a loss to find any known relatives.

"May I speak with you, Reverend?"

Jeremy winced at the title. He had never attended seminary and was unsure what the Methodist church would have thought about him, a conflicted half-agnostic and lapsed member of the Church of Christ.

Half the time he wasn't sure he believed in God, but it sure seemed to reassure some of the older crowd. "Please, call me Jeremy."

Karen smiled, "Well, I guess, considering you and Grace and everything." Jeremy winced; he knew what was coming next. "Grace turned nineteen last month, you know."

"Yes, ma'am, I know."

"Don't you dare, ma'am me, Jeremy Deeds, I'm barely two years older than you and you know it." Jeremy's discomfort grew. Karen smiled again, perhaps to show him her words were just that, words, and that she wasn't offended. "It feels strange coming here, though, because it should be Anthony here, the right of the father to speak about his daughter, and all that." She looked around the tiny room, and tugged at her clothes which were clinging from the miserably humid heat. "Shall we go outside?"

"Sure." Jeremy stood up. The heat actually felt good in his legs; it was the winters that were the worst for him. He could predict bad weather better than the old-timers from the strong aches he felt in his damaged legs, but in the summer there was some relief, as if the sun could reach through skin and muscle and warm the irrevocably damaged bones beneath. Still, it wasn't easy to walk far, no matter what.

They walked slowly out the door; the sun was bright overhead and the waves of heat rippled across the empty parking lot. Grace and the orphans were nowhere to be found; perhaps they had gone to the creek to swim. It certainly was a good day for it. Karen pointed to a tree a hundred feet away and they walked over to it and sat down. Before Karen could say anything, Jeremy said, "Mrs. Wilkes…"

"Call me Karen."

"Um fine, Karen, I…I just wanted you to know…that I…I've never done anything inappropriate with Grace," he said, fumbling over the right words to say.

Her loud peal of laughter surprised him. "And well I know that!" She smiled and looked concerned, "Is that what you thought I was doing here? Warning you away from her?"

Jeremy had a hard time meeting her eyes. "I just…"

"Do you like Grace, Jeremy?" Her question was soft.

"Of course I do, I mean, she is a great help around here, the kids love her, and…she was a great comfort and help with Reverend Thomas, especially in those last days."

"But do you *like* her?"

"Mrs. Wilkes," he couldn't manage the informality of her first name to such a serious question. This was Grace's *mother* he was talking to, "I'm thirty-nine years old and Grace is…"

"And Grace is an adult, capable of love," Karen interrupted. At his shocked expression, she smirked a bit, "I didn't choose you; she did. And twenty years between you is a sight better than the 23 years that

separated me from my Anthony. That marriage
worked just fine," her eyes filled, "right up to the
end of our time together." She shook her head,
choking back the memory of her husband lying dead
on the ground.

It had been six years, and yet it had been the
blink of an eye. The loss of him had not abated; she
still expected to see him walk through the door, or
be there in bed with her when she woke up at night.
"I'm not in judgment of you and I'm less worried
about the age difference than you apparently are."
She stared into his eyes, "What I want to know is
this: is the love that Grace feels for you returned?
Do you feel for her as she feels for you?"

He started to stammer out a response and she
stopped him. "I've put you on the spot, and that
isn't fair. So listen to me, and think about it. Grace is
in love with you. She has been for years."

He started to disagree and she stopped him with
a wave of his finger, "You think she is too young to
know what she wants, but she isn't. She was
practically a mute when I sent her to you. The only
time I heard anything from her was at night, when
she would scream from the nightmares of
remembering that awful day. I didn't know what to
do, but I knew she was lost and I hurt so much from
losing Anthony that I could barely help myself,
much less her."

Karen stopped for a moment, collected the
emotions threatening to burst out now. Even after

all this time, the wounds were fresh. She gazed at the horizon, and in the distance they could see the children returning, tumbling through the grass. In a few moments they would be back in the church parking lot.

"I sent her to *you*, Jeremy, because I remember your face when you saw her that day, sitting out on the back porch. And you helped her; both you and the Reverend did, but mostly *you*. She focused in on you like you were her own private lifeboat. At first, yes, when she first talked about marrying you I dismissed it too. She was a child, with simple beliefs and a good heart. But as these years have passed, she's grown up and never deviated from it. She's waiting for you to reciprocate. So you think about that, Reverend Deeds, and let me know if my daughter's feelings for you are something you can return."

Jeremy squirmed again at the title of Reverend. "Please, I really wish everyone would stop calling me that."

Karen shook her head, "You are the Reverend here now, you know. Long before Reverend Thomas passed you were doing his job and we all know that. Let your parishioners call you Reverend Deeds; it's for them, not for you." And with that piece of advice she hugged him, then got up and walked off, leaving him to sit under the large oak tree with a completely new point of view.

She was gone before Grace and the kids returned

and he couldn't help but smile when one of them flung herself into his arms, half-damp and covered in grass. Collette, the youngest, just an infant when her father and mother died during the assault by a faction of the Western Front on the tiny town of Tiptonville, giggled as she squirmed in his lap. She was an adorable child, with curly red hair and lively brown eyes.

"Mister Jeremy, we went swimming in the creek and I catched a crawdad but Miss Grace said I hadda put it back." She pouted slightly, her eyes dancing with mischief.

"Quite right," Jeremy smiled down at the child, and then flashed a smile up at Grace, "Leave that crawdad in his home. Besides, you are lucky he didn't *pinch* you," he said, eliciting a scream as he tickled her side. And with that, the rest of the kids dove in and began wiggling, tickling, and shrieking in Jeremy's lap while Grace looked on and shook her head in mock disapproval.

Jeremy looked up during the ruckus and caught Grace staring at him with a look he hadn't seen before. Or perhaps it was better to say, he hadn't bothered to notice. It seemed that, when Grace came around, he spent a great deal of time looking at everyone else *but* her. And why was that? Why was he so worried about what others thought of him? Or of her?

This thought continued to plague him, through an early dinner, through the evening games and storytelling, through the baths and bedtime rituals, and he found himself sneaking glances at her throughout the evening. Grace was petite, like her mother, with curly brown hair and big blue eyes. She still slept in the girls' dorm every Monday through Thursday night, and went back to the family farm Friday evenings after supper, returning early Monday in time to help him fix breakfast for the kids. Today she was wearing a pair of patched and tattered jean shorts and a short-sleeved top. She was slim, and seeing her in a new light after Karen's visit still had him feeling like he was some kind of pervert. There were twenty years between them, for crying out loud, and he felt wrong just looking at her that way.

Just then, as the last of the kids were put to bed and they were alone, tidying up the communal living spaces, Grace turned to ask him a question and caught him staring at her. Jeremy's face flamed red and he quickly turned away. For crying out loud, he was thirty-nine years old, and here he was, blushing like a pimply-faced teenager trying to get to first base. He was so busy trying to hide the flush on face that he missed the big grin that lit her face at his sudden interest.

It would be two weeks before he mustered the courage to visit Karen Wilkes and answer her question on how he felt about her daughter and another five more before the church was able to play the wedding march for the couple. Despite Jeremy's fears, none of the townsfolk or members of the church had concerns about the age difference. Too many things had changed in the world, and if the Reverend was happy, and Grace was happy, then they were too.

In the years to come, the disparate age gap would matter little, and the couple, their adopted children, all orphans, and their two biological children would be instrumental in bringing healing to the community.

CHAPTER FIFTEEN

TO EACH A TRADE

"The idea of apprenticeship was a term that seemed to hark from the Middle Ages. But here was this opportunity, for Tina, for us, and we accepted it. I think it was one of the best decisions we made as a family, but it was hard, real hard. Watching her leave was hard for me and hardest by far for David. But we were facing a bleak, cold winter. A late start to the spring planting, along with a freak frost in mid-May had wiped out all of the fruit tree harvest and a freak cold snap in late August had wiped out most of our remaining crops. We were in bad shape and we knew it. So we said our goodbyes, watched her walk away with her hand firmly in Penelope's, and hoped we would all survive our first winter apart." – Jess's Journal

Jess didn't like the smell of the lamb's ear. She had cut the dried, dead flower spikes off of the plants and began trying to extract the seeds. Jess had done this with all of the plants currently in the garden. So far she had managed to harvest hundreds of sage seeds. The sage hadn't bothered Jess a bit, but David had run out of the house protesting the strong scent and howling that his eyes were burning.

It was early September, yet the days were still quite warm. The sun beat down and there was a light breeze, keeping it from being unbearably hot. Everyone was busy with something, making use of the slightly cooler weather to get a long list of needed tasks done. At the moment, it was almost impossible to imagine the impending winter. The tomatoes were still producing and the apples that had escaped the late frost were just about ready to harvest. David had announced he would be clearing an area on the other side of the block where they hoped to start a new orchard and plant the ten small apple trees he had helped Mr. Banks graft last year. There were also a large number of peach and cherry trees that Jacob and Tina had planted as seeds which were now in their second year of growth and ready to be transplanted as well. They had all headed over to the area that morning and were clearing areas of weed cover and prepping the soil. That left Erin and Jess and Quincy behind.

Erin sat quietly next to Jess, her red hair shining

in the sun. It was curly, just as Erin's had been.
Sometimes Jess found herself wanting to believe that
she *was* Erin, or even Erin's daughter, a piece of her
best friend come back to her, a piece she could keep
close.

She had seen her friend die. But it didn't matter;
she still caught herself hoping for a different reality.
The little girl was so quiet, still mute, unlike her
namesake in so many ways, yet Jess loved having her
near. The child had a gentle, kind spirit, which spoke
louder than words ever could.

Jess had also harvested the dried pods from the
kale plants that had flowered. She had uncovered a
garden three houses down beneath a dense carpet of
weeds and discovered a persistent kale plant in the
mix.

That little gem had yielded hundreds of seeds.
She had planted handfuls of kale seeds in areas close
to the chicken coop where the chickens could feast
on them. Then she had planted long rows of kale
two houses down, which still had a privacy fence
mostly in place. The flock never strayed too far from
their coop and, hidden behind the tall fence, the
rows of kale grew thick and lush. The plants would
be perfect for adding to salads and soups, and for
trade as well, since most of the townspeople still
seemed to be in a rut of growing the tried and true
vegetables, without thought to nutritional
powerhouses like kale.

She didn't know what to do with all of these

lamb's ear seeds, didn't even know if it was worth her time to do this, but she persevered. Jess gathered every seed she saw come available; basil looked to be next, and some lettuce that had bolted in the rows next to the kale. She wrote on scraps of paper and shoved the drying plants into bowls, boxes, anything that would hold them. She sat on the front stoop, slowly picking at the stalks of lamb's ear, trying not to breathe through her nose. The flower stalks of the plant had an odd smell that made her almost nauseous.

The smell seemed to bother Erin equally. She wrinkled up her nose and made a face at Jess, which made her laugh out loud.

Quincy let out a small whine and one short bark. This usually meant that someone familiar was approaching the house. Jess looked up, surprised to see a stranger approaching. The woman looked to be in her late 40s with slim, long legs, and she was tall. Her hair was long, straight, and dark and she had it braided in one thick rope down the middle of her back. Her temples showed gray, as did one long streak that ran the length of her long hair. Despite the cool fall day, she was wearing shorts and a sleeveless tank top with a durable rucksack resting on her shoulders.

She met Jess's gaze and smiled, raised her hand in greeting, "Hello there! You must be Jessica Aaronson." She reached down and scratched the dog's ears, "And this must be Quincy."

Quincy licked the woman's hand, then settled down at Jess's feet again, her tail a steady thump against the ground. Her latest litter of puppies squirmed on a blanket nearby, mainly sleeping, and Quincy didn't seem alarmed at all by the stranger. Jess had long since come to rely on her dog's instincts—she had found them to be quite accurate.

Still, Jess knew nothing about this strange woman, but she already seemed to know a great deal about Jess and her little family. "Uh, hello." It sounded lame as it came out. Who was this woman?

"I'm Penelope," the woman said, sticking her hand out to shake Jess's. Jess fumbled with the lamb's ear and quickly stood up to shake Penelope's hand. "I see you are collecting lamb's ear seeds." Her eyes were a dark brown color, full of warmth as she asked, "Do you work with other herbs?"

Jess nodded, and did not elaborate. The truth of the matter was that the lamb's ear, along with the basil and some other herb seeds she could barely identify, would probably be handed over to Tina. Despite being just ten years old, the girl had become a font of knowledge.

Penelope smiled, "Do you know anything about the properties of lamb's ear, Jess?"

"Only that it's making me feel sick to my stomach. I don't like the weird smell."

The woman laughed then, and it was soft and free. "Stop for a while and I'll take over. I've gotten used to it." She sat down on the stoop, took the

Page | 191

bucket from Jess, and began plucking at the dry flower heads. Jess could hear the intermittent scatter of seeds as they fell and hit the bottom of the bucket. "The leaves can be picked early, before it flowers and can be dried and used in tea. You could also eat it in salads, or steamed, but most people object to the furry aspect of it. The best use of lamb's ear is for small wound care—it is absorbent and soft, and plentiful. But that isn't why I came here." She finished with one stalk and started on another.

"I've come to speak with you and David about Tina and a possible apprenticeship."

Jess looked at her, trying to gauge whether the woman was joking, "Tina's only ten years old."

Penelope's hands didn't stop moving as she turned toward Jess and gave her a long, appraising look. She had spent time in the heart of the town, talking to Sarah Turner. She had described Jess as the go to person for information on the town and its residents. After a few days of trade and work, Penelope knew enough of the girl's history to know that she and her house full of kids had struggled through some pretty tough times in the past six years. Sarah Ann had been forthcoming with details about Jess, informing her that Jess was busy writing down the lives and accounts of most of the residents of Warsend and compiling a history of the area.

"She goes from house to house, usually during the winter when there's not so much to do," Sarah

Ann had said, "She writes down whatever memories they have—of this war, of their families, of the time before—whatever someone wants to talk about, really." The woman had shrugged. "I wasn't born here, but she even wanted my story."

Penelope had been as circumspect as possible. She had been searching a long time for the author of the letter she had found in the cave. She was sure, however, that this Jess Aaronson was the one that had seen Mom through her final days, and buried her in the cairn outside her beloved cave.

If you are reading this, then you undoubtedly know Madge. My name is Jess Aaronson. I'm sixteen years old.

The letter was crumpled and tattered now, worn from reading and re-reading it over and over.

"Well, I've heard from Dr. Ridley that she knows a lot about herbs and healing." She smiled and turned back to the lamb's ear. "I've also come for a different reason. I've been looking for you for a long time now, nearly five years. You see, you knew someone very important to me."

She let Jess digest this in a long moment of silence. Jess's fear was rising slowly. This woman wasn't a soldier; she had no weapons…could she have come from the camp? Her memories of Tent Five and the camp haunted her dreams each night, but her days had been bright and full of love for long enough that she had learned to cope with the nightly terrors.

Penelope must have sensed her fear, as she

stopped and said, "I'm sorry; I didn't tell you my full name. It's Penelope Falling Water Aster…Dr. Madeleine Falling Water—you may have known her as Madge—she was my mother."

"I, she, oh my God. Grandmother Madge. She…" Jess couldn't put the words together. And the tears came then.

Penelope watched her for a moment. She had read the letter so many times, but she had still had her doubts. Had this girl and the other children truly loved her mother? Had Madge been at peace, surrounded by someone, anyone, who may have cared for her? Had they said the prayers the old woman's spirit required in order to find peace in the hereafter? Watching Jess now, it seemed that the letter had spoken true.

Before I tell you how your friend or mother died, I want to tell you how she lived. How she gave us sanctuary and saved our lives, by leading us here, to this cave…

The four of us, my newborn son Jacob, David, and Tina, both orphans from Clinton, and I have been here since September.

Penelope reached out and hugged Jess to her as tears began to slide down her nose. David found them that way a few minutes later and just stood and stared at the two sobbing women. A moment later, Tina also wandered up and took in the scene.

I am sure I do not need to tell you how special Madge was —or how much she came to mean to us. I lost my best friend in the world just days before she found us. I couldn't think; I

Page | 194

was scared and lost.

"What's going on? Who is she?" Tina asked her brother. He just shrugged and kept staring at Jess and Penelope. Tina's voice, however, was enough to reduce the crying and elicit some basic explanation of who Penelope was. This was followed immediately with an invitation to dinner.

Two hours later, the sun had slipped low on the horizon and dusk was gathering. Penelope's husband Kip had joined them and they had just finished nibbling the last kernels of corn off of the cob.

Penelope had been fascinated by little Erin, who at nearly four years of age was in a growth spurt and had lost most of her babyish looks. The young girl was slender and pixie-like, her freckled skin slightly sunburnt, and her hair a mass of bright red curls. She still did not speak, and Jess wondered about it from time to time. Would she ever? She had been with the family for just over six months and was obviously happy with everyone. She understood what was asked of her, nodded, smiled, and shook her head when she disagreed, but never spoke a single word, except for the occasional giggle when David tickled her.

As dinner wrapped up there was a quiet silence that descended upon the group. Penelope looked at the bunch of them and marveled at their resilience. Jess was tall and graceful. Her skin was tanned a golden brown from working in the sun, and her hair fell in long curls down the middle of her back. David was in his mid-to-late teens, and his arms and chest were muscled and lean. They had served some stew with turkey and wild greens in it and Jess had pointed to David, noting that he was the one who had landed them the turkey using his bow. It was the same bow that Grandmother Madge had taught him to use.

The end was peaceful. We were with her, holding her hands, and my baby Jacob nestled beside her. She loved to hold him, and he adored her. We all did.

The sun had slipped down beyond the horizon, pink and red streaks colored the clouds, the crickets had begun to sing, and the evening had a chill. They had spent hours describing their time with Grandmother Madge in the cave. Penelope and Kip had asked many questions, Kip especially, amazed that they had all spent a winter there. As dinner had wound down, they had put a pot of chicory coffee on to boil, sweetened with the sugar beets Jess had cultivated in the yard two houses down.

They had expanded their gardens to several yards, those they identified as having good soil, and others that simply had intact tall fences. Especially when it came to foods that deer liked, the high fences had been effective in keeping out the local deer population that was exploding in spite of regular hunting.

"Grandmother Madge said you were in Europe, or was it Africa?" Jess asked, dying to hear about the outside world, "How did you get here?"

Penelope and Kip's faces grew grim. They glanced at each other for a moment and Penelope held out her mug to Kip for a refill. He was nearest the coffeepot. "That has been an adventure, let me tell you. Have any of you heard much of what is going on in the outside world, outside of the former United States?" she asked Jess and David. The word "former" raised David's hackles a little. What did she mean *former*? They were still the United States… weren't they?

Jess answered, "We heard that The Collapse spread past our borders. That it was kind of like a domino effect. First the economic collapse and then multiple civil wars and uprisings in places like Greece, the Middle East, even China after the U.S. dollar collapsed."

She dug into old memories, from before the invasion by the Western Front, "There were a lot of problems with the Euro before the Collapse. But afterwards," she shrugged, "we lost power and internet and my parents stopped talking about what was happening out there."

She stared into the gathering darkness, "Maybe it was too big, too frightening even for them. And then afterwards, after I returned with David and Tina and Jacob, well, we haven't exactly welcomed outsiders in Warsend until more recently. The world has changed, I'm sure, but we only know what is nearby. There have been plenty of false starts into reasserting government on a broader level, but nothing that's stuck." She gestured toward the town center, "We have a militia, a mayor…"

"For whatever they are worth," murmured David in disgust.

Jess shot him a glance, "…and a basic town government in place. Every so often someone gets their britches in a knot and wants something more, and starts talking about money and taxes and the federal government. That doesn't last long."

Penelope nodded. "When the United States collapsed, much of the world was already on the brink of complete chaos. The riots in Greece were just the beginning of what became an uprising, civil war, and eventually a full war through Europe."

She gave a dark laugh, "Even Switzerland couldn't sit this one out. And Africa had already been a hotbed, right along with the Middle East; so much infighting, along with the scourge of HIV and so many young people growing up without any parents, without any direction in their lives."

She took a sip of the dark, heavily sweetened chicory and continued, "We were traveling with an independently funded humanitarian aid mission in Uganda. The Lord's Resistance Army controlled much of the north at the time. The word got out that every American had better get out now, or else." Her face had a wry look, "As if it were that easy."

Her husband Kip, who had said little until this point, took up the story, "It took us nearly two years just to get out of Africa. Everything that could break down did—communications, monetary systems, and the American embassies, or any embassies friendly to United States interests were either closed, burned to the ground, or abandoned. The fact that we were Americans was suddenly a very bad thing. Luckily we had friends, those who had been helped by our organization, by us. We stayed with a string of them, until it became dangerous for them to keep us there. We eventually found our way to the Mediterranean and tried to enter Europe via Italy, and later Spain." He shook his head.

Penelope continued, "It seemed that all of Europe was either involved in uprisings, civil war, or fighting each other. More than anything, though, we, well, *any* Americans were turned away. We ended up with several others from our aid group on a freighter, bound for Port-au-Prince. It was the closest thing we had to the U.S., although anyone we spoke to told us there had been nukes set off in the south and there were plenty of pointed fingers."

She took another sip of the chicory, now cooled in the mug, and continued, "In the end, we don't know how it started, or who pushed what buttons, but there were nuclear detonations recorded in Austin, D.C., and Los Angeles. It looks as if the Star Wars defense program took out most of the satellites in space at right around the same time—effectively ending world-wide communications."

David remembered some of the talk, overheard through closed doors and muffled conversations between his parents. Hearing it so clear, so real from two people who had experienced it, it was surreal.

Jess remembered more, and hearing Kip and Penelope describe it, brought back the memories of the internet, intermittent, and her father shouting about the nuke in Austin before everything went down for good.

Penelope stared at the bottom of her cup, her vision clouded by the events that came next.

Kip waited for her to speak and then he continued the story, "We knew the chances of finding Madge were unlikely. There had been such chaos in the cities, we wondered if she ever even made it out. Not to mention that she had told Penelope and her other children of her illness and that she didn't have long. Penelope had been scheduling a trip back to the States when everything went to hell. We just didn't hold out much hope. We stayed in Haiti for nearly eighteen months trying to stay alive and figure out where to go next."

Penelope sat there for a moment, her eyes and mind miles away, lost in memories of Haiti. She didn't want to tell them of the disease, the murders, or how many times they had fought for just enough food to survive. She didn't want to talk about the children she saw lying dead in the streets.

Penelope roused herself, "Florida was impossible —there were nearly a dozen naval bases there that banded together once communications with D.C. ceased. They patrol the waters and allow no one in.

It's a fire first, ask questions later situation. We couldn't get close enough to tell them we were American, not that it would have mattered. They had locked it down to Florida residents anyway. Texas was a fallout zone, as was much of the Caribbean and the southern states," she pursed her lips, "Not that they told Florida citizens that. They were actively denying it even after the first reports of radiation sickness. Once the Western Front started moving east into the Plains states, other factions of former military, along with extremists, rose up to define their own areas of control."

Kip chimed in, "The Allied South struggled to consolidate Louisiana, Arkansas, Mississippi, Alabama, Georgia, and South Carolina. Mexico had surged into Arizona, New Mexico, and the most southern section of California and there was chaos there—lines drawn between the white, Hispanic, and Native American populations. The drug cartels made a move for power. The east coast had three different contingents—the Northern Allies who were struggling to define the borders of half a dozen small states, the Unionists that controlled some parts of the southeast, and the Patriots who were hopelessly divided through infighting in Kentucky, Ohio, and Indiana."

Even Jacob and Becka, who understood little of the states being discussed, having been born after the Collapse, were silent. Erin, just four years old, had curled up in David's arms, and was sucking her thumb, listening intently to Kip and Penelope's account.

Penelope continued, "We finally found entry just west of Biloxi, Mississippi. There had been a radiation fallout scare and much of the area was deserted. We headed up Highway 49. After that it was a zigzag route, we entered Tennessee, tried to go through the northwest section, but there were a chain of small towns, all with militias, and we were turned back at Tiptonville." She took another sip, "The Western Front had torn through that region and everyone was on edge. If you weren't a resident they turned you away, no questions, no argument." She smiled wryly, "After all, they were the ones with the guns. You can't argue much with the business end of a gun."

Kip spoke, "We spent a winter in Arkansas. There were migrant groups moving through the areas, many of them working crops, building or reinforcing town borders, living like gypsies as they searched for a place to stay. We moved in and out of these groups—diseases we hadn't seen in decades in the Western world ran rampant. Cholera, bouts of dysentery, and a host of other illnesses could be found in any group we joined. But the alternative was to go it alone, without some of the protection a group could provide. Sometimes it was worth it, other times it wasn't."

Penelope spoke, "And eventually we moved through parts of Oklahoma, Kansas, and then finally

Missouri. Once we hit Missouri I was determined to find my mother. I had thought about it a lot, wondering what she would do, where she would go if she knew she only had a short time to live. I doubted that she would have stayed in her home there in Kansas City, and we were close to the archaeology site she had been working on for the last few years. I had been given the opportunity to visit the site the first year they had begun work, so I was familiar with where to find it. I figured if she wasn't there, I would try finding her in KC. I wasn't holding out much hope either way."

She paused, drained the last of the chicory from her cup, and said, "I noticed the cairn immediately. When we arrived at the cave I was convinced that the full team had to have been there, since there was evidence of more than just Mom. It took me a while to go deeper into the cave. I was wondering where everyone went, even though it was obvious it had been a while. I had completely forgotten about the long passage. Finding your letter, even as it raised more questions, gave me some measure of peace."

Her eyes brimmed with tears, "She wasn't alone when she passed. That means so much to me to know that she had someone with her as she passed into the world of spirits." She wiped at a tear that had escaped and began trickling down her cheek. "And eventually we came here, looking for you, Jess."

Jess realized then that her own cheeks were wet

with tears. The few months they had spent with Madge had been beautiful ones. The old woman had given her so much—love, acceptance, and peace—even now, six years later, she remembered it like it was yesterday. Just when her faith in humans and life in general had been so sorely tested, Madge had reminded her of all she had to live for, all that she could be for Jacob, the others, and for herself. Healing during those months in the cave had allowed her to have some trust in others again. She had emerged from the cave as more than just a ghost filled with grief over the loss of her friend, Erin.

Grandmother, that is what she asked us to call her, took us in, and taught us how to survive here, in this cave through the winter. It is now March, late March, and no snow has fallen in several weeks. The temperatures are rising and it is time for me to try to finish my journey home.

"I have her journal. The personal one that she kept," Jess remembered suddenly. "I can get it for you."

Penelope held up a hand, "Tomorrow. Can I come again tomorrow?" The sun had set and the darkness had closed in. "We are staying in town. That they let us in at all was a surprise, but apparently the militia is allowing traders and migrant workers in these days, so we will be here for another day or perhaps two."

Jess nodded, "Yes, yes of course. Come by tomorrow." They said their goodbyes and she watched Penelope and Kip walk away into the darkness. It was a new moon in the sky, and the darkness seemed overwhelming as they disappeared into the night. She gave a small start when David put his hand on her shoulder.

"She wants something, doesn't she?" he asked, his voice quiet in the gloom.

"Yeah…" Jess didn't know how to say it better, "She wants Tina."

"What?!" David sounded outraged and he looked as though he was ready to run after the couple and confront them.

Jess hastily explained, "There's a group of doctors, healers, working together in the city, or what's left of Kansas City, to create a new learning center for the healing arts. Sarah Turner told her about us, about Tina, and Penelope says it would be an apprenticeship." She grabbed his sleeve, "They are coming back tomorrow. We will learn more about them then. Okay? Let's not jump to any decision right now. They seem alright, and you can say no, but at least let's hear them out. It might actually be a chance for Tina to become a doctor… someone necessary…a future she might want."

David pulled away. "She isn't your sister, Jess. You can't just make this decision for her, or for me." His tone was defensive, even bitter.

Jess felt a surge of pain. They had spent years together, and she loved Tina just as much as she loved David or Jacob. "Of course not…I'm not trying to make a decision for her. I'm just…I'm just saying we should listen to what they say."

David walked in the opposite direction, away from where Penelope and Kip had headed into town, away from the house and Jess. She watched him go, feeling hurt and defensive. She knew he had a right to his feelings, but his abrupt departure wounded her. The last thing in the world she wanted to do was suggest that *she* wanted Tina should go away.

I don't know you, and you don't know me. But I'm writing this letter and then hiding the box where only someone who knows Madge and inner twists and turns of this cave will be able to find it. I have to be sure, you see. It still isn't safe. They have sent out soldiers hunting for us and I don't know that they aren't still out there, looking.

The next day, David seemed better. They had worked on the house, repairing a section of the roof, and then weeding several of the beds of potatoes and lettuce. Jess had made up her mind to tell Penelope they weren't interested, that Tina was far too young. What possible apprenticeship could apply to a young child? As she watched Penelope approach, her long-legged stride fluid on the broken pavement of the street, Jess could see that Sarah Turner had joined her and that Penelope's husband, Kip, was not with them.

Sarah was a kind woman. She had always treated Jess as an equal—and during those first months and years, she had championed the younger woman's cause, and that of their motley group of children more than once. Sarah was quite protective, in fact, which made Jess wonder about the older woman's past, and that of her children, who were nearly the same age as Jess. Sarah had always been rather close-mouthed about where she had come from, or where Cody and Laura's father was.

What would Sarah have to contribute to all of this? Jess wasn't sure what to think. A quick glance at David's face signaled trouble. Tina was *his* sister, and he had a right to his opinion, but for the first time Jess wondered what Tina wanted. Stay or go, wasn't it up to her? After all, Tina was nearly the age that David had been when they all first met in Clinton. He had been old enough to make a decision then, a decision that taken him away from everything familiar, everything that reminded him of home. Shouldn't Tina have the right to make that same decision? Even at the age of ten years?

Jess was conflicted and she knew it showed in her face. Sarah took it in, smiled at her, and gave her a warm hug. "Good morning Jess!" Since her daughter Laura had married Todd Stevens the laugh lines on her face had deepened. The births of Laura and Todd's two boys had brought happiness, along with something Jess could only describe as longing to Sarah's face. Jess wondered if Sarah was thinking of the husband she had left behind. Jess had listened to so many stories, so many unfinished, unknown fates of loved ones. It was perhaps the most haunting part of her job as historian— the unknown fates of so many. Sarah's story was one of dozens.

It was hours before dinner and they had had lunch just two hours earlier, but Sarah produced a loaf of her sourdough bread, a favorite of David's. That was combined with a bag of fruits that Kip had sent along, payment for some picking work they had both done earlier in the day. Jess and David, along with Tina, Sarah, and Penelope, sat down for a bite to eat and some conversation. It was stilted at first, mainly due to David, who felt cornered and resentful. Jess laid her hand on his knee, reminding him silently that she was his ally. He stared at her hand as she made small talk with Penelope and Sarah, concentrated on the long, tapered fingers. They were rough with callouses, but still delicate. He looked at them and tried to calm his fears—of losing his sister, knowing how much she wanted to go.

Tina had come to him that morning, the sun barely peeking over the horizon, and quietly folded herself on the floor of his room, quietly so she didn't wake Jacob. Her room was right next door, shared with Becka and Erin, when one or the other wasn't curled in bed next to Jess. "I want to go with her," was all that she had said when he opened one bleary eye and focused on her. They had engaged in a silent contest of wills, him glaring, her just staring back, until he had finally turned away and pulled the covers over his head and tried to ignore her. When he had turned back over a few moments later she was gone.

The small talk had progressed while he was woolgathering. Penelope was describing her mother's house in Kansas City. "It's over 130 years old and solid brick. Surprisingly, it's rather intact considering the dire situation that most residents were in before and during the collapse. Most of her books are still there," Penelope smiled at Jess, "she wrote about all kinds of recent history, as well as anthropology. She had quite an obsession with Jesse James and also had notes on Pendergast, a corrupt political boss in the early 20th century." She turned toward David, who just shrugged and shook his head. He had never heard of Jesse James or Pendergast.

"In any case, the house was gone through, but not much was taken and it was empty when we visited it last week. We are planning to stay there and work with a medical group that is forming." She looked at Tina and smiled at her, then back to David where her smile faltered a brief second, "If it would be all right, Tina could come with us to Kansas City, and stay in the house. There is plenty of room and there are other students who she would be learning side-by-side with. You could come too, David, to see for yourself, if you liked."

A long silence ensued. All eyes were on David, until Tina spoke up, "I want to go to Kansas City with you, Penelope. I want to learn how to be a doctor. It's all I've ever wanted to do."

David closed his eyes for a moment,

remembering her tiny hand in his, her matted hair in those weeks and months that had followed the deaths of their parents. The feel of her tiny body nestled against his. He remembered farther back, the first time he had seen her in the hospital, a tiny red face, impossibly small, mewling cries that sounded like a tiny, sad kitten. They had never fought; with nearly eight years between them he had always been the oldest, the one she looked up to. And when they had been alone, lost in the rubble of a dead and broken town, she had depended on him for everything.

It was only here, in Warsend, that she had come into her own, as young as she was, defining her future, writing it on the wall with nothing short of indelible marker. Her abilities, her intuitive understanding and curiosity of the healing arts had given her this opportunity. And who was he to say no? How could he? David thought of her being absent, not someone he saw every day, not in the garden or walking into town with freshly picked herbs for Dr. Ridley, and something deep in his chest twisted and pulled. She was all that he had of their former life. The only evidence he could show of the parents that he had lost. The words to say all that seemed to elude him.

In the end, he simply stared at Jess's hand, still on his knee, and said, "If Tina wants to go, then, I guess that's what she should do."

But if you find this, know that she died surrounded by

Jess, David, and the kids stood there for a long time the next morning and watched Tina walk away, her tiny hand in Penelope's, Kip alongside her. They watched until all three became dark specks that simply disappeared over the horizon.

ASCENSION

"Good can imagine Evil; but Evil cannot imagine Good"
– W.H. Auden

Sulwyn leaned back in his chair, his arms crossed in front of him, and shook his head. His gray hair had been cropped close—there was an outbreak of lice going around the camp—and even some of the women had chosen to cut most of their hair off rather than scratch all day. "Slaves? I just don't see how it's gonna work. Slaves have to eat."

Cooper had surprised everyone by returning with three black women from the last raid. He had insisted on putting them in a half-burned cabin where they huddled, tight-lipped and bloody, under armed guard. The raid had been quick, brutal in its efficiency.

The cabin had belonged to one of Sulwyn's chief lieutenants. Two weeks before, deep in the night, a fire had sparked, and others woke to the cabin fully engulfed in flames. The man had burned to death while the rest of the camp had concentrated on making sure the fire didn't spread to the rest of the nearby cabins and tents.

Despite part of the roof missing and some gaps in the charred timbers, the body of the cabin was intact. They threw a tarp over it, chained the captives, and attached a lock that opened only from the outside. Situated in the middle of the clearing, the captives would have to run by scores of armed Amerika Reborn soldiers in order to escape.

Cooper shrugged in response to Sulwyn's question. "Who says we need to feed them well? Slaves are for working, and if one or two dies," he shrugged again, "oh well, there's more out there." Sulwyn thought about this for a few moments and while he did, Delwen came to the door of the cabin.

In her arms she held a small baby. Cooper felt a wave of disgust wash over him. He didn't know who he despised more, the mewling brat that was his daughter or the unattractive woman who held her. He found himself wondering how his life had gone so wrong. In the Western Front, he could have had any woman he wanted, he could have ordered any man's death, or done it himself with impunity. And here, he closed his eyes; here he was bound by Sulwyn's rules.

It had been hard to break into the upper echelon of leadership—there was Sulwyn, his wretched daughter Delwen, and several others that had been with Sulwyn from the beginning. Albus had been as close to Sulwyn's right hand man as you could get, and Cooper had made sure to get rid of him when the short-sighted man had refused to align with him.

Albus had been the one Sulwyn listened to the most and Cooper had gone to him with the idea of capturing slaves and eventually using them for drug production. Plenty of people wanted an escape from what they saw as a dark new world. Cooper would never understand that thinking, but he was certain he could benefit from it. Manufacturing the drugs that gave them those ways to escape could be very profitable.

Albus had been fine with the slavery part, but the drugs? "No way," he had said, "what kind of an idiot are you, Cooper?" Drugs had killed his wife and young daughter over a decade before, something he said little about, but the images of the crumpled car and blood haunted him even now. He warned Cooper that if he persisted in his plan, that he would push Sulwyn to throw him out, whether he was married to Delwen or not. Cooper held himself back from doing violence to the man. A week later he made sure that Albus would never bend Sulwyn's ear again. The flames had destroyed all evidence of the crime.

Delwen's hard-edged voice broke through his reverie. "I ain't seen you around much these days." Her tone leaked resentment in every syllable. Her face and body was heavier now; she had put on a few pounds with the brat that hadn't come off. Perhaps if she actually did something besides sit around and feed her fat face she'd get back her body, which would be some improvement, but not much, to her looks.

He stared at her, wondering if there was any way he could get away with killing her in some handy accident. "I've been sleeping in the hammock outside. I thought that would be better than disturbing you when I got back late." The raiders, led by Cooper, had returned late the night before. It was September, and the nights were still quite warm. Sleeping outside in the hammock had meant he didn't have to listen to the squalling baby, or to his wife's snores, both of which disturbed his sleep and peace of mind.

They reminded him all too often of his new disturbingly domestic life, which he didn't want and certainly hadn't asked for. A few wordless meetings in the dark, the only ever instigated by a woman instead of him, and he had ended up facing Sulwyn, and a quietly smug Delwen, one cold March morning. "My daughter tells me she's pregnant, and you are the father."

Cooper hadn't known what to say. Scuttling through his brain had been the question he'd wanted to ask but didn't. *How do I know she's just slept with me?* But he knew Sulwyn well enough by now not to ask a question like that. In another time and place, this man would have been a baron. He was a good leader, yet he was definitely removed from the others. And after four years with the Amerika Reborn, dealing with Sulwyn nearly every day, Cooper knew that questioning whether the man's only child was sleeping with multiple men would have been a mortal mistake.

Sulwyn had given Cooper a minute or two to realize how badly he was hosed before saying, "We don't have a preacher, so I guess I'll have to do. We'll have some kind of ceremony tomorrow." And with that, Cooper's fate was sealed. Once the leader of a hundred plus faction of the Western Front, and now a lackey of Sulwyn's. With every caterwaul that came from the brat he had sired, he thought of where he had been, and where he was now, and regretted it. Somehow he needed to take back his life—and that meant that Sulwyn had to die. But before he could just kill the man, without question or retribution, he had to make this group into a fighting power that the region had not seen before. They had to see him as a leader in his own right—then, and only then, would the men follow him. When that day came, he could and would kill Sulwyn with impunity.

Delwen just glared at him and jiggled the infant.

From the sour, scrunched-up look on the baby's face it appeared as if she was getting ready to begin howling any moment. Cooper hadn't had any say in what the child was named, not that he particularly cared anyway, and Delwen had announced that the baby's name was Sulwen, the feminine version of Sulwyn, which meant white sun in Welsh.

Once she had come out, Cooper had been convinced she was his kid, but it hadn't changed his mind about children in general. He despised the mewling brat. At least Armando had been quiet, but this creature screamed all day and all night, given the opportunity. Sulwen's name was quickly shortened to Sully, in order to differentiate her from her grandfather more easily.

"Well, I want one of those women you rounded up to help with Sully," Delwen said, "I can't get any sleep and you sure aren't any help." And with that input, it was decided. The slaves would be put to use, and the first part of Cooper's plan fell into place. First slaves, then drug production and sale, and then he would find a way to get rid of Sulwyn, along with Sulwyn's daughter and grandchild. It all felt perfect.

Camelia didn't just handle the doctoring; she had also been put in charge of bodies and burials. Two weeks before, Armando had watched with grim fascination as his mother gave the grisly burned remains a cursory examination, her focus honing in on the skull for just a second longer than normal, and then turned back to the business of digging the hole. Later that night, when the others were gone and Armando was alone to snuggle next to his mother he asked her in a tiny whisper, "Why did you look at his head, Mamá?"

Camelia pulled him close, "Promise you won't ask again? I'll answer, but you must promise not to speak of it to anyone."

Armando wondered who she thought he might talk to, since he had been ostracized from anyone his age due to his 'color' and nodded, "I promise, Mamá."

"Someone killed him," she said flatly.

"Why?"

"Because he was in the other man's way—then he burned the cabin to hide what he had done."

"It was Cooper, wasn't it, Mamá?"

The conversation had been conducted in whispers, and all of it in Spanish, but Camelia had flinched at the name and pulled her son even closer. "Shhh, do not say his name."

"Well, was it?"

"Yes, I think so. Now go to sleep."

Part Two

"Love is the emblem of eternity: it confounds all notion of time: effaces all memory of a beginning, all fear of an end." — Madame de Stael

CHAPTER SEVENTEEN

MORNING

"Like a morning dream, life becomes more and more bright the longer we live, and the reason of everything appears more clear. What has puzzled us before seems less mysterious, and the crooked paths look straighter." – Jean Paul Richter

Light peeked in through the boarded-up window in Jess's bedroom and she opened her eyes instinctively, knowing that the daylight was wasting and there was much to be done today. Becka lay curled up next to her, hair sticky and moist with sweat from the fever she had been fighting for days. A small hand fisted the covers, and one leg lay over

Jess.

She slowly slid from the bed, quietly cursing the bitter cold that cut into her as soon as she left the warm layers of bedcovers. Becka murmured and shifted, curling into a small ball. Jess pulled on a thick sweater and slid her socked feet into tattered and taped-over work boots.

Her feet guided the way to the hall where the light did not, for the years spent in this house were many and she knew each squeaky floorboard, each corner of furniture and doorway within it. Her hand was reaching for the doorknob of the door of the bedroom at the end of the hall when it opened and nine-year-old Jacob spoke quietly in the darkness, "Mornin', Mom. How's Becka?"

Jess sighed, "No change. I left her sleeping. Breakfast or barn?"

"Breakfast…eggs okay?" he replied.

"Sounds fine," Jess reached out through the gloom and smoothed his hair with her hand, "Wake up the others, but tell them to be quiet and let Becka sleep."

She walked through the living room and on through the kitchen and small pantry next to it. Next was the door leading to the barn. In a former life it had been an attached two-car garage, but now it was a shelter for the family's two goats, a large rabbit hutch, and feed supplies.

Sounds of the others moving about in the house could be heard dimly through the walls as Jess set about feeding each of the animals. Later she would let the goats out into a corral to stretch their legs. After feeding came cleaning, and after that came her daily war with Satan, their female goat, for her meager pitcher of milk. Satan, as her name implied, came straight from hell and was meaner than any goat had any business being. Jess once again resolved to finish off the wretched creature as soon as she produced female offspring. Satan was also resolved not to ever produce anything but males. Consequently, her life and future seemed safely assured. Apple, the male goat, kept out of Satan's way and always seemed to have a henpecked, desperate look about his whiskered face.

"Damn it, Satan," Jess exclaimed as she wrestled the goat into place only to be sprayed by the first drops of milk she squeezed out. The goat had moved suddenly. As she wiped her boot off, the goat took the opportunity to swiftly nip the unprotected finger.

"Sonuva…aw jeezsus!" Jess held her bleeding digit to her lips. "Goat curry! That's what I'm gonna make you!" She waved her fist at the goat half-heartedly, knowing the threat was empty.

The door to the garage swung open and Erin stepped through, shutting it quickly so as not to let out what small amount of heat was emanating from the kitchen. Erin was now six years old. There was a quiet maturity about the child that belied her tender age. Without a word she took hold of Satan's head and offered the beast a withered crabapple. She was the only one in the family who could coax the blasted goat to stay still, and she also was the only one of them to never have been nipped, stepped on, or even so much as butted by Satan.

Jess smiled and quickly began milking the goat, stopping only after the last drops of milk were squeezed out. Satan had long since finished the apple and was standing still patiently, as Erin stroked the recalcitrant beast's head and whiskered chin. The girl's eyes held the goat's gaze steadily and it was as if they were speaking a silent language, telling secrets and exchanging memories with each other.

"All done," Jess broke the silence, Erin let go of Satan, and the goat instantly left to graze on the fresh feed set out for her. Jess reached over and smoothed the child's tangled hair with her hand and smiled down at Erin. "Any words for me today, sweet Erin?" she asked the girl, cupping her chin in her hand.

The fey child only smiled and shook her head, saying nothing at all, and instead she held out her arms to be picked up and hugged. As always, Jess took Erin in her arms and hugged her gently against her, marveling at how such a small creature could so silently charm all those around her—man and beast alike.

Erin had appeared on the doorstep over two years ago. Jess had rounded the front of the house, saw her crouched there and instantly drew near, crouched down, and gathered her in her arms. The trembling creature had wrapped her arms and legs around Jess and buried her face in Jess's neck. She had not uttered a word then, or in the two long years since. But where her voice failed, her eyes and hands spoke volumes, and she had instantly become a part of their family, without question or reservation.

The spring following Erin's arrival, a body was discovered a mile to the east, along the creek bank. It was the remains of a man with red hair much like Erin's. He had been shot. There had been a well-loved teddy bear tucked inside a child-size knapsack lying nearby.

Thurman Banks had found the body and told Jess about it the following day as he brought by some potatoes in exchange for fresh eggs from the chicken coop Jess and the kids kept in back of the house.

He had buried the body where it lay, he said, and put up a rough cross for the unknown man. He looked over at the small, silent child sitting in the garden patch, placed the bear in her lap and went away quietly with his eggs. He visited often, and never failed to bring by something special for Erin when he did, for the child had enchanted him.

Jess gave Erin another quick hug before setting her back on the ground. "Go help Jacob, sweetheart, he's in the chicken coop and surely having trouble with Maude and Beulah by now," she directed the child, envisioning her son struggling to get the eggs from two of the older, more aggressive hens.

Maude and Beulah, like Satan, were destined for the stockpot one of these days. But they were still quite reliable layers, so Jess held off from ending them, despite the inevitable pecks and scratches they handed out so liberally. Erin slipped away silently and headed out the side door toward the back of the house.

Jess headed back inside the house and promptly ran into David, who was still rubbing his eyes, trying desperately to wake up. "Mornin' Jess," he said yawning, wincing as he saw her bloody finger, "Satan git you again?"

Jess nodded and headed for the medicine cabinet to dose her injured finger with iodine, leaning in first for a peck on the cheek from the young man as she passed by. David was now twenty years old, and his hair was nearly shoulder length, dark brown, and tousled, his eyes a soft, friendly brown. Like the rest of their hodgepodge family, he was of slender build —obesity had all but disappeared in the past decade when food was scarce and most lived at bare subsistence level. Though harvests were better now, they were still far from being safe from starvation if a winter came early enough or lasted too long.

"So what's on tap for today? Lessons, huntin', or washin'?" David asked as Jess busied herself lighting a small fire under one burner.

"Well, we could use some meat, or even fish if you could get them to bite. Take Jake; he's itching to get out there and do 'manly' things." Jess winked at him and David snorted and nodded. "I'll see how far Erin and I can get with the wash, but make sure and gather it up for me, okay? Then maybe some lessons for Jake tonight if you two don't get back too late."

Jacob slipped in as she was talking. "Huntin'? Really? Right on!" Then his face managed to twitch into a somewhat serious expression, "But Mom, you know how far we have to go out to get anything; it might be real late when we get back. We might not have time for lessons tonight." He tried unsuccessfully to look disappointed.

Jess turned and gave him 'the look.' "Well then, perhaps, young Jacob, you should stay here with me and help with laundry and still have plenty of time for your lessons afterwards. It seems to me that you should be farther along in that book by now, and your math needs work too."

Jacob practically stumbled over himself getting his objections out, in the end it was a wail, "But Mom!"

She raised an eyebrow, "So I can depend on you being back by sundown?" He nodded excitedly. "Glad to hear it. Now be sure to pack a lunch for the two of you while breakfast gets cooked and wear your warm wool socks that I made you." As he prepared to launch himself like a rocket into the living room and on through into his bedroom she called out in a loud whisper, "And quietly! Becka's still sleeping!"

CHAPTER EIGHTEEN

SAYING GOODBYE

"I can't stay here. It isn't home without him. Chris will say, 'What about our babies?' And what about our babies? Our babies are gone, gone before they drew their first breaths. If I stay, here where I have lost so much, I will taste the ashes of regret in my mouth forever." – Carrie's Journal

The little graveyard didn't have much room left. Not with its newest addition. And unlike the four previous, mostly private, ceremonies, this one was well attended. Practically everyone in Tiptonville was here. Carl had whispered to Chris that they had even shut down the Trade Mart for the day.

To the right stood Joseph, looking quite tall and

somber for his fourteen years. Beside him, seated in a well-padded chair with a blanket was Mr. Liles. The man was 116 years old and looked so frail and thin that Chris feared a stiff breeze would blow him away. His rheumy eyes watered and he clutched a much-abused handkerchief in one hand while the other plucked randomly at the blanket that swaddled him. Joseph said that Mr. Liles slept a lot these days and ate little.

The teen had volunteered to stay with the old man after a recent fall had left him weak and fragile. Joseph had developed a knack for working with motors and he had begun helping out Mr. Liles a few years earlier in the shop. Now he stayed and cared for the old man, fixed meals, and made sure the stove stayed lit. He also manned the store and helped the infrequent customer.

Despite the attention, Mr. Liles had declined steadily during Fenton's illness. Chris wondered what it must be like to outlive your children, your grandchildren, and to see your friends pass before you. How many funerals had Mr. Liles attended? How many goodbyes?

Liza and Carl, along with their three children, Molly, John and little Abby, stood on the left. Liza's face was a mask of grief, her eyes red-rimmed, and her nose blotchy. She would not cry, however, in front of the children. Abby, not quite two years old, wriggled in her arms, itching to be set down so she could run through the tall grass. Little John, just three and a half years old, stood holding his dad's hand and looked puzzled by all the people and the mournful tone in the air. Molly Ann, who would be six in less than two weeks, clutched Carl's other side, her tiny face sad. She had been Fenton's favorite, the first of his great-grandchildren and he had doted on her.

Outside of immediate family and Mr. Liles, it appeared that the rest of Tiptonville stood outside of the waist-high metal gates. Everyone wore black armbands. Mrs. Jennings, the town librarian, stood close to the fence, grasped it with one frail hand, and wept softly into her handkerchief.

Reverend Deeds stepped forward, leaning heavily on his cane with one hand, the other arm around his young wife, Grace. He opened a well-worn Bible riddled with tabs and papers marking different passages.

Carrie leaned against Chris. She had miscarried just a week before, and was still weak and tired. She closed her eyes, trying to stop the tears from sliding down her face.

Gramps had suffered for so long, and Liza had done everything she could. In another time, when the world had been whole, Gramps could have had bypass surgery. The doctors would have been able to open him up, clean out the clogged chambers, and give him a decade more.

But that time, like the country they had long identified with, was gone. The recovery and founding of the new nation was taking its time. This had all taken too long for Fenton. This life they led was harder, with no time for the weak or the sick to heal. Not when there were fields to be plowed or the basic necessities to be met. Slowly, his heart had reduced his ability to walk very far or exert himself in much of any way.

There were rumblings of a Reformation, now that the Second American Civil War was officially over. Life was slowly going back to normal. However, that seemed to be happening with more speed on the east and west coasts, not here, not in Tennessee, or even the larger southern cities. The citizens of Tiptonville, along with so many other small towns, were still on their own.

It had been a difficult thing to see, watching Fenton slowly succumb to heart disease. It had been especially hard for Liza, there in the house, pulled in so many directions. She had three small children, the duties of the farm and the townspeople, who now regularly visited for their doctoring needs.

Jeremy—Carrie still had a hard time thinking of him as Reverend Deeds—stepped forward and began to speak.

"We are gathered here today in memory of our friend, a beloved grandfather and member of this community, Fenton Perdue." He opened it to a marked page and began the sermon, "Jesus tells us that we will know not the hour of our death…"

Carrie's attention wandered from Jeremy to the

markers in the small family cemetery. Her gaze came to rest on her father's and mother's graves. Her heart ached at the memory of them, especially her mother, Amy.

That last time she had seen her she had been in the hospital bed looking so thin, so insubstantial. Carrie had been afraid to hug her, afraid that Joseph, who had just begun crawling, would hurt his frail mother as he wiggled in her arms. It had been three days before Thanksgiving and the hospital reeked of turkey and disinfectant, an unpleasant and disconcerting combination.

Fenton had stepped out of the room with Liza and baby Joseph to get a bite to eat at the cafeteria and Amy had beckoned her daughter closer. "Carrie, sweetheart, come here." Her bony fingers were cold in Carrie's hand. A tear trickled down her mother's pale cheek. "You are so beautiful and I love you so much. You know that, don't you?"

Carrie had nodded, unable to say anything. There are moments when you know it, whether the words have been said or not, that things are not going to get better, that life will never be the same again. Dad was gone and now Mom was dying too. Carrie could see there was little time left, but her voice seemed to have deserted her. She wanted to tell Mom everything and beg her not to leave, to just fight harder.

"Carrie, sweetie, your sister and little brother need you right now. Even Gramps needs you. And these next few weeks and months will be hard. I know they have already been hard and that you feel lost and scared right now." Her mother stopped, struggled to breathe, and then continued,

"Someday though, someday you will find love. You will make a family of your own and you will have babies and you will laugh and love. Promise me that you will do these things—that you won't wait for the perfect moment—but jump into life and live it and love every moment of it. Promise me that you will find happiness and that when the time comes to leave, you will do it, and you will go where you need to go and be who you need to be."

Carrie nodded, her eyes full of tears, "I promise Mom." A moment passed before Carrie mustered the courage to admit, "I stole five dollars from Dad's wallet the day before... the day..." her voice faltered.

Her mother managed a small chuckle. "I know you did. Your dad told me." She squeezed Carrie's hand with remarkable strength. "Anything else you want to confess?" she asked, her voice cracking with the effort.

Carrie struggled for a moment to form the words, "I blamed Joseph at first. For making you weak, for making you get sick. But...I know it isn't his fault and I promise I will be a good sister and not fight with him or Liza." She could see her mom slipping into sleep, exhausted from their brief discussion. "I love you, Mom."

Jeremy's words interrupted Carrie's reverie, "Even though I walk through the shadow of the valley of death I will fear no evil, for thou art with me." He continued the Lord's prayer, and she could hear the others murmuring it softly all around her.

Gramps had loved them, grouched at them, guided them…and now he was gone. The memory of her mother's words fell like arrows on her heart.

Jump into life and live it and love every moment of it. What had she been doing?

Carrie couldn't help but feel she had ignored her mother's advice, at least some of it. She had found love and embraced that, but she had somehow lost her way on the rest. As the coffin was slowly lowered into the ground, and her tears, along with many others', flowed freely, Carrie could not shake the feeling.

Somehow, I need to change. Somehow, I need to be more *than I am right now.*

CHAPTER NINETEEN

LOVE FINDS US

They say, those soft-spoken romantics, that love finds you when you least expect it. Somehow sneaking up behind you after all of that loneliness and searching. It hits you dead on in your brain-pan and touches your very soul. It sucks you in and steals your heart. It is a moment when you are looking down at the ground, trudging forward, innocently aware that fate is coming down the highway, barreling along, making time, a load of bricks on its back. This deep and great love, it takes you and sweeps you away with no regrets or time for compromise. – Christine Shuck

In the end it was really Satan's fault. If it hadn't been for that awful creature, and a very bloody finger, who knows how long it might have been before Jess realized that she was in love with David and he with her? So in the end, that damned goat got to live, despite her violent tendencies.

Satan grunted and her bloated stomach convulsed and twisted. David stared at the rear of the animal, "I think I see the head!"

Jacob sidled up next to him and stared as well, "Oh gross! That is so cool!"

Jess had had enough of everyone. "Out! Out!" she ordered Erin and Jacob. Satan had been laboring for well over four hours now and Jess had missed breakfast and lunch and was hungry and cross and done with the circus act the pregnant goat seemed to be putting on.

David eyed her warily, "You all right?"

She just glared in return and eyed the retreating kids. Jacob foolishly spoke, half inside the sanctuary of the house, half of him still in reach, "But Mom, I…"

"I said OUT!" The door slammed shut and she relaxed somewhat and turned back to Satan. "This effin' goat had better have a girl this time."

"Still going to turn her into stew?"

"You're damned straight I am!" Despite her tough words, she stroked the pregnant goat as the kid's head slowly began to emerge. "C'mon Satan, you can do it!"

Out slithered a kid, covered with blood and definitely, oh quite definitely, another damn male.

Jess cussed low and furious. "Damn you, Satan, *another* boy?"

The goat's stomach convulsed and writhed again. David stopped staring at Jess's tousled blond hair and turned back to the goat. A few seconds later he was holding a tiny, damp newborn kid and grinning.

"Looks like a girl to me!" Satan made a strange sound and David's grin slipped as he stared at Satan's rear in puzzlement.

"What is it?" Jess asked, sounding concerned.

"I…uh…think she's having triplets!"

"You are shitting me." David arched an eyebrow in mock shock. It was a rare thing to hear Jess curse and she was always after him to watch what he said in front of the kids.

"No…I'm uh…ah crap, here it comes!" David shoved the slimy, damp newborn kid into Jess's arms and reached up in time to catch the third one before it slid out onto the hard concrete. He examined it quickly and looked up with a grin, "Would you believe it's another girl?"

As if sensing her days were numbered, Satan reached back and bit down hard on the hand resting near her flank. Jess dropped the floundering newborn kid and recoiled away from the vicious animal. Blood flowed freely, and brought tears of pain into Jess's eyes. "Oh damn it all to hell, that really hurts!"

David was at her side in an instant, applying pressure and wrapping the finger in a clean cloth.

They had a pile of them there on the floor for toweling off the newborn kids.

The minute he touched her, smelled her hair near his face, it made him crazy. And today was no different. He'd been avoiding being alone with her for weeks now. It was just too much, these feelings he had when she was nearby. The slightest touch, the smell of her, even her *smile*—and his body would vibrate from deep inside.

And all the while he wondered if she even knew how much he wanted her. At first he had told himself he was just horny. It was natural, normal, and they weren't related after all. But it seemed as if they had known each other forever. He told himself that she couldn't see him that way, because he was younger and she'd taken care of him when they first met.

He'd only been eleven and her fifteen and pregnant and both of them as lonely and scared as could be. For years he'd thought of her just like that, just like the moment they had met. A big sister figure, alone, just like him and Tina.

But something had changed. First the dreams had come, bringing visions of soft lips, deep blue eyes, fantasies of her lying naked in his arms. After a few of those dreams and blushing furiously when he looked at her across from him at the breakfast table, he'd headed east on a week-long hunting trip hoping to get his head (both of them) screwed on straight. Along the way he had found Elle Beringer alone picking mushrooms in the woods and she'd showed him what he'd only dreamed and fantasized about. It had taken the edge off for a while.

Whenever it got bad, he went on another hunting trip and looked up Elle at her cabin where she lived alone and traded mushrooms and wild carrots for some fresh goat's milk or eggs. She'd asked him to stay once, and he was tempted—the sex was phenomenal—but something kept pulling him back to the little house in Warsend.

One day, after many months away, he'd stopped by Elle's to find her with a swelled pregnant belly and a man by her side. The tiny cabin had doubled in size, new wood gleaming in the sun. Elle was a good woman; he was glad to see her settled and happy. She introduced her man, Mike, and they sat and ate supper together before parting ways.

"You're a million miles away," Jess's voice brought him back to reality, his face inches from hers, "you okay?"

He looked into her eyes, they were a deep crayon blue, and before his brain could come up with a million reasons not to, he leaned in, reached one hand up into her soft blond hair and pulled her close and kissed her. The kiss lasted several seconds, her lips were soft and she made a quiet almost purring sound in the back of her throat. He found it to be incredibly sexy.

When they broke apart he was terrified to even look her in the eye. What if he looked up and saw pity? What if he saw a look that said 'sister' or 'friend' and not lover? He had wanted to kiss her, to know the feel of her skin and lips against his own for so long. He could not bear the thought of her not wanting him back.

Jess was stunned by the kiss. More than anything, she was shocked by her response to it. Her whole body thrummed! She had avoided men for so long, kept herself safe by sticking to the family, hiding behind the children and their needs in order to never have to be attractive or attracted to another man for the rest of her life. So why did she want to grab him by the shirt, pull him back up against her, and have him kiss her again like that?

At that moment, the door to the garage opened and saved them both from whatever foolish words they might have uttered next.

Jacob flew into the room, "Oh wow! THREE baby goats. Satan had triplets!!!!"

Becka was at his heels, bouncing up and down, and Erin followed silently. Although she could speak, she still chose silence more often than not. Old habits die hard. Jess and David had practically jumped apart when the door opened and while Jacob had eyes only for the newborn kids, little Erin gave them a once over and smiled secretively at them before turning her attention to the newborns. She was a perceptive little girl.

The rest of the day was consumed with cleaning up the afterbirth and making sure all three newborns were nursing well. Satan was looking fine, despite the strain of multiple offspring, and Apple kept his distance from the tiny family unit after Satan bit his neck when he sniffed the newborns.

Jacob was singing some impromptu song about goat curry, stopping only to ask what exactly curry was and Becka had asked to name the newborns Damien, Lucifer, and Beelzebub. When reminded that Lucifer and Beelzebub were both male names she was quick to note that angels were androgynous and after all, and that Satan wasn't particularly a girl's name either. So the names stuck.

In later years, their names would prove to be frighteningly accurate. Both girls took after their mother and exceeded her in viciousness. Damien ended up being the gentle one. Lucifer and Beelzebub ended up in the stewpot long before their mother did.

Jess and David avoided each other's eyes and busied themselves with chores and dinner and cleaning. Jacob and Erin ran and played for most of the day outside and fell asleep, dead asleep, in the middle of the living room floor by the fourth page in the book Jess had begun reading to them, *Harry Potter and the Half-Blood Prince*. Jess's voice faded to a whisper as she surveyed the limp bodies at her feet. They were wrapped in blankets and breathing even and deep.

She raised her gaze to meet David's. He had been staring at her steadily for the past ten minutes, slowly convincing himself that she hadn't said "no" to that kiss, she had even touched his hand lightly, caressingly, earlier when asking him to pass the salt. She smiled at him nervously, broke eye contact, and stood up. Negotiating around the limp sleeping bodies was difficult; the floorboards creaked noisily and caused Jacob to shift and mutter in his sleep. Jess negotiated her way to the dark hallway and the open door to her bedroom. Her heart gave a thump of surprise as she realized that David was inches from her.

He had been silent in his approach. Standing this close, she realized he was nearly half a foot taller, "*When did that happen?*" she asked herself. Damn it but he was close; mere inches separated them.

"Maybe we should talk about this…" she began to say to him, her body beginning to thrum.

"Mm hm," was his only reply. He pulled her against him gently, sought out her soft lips in the darkness, and kissed her. Unlike their first kiss, there was no question in this one. Their tongues met, entwined, teased, and intensified.

She made one more attempt, "The kids, they might wake up." She felt annoyance, not at David, but at herself for even mentioning the kids. It wasn't what she was worried about, not really. By this time they had somehow made their way inside of the bedroom. He closed the door firmly and quietly behind them and pulled Jess close to his body.

He threaded his fingers through her soft, blond

curls. She had cut it short just the one time, before their journey back to Warsend. Ever since she had let it grow long, only trimming the rough split ends away, and it was now past her back, a riot of curls and waves.

He leaned into the curve of her neck, whispering against her skin, "This has nothing to do with the kids. This is between you and me. The kids will be fine out there."

Before she could protest any further he pulled her down onto the bed and covered her mouth with his. She found her hands moving along his body, pulling at his shirt, sliding her hands along his ribs. Clothing melted away, her shirt tossed over there, a shoe clattered to the floor. His tongue and mouth moving along her neck, down to her breasts, sliding a hand into the hem of her pants. She stiffened, almost imperceptibly, but he felt it.

He stopped, his voice was soft in her ear, "I love you, Jessie, and I would never hurt you. You know that, right?"

She nodded, unable to trust her voice; the fear and memories had just hit her and then, just as quickly, passed through her. And a few moments later, the unexpected pleasure of lovemaking, not just sex, was mind-blowing. For years she had avoided men, avoided the thought of ever being close to another. But this, this was physical love, with someone she had spent the last ten years living and working next to. It was familiar, yet completely new, and she hadn't felt anything like it before.

Tears followed. There were so many tears that he became confused and worried he had frightened or hurt her, until she told him that she loved him too. He held her then, covered her with a quilt and pulled her close to his body until she stopped crying and fell asleep in his arms. It was now that he could see so clearly the horror that she had experienced in the enemy camp those ten years past. Nothing could erase those memories, and he knew there had been no one since, no man to show her any different. He fell asleep that way, holding her close, listening to her soft breathing.

David was having an amazing dream; more of a fantasy, really. In it, Jess was running her mouth and tongue along his neck, stroking his chest.

"Wake up." He opened his eyes and saw her above him in the gloom, her hands on his chest. She nibbled his fingers and smiled at him in the dim moonlight, "I promise I won't cry this time."

They made love again, her body writhing in pleasure beneath his. His heart was racing and her body, dear lord, it felt so good to be inside her. He held her close afterwards, their bodies wrapped around each other, legs and arms entangled.

"David?"

"Mm?" he had been slipping back into sleep again.

"Is this…" Jess's voice faltered, "Is this for real?"

"God, I hope so," David laughed, nuzzling her

neck, kissing her shoulder lightly.

Jess squirmed a little; his face was scratchy and it tickled a little.

"How long have you, I mean, have you felt this way for me for a while?"

"The last year, give or take a few months," he said, kissing her again.

"How did I not notice?" her tone was tinged with wonder and exasperation.

He shrugged, "I did my best to hide it. I figured you wouldn't take me seriously."

Jess laughed, "Wow. If that's what I've been missing out on for the past year, I…I don't know what to say."

"You don't need to say anything." And he leaned over and kissed her again, his hands caressing her body. "Not a single thing." Their lips met in the dark and after that there were no more words until morning.

CHAPTER TWENTY

DARK HORSE RIDING

"Betrayal is the only truth that sticks." – Arthur Miller

Delwen rolled over, leaning away from Heimdall, and reached for the half-smoked joint. She struck a match and lit it. She had to pull hard on it; the weed was still a bit wet, the taste harsh. They had started growing the plants a few years ago. They had the slaves tend it, along with working the meth lab, and Amerika Reborn had a decent "honest" income going now that the Reformation was spreading.

The Reformation, however, was a double-edged sword. With a return to normal life, or some semblance of normalcy, the demand for drugs that

Amerika Reborn had become so good at supplying had begun to climb. However, the ways in which they produced the products, namely using the slaves, was beginning to garner the wrong sort of attention. The raids, something that had diminished significantly in the last year as more and more of the localities began to solidify their loyalties with the Allied South, were also attracting the wrong sort of attention from militias and local governments re-forming to the east. The group had begun as a few remnants of military units in the region and slowly evolved into a large governmental unit with tentacles in nearly all of the larger towns and cities that stretched through Louisiana, Arkansas, Mississippi, Alabama, Georgia, South Carolina, and the eastern edge of Texas.

Soon Amerika Reborn would have to give up the slaves and possibly move to a different part of the country if things continued on their current trend. It wasn't time to close up shop though; the demand for drugs was higher than it had ever been before. It seemed like everyone needed an escape from reality at some time or another.

Heimdall's acne had faded over the past ten years, but the scars remained. So, it seemed, had his lovesick obsession for her. He'd had it bad since they were kids, always following after her, with his greasy, lank blond hair, the occasional whopper of a bruise from his volatile alcoholic mother, always volunteering to go on guard duty with her.

When she had first pulled him aside in the woods after a mission a few months ago he had been surprised, but responsive. He wasn't a bad lay, she mused; he had been attentive to her needs, something that Cooper never was, and had kept his mouth shut about it, something she needed him to do until the time was right. When the first encounter hadn't produced the desired outcome, she had pulled him aside again.

Later, she had done it for fun, even after she was sure. Getting pregnant was her insurance policy—and finding a guy like Heimdall, all muscle, not much brains, was essential.

Delwen's father, Sulwyn, had made a big mistake. Despite all of her hard work, her dedication to *proving* to her father that she could lead, he had given the reins of power to Cooper. But that was about to change, for Sulwyn and Cooper both.

While Scott Cooper had never truly liked her, or even trusted her, over the years she had learned to read him better than anyone. Delwen knew he was planning something, and it probably had to do with taking Sulwyn out of power…permanently. Cooper wasn't the type to take orders. From what he said of his time with the Western Front, he had made a determined and calculated effort to kill his way to the top, and she knew it was just a matter of time before he took her old man out, and probably her as well.

Delwen had her own ideas about who should be

in charge—and after years of being ignored or marginalized by her father, just because she had breasts and baby-making equipment instead a dick and balls—well; it was time for a change. She smiled to herself, her homely face curving. Sulwyn had made a big mistake underestimating her. So had Cooper, for that matter. And she was nearly ready to give them both what they so richly deserved. Just a month more and she would enter into her second trimester. Her father would be dead. Cooper would either be dead or on the run, and she would hold the scepter of power in her hands.

Heimdall reached his hand out and caressed her hip. His hand was rough with callouses, but he had a gentle touch. Delwen handed him the joint and was about to reciprocate when there was a scratch at the door.

"Shit!" she whispered, grabbing for her clothes. They had used Heimdall's cabin for their tryst, and she felt stupid for allowing herself to relax. Who could have followed them? Was it Cooper? Or one of Sulwyn's cronies?

Behind her, Heimdall stubbed out the joint and was hurriedly pulling on a pair of pants. He went to the door first, easing it open, and then opened it all of the way to the person standing on the other side. It turned out to be Sully, Delwen's six year old daughter, looking every inch of her father. She was a pretty girl, with ice blue eyes and black hair, just like Cooper.

The girl was quiet, reserved, her intelligence kept hidden from most. With neither of her parents particularly interested in her, she had naturally gravitated toward her grandfather, Sulwyn, after Camelia had died in the outbreak of dysentery that had halved the ranks of Amerika Reborn four months ago. Camelia had become nursemaid to Sully a few months after her birth, just as Camelia was weaning Armando. Delwen hadn't had enough patience to nurse for long, and with no formula, there hadn't been any other real option. Long after the child was weaned, Sully had stuck close, as if sensing that Camelia cared more for her than her own parents did.

Camelia had found it ironic, the similarities between the two children, who were, after all, half-siblings. They were the only children in the camp and Armando and Sully did everything together, something that was often frowned upon by the Amerika Reborn leaders, yet no one challenged it, no one wanted to take care of a small child. But it had all changed when Camelia died.

Delwen and others blamed the Hispanic woman for the disease, despite the fact that several members of the AR had sickened first, and inevitably transmitted the dysentery to their one and only doctor. Alenoush, who had studied for several years under Camelia, had gotten sick as well and died just two days after the Hispanic woman, leaving no one with any medical knowledge. The Reformation's tentacles were spreading, though, and the group hadn't had any major illnesses since the dysentery's spread had been halted. There was a town a few miles away that still turned a blind eye to the group's unsavory aspects—in no small part thanks to the mayor and his 'town council,' who were happy to indulge in the AR's samples of meth and weed. They had a doctor available if the AR suffered another medical emergency.

Sully had missed Camelia deeply, but she said nothing; even at the age of six she could see the way of things. She feared her father, avoided her mother whenever possible, but had found a small measure of kindness from her grandfather Sulwyn. She stood at the doorway, understanding on a level that belied her years that her mother was engaged in something she wished hidden.

"Grandpa is looking for you," she told her mother, staring at the dirty wood floor of the cabin.

Delwen nodded to her daughter, "Go to the woods out back, stay there, and pick some of them greens. Don't come back until you have a good armful. If anyone asks, I was there picking and gave 'em to you to take over." She said it tersely, and stared at the girl until she nodded and ran toward the woods.

After the girl disappeared, Delwen shut the door, finished dressing and grabbed a handful of mint from a patch growing near the cabin to chew on and stuff in her pockets. It wouldn't do for Sulwyn to smell either of her two sins on her.

He knew what a bastard Cooper was, but had told her many times over the years, "You made your bed girl, now you are going to damn well lie in it."

Having an affair with Heimdall, no matter how careful they were or how uninterested Cooper was in her (he hadn't slept with her in well over two years), was simply unacceptable in her father's eyes. And as for the weed, her old man thought it was all well and fine for others, for the "weak" ones to do that. But heaven help her if he caught her at it. Her mother had been a crack whore on the avenues. Sulwyn reminded her of it time and again.

"She was weak and stupid and wanton, and I did what I could to save her from herself."

Her mother had died when Delwen was a baby, long before she had held the name Delwen Kingmaker.

When she arrived at the central cabin, a large meeting room that doubled as their communal dining area, she watched the old man carefully. He had sent the one lone guard away and he was looking bad, sipping at the tea she had begun lacing with belladonna months ago, his skin pale and sweaty, his pupils large. He blinked when the door opened, letting in a surge of light, and turned away. The light hurt his eyes and Delwen couldn't help but smile; he was steadily worsening.

Sulwyn was alone in the dark room. He barely glanced her way when she shut the door behind her and advanced toward her father. The older man's hand shook as he waved her closer.

"You kept me waiting a bit, girl; where were you anyway?" His speech was slurred, and he compulsively licked his lips.

"Pickin' greens, sir," she answered him promptly, in the way he expected her to. He lifted the cup of tea. It settled his nerves, at least for a while, which seemed shot these days. He hated watching his fingers shake, the cup slopping liquid out as he brought it unsteadily to his lips. It seemed to him as if he was always thirsty these days, and tired, so tired. The dreams were the worst, waking nightmares of the Collapse but different. Instead of human beings, the military were actually monsters, hiding in their uniforms, pretending to be saviors and instead eating their victims alive.

"I need that damned slave woman to come attend me," he said, slurping at the tea and trying to ignore the stabbing pain in his head.

Delwen wondered if she had made the last batch too strong—Sulwyn was degrading fast.

"Camelia?" she said and tried to think fast, "She's off with Cooper on a raid, don't you remember?" Now was not the time to remind him that the Spic had been dead for months.

Her old man blinked, confusion filling his haggard face, "A raid?"

"Yessir, you said Cooper couldn't be trusted and neither could that colored woman, so you sent them both off on a raid. You said Cooper wanted to kill you, remember?"

His jaw was slack, his eyes confused, and he reached up one hand to his head. Everything was so confusing these days, like some kind of waking nightmare. Delwen looked at her father and realized it was now or never; he was suffering deeply from the effects of the drug, and he was now susceptible to her influence as he never would have been otherwise. She knelt down beside him and began to whisper quietly in her father's ear.

CHAPTER TWENTY-ONE

PAINTING DISAPPOINTMENT

"I know he loves me, but this pain is mine. It's mine to keep, mine to bear. If I cannot bear his children, at least I can bear the brief memories of their existence, their time inside of me. They are the faces I see on the canvas. Chris doesn't understand why I paint. It's to remember them. How they would have been, how they come to me in dreams. I will never get to hold them, never hear them say they love me or watch them grow up. The paintings are all I have of them." – Carrie's Journal

It was her weeping that woke him. Muffled sobs in the dark. Chris fumbled for a candle and matches. Back at the main house there were solar panels and a

Bloom box, signs that the Reformation was slowly trickling into the backwater towns. As the town doctor Liza had qualified for the latest in gadgets that were making their way from the East Coast, but here in the old homestead they were roughing it. The simple four-room stone structure had been steadily rebuilt over the past five years. After Liza and Carl had married and began having babies, it was easier on all involved for Carrie and Chris to make the old homestead their home.

After all, they didn't need as much room. In all, they had suffered four late-term miscarriages and countless others earlier on. It had left Carrie devastated, and she grew thinner and frailer with each failed pregnancy. Liza and Carl's two oldest children, Molly Ann and John Fenton, absolutely adored their Auntie Carrie, which made seeing them even harder on her. Chris could see it in the tight line of a smile and stiffness in her shoulders; even as she opened her arms and let them barrel into her. How she wanted just one to call her own.

She hadn't argued at all when Chris first suggested rebuilding the old homestead in the woods. It had been Fenton's childhood home. The old man had looked positively touched when Chris first asked him for permission to rebuild, and eventually add on, to the crumbling ruin. The plan had been simple—just one bedroom, a kitchen, bathroom, and living/dining area. It followed the original plan of the building and included a loft, which had been semi-private, open to the living room below. The loft area had been Fenton's, but now it was a place for Carrie to write and paint in. A large bank of windows, different from the original design of the house, allowed plenty of natural light in. She had taken up the writing and painting after her second miscarriage nine years ago. It seemed to help distract her and ease the pain and loss.

Chris fumbled over the matches and struck one, lighting the lantern by the bed. "Baby? You okay?" His voice cracked and his eyes were still encrusted with sleep. Outside the darkness was absolute. He picked up the lantern and headed for the tiny bathroom. Inside it, Carrie had pulled off her nightgown, and large blotch of red stained it. "Oh, Carrie, I..."

Carrie's voice was strained, "Please don't say it, Chris. Don't say anything. Okay?"

Chris reached out a hand to her. "Carrie…I…"

She pulled away. "I have to clean up. Just, just, please go back to bed. I'll be fine. I, I just need to be alone, okay?"

With each loss, the gulf between them seemed to widen. She kept the pain close to her, embraced it like a friend, and pushed away Chris, Liza, and anyone else who cared. Chris didn't know if she was trying to spare them from it, or if retreat was just a coping mechanism, but each time his own misery grew. How much more of this could their relationship take? This terrible feeling that they were growing apart, isolated from each other, lost in their own private pain?

Chris retreated back to bed. She hadn't even told him this time. And how long had she been pregnant this time? A few weeks? A month? With Fenton's passing and Liza's new baby on the way, work on the farm was busier than ever. Usually he tried to pay attention, to know, so that he could be some kind of support for her. But he had been so busy.

The lantern light was blown out and he heard Carrie navigate her way back to the bedroom. She moved silently across the floor—only one or two creaks gave her position away—and then she was sliding into bed beside him.

"How long?" he asked her.

"Two months, six days," she replied, and her voice sounded hollow. "I didn't want to get your hopes up."

Chris closed his eyes in pain and guilt. He hadn't noticed at all. *Two months, and I didn't even notice.*

"Sweetheart, I…" he began.

"Please Chris," she cut him off, "I'm just really tired right now."

He pulled her close to him. She stiffened at first, sighed, and let him pull her against him. They lay there, unmoving, for a long time before either could sleep again.

The next day dawned, sun bright over the tips of the trees and the warmth of the early summer sun already warming the tiny homestead. Chris awoke with a start, realizing he had slept late, later than he had in a long time. He could smell hot chicory percolating on the stove and quickly dressed. Usually he was the one who rose first.

After splashing some cold water on his face, he walked into the kitchen, poured himself a large mug of the brew, walked into the living room and looked up. Sure enough, there she was, sketching away. She usually threw herself into a new project or series right after a miscarriage. He could see her now, intent on sketching out the details on the canvas, which she would then fill in with the paints she made from plant extracts. *I'll have to let Liza know,* he thought, *have her check in and see if Carrie needs any extra iron supplements and also to keep the kids away for a week or so.*

He knew he would also have to push Carrie to stop working, to eat something and even to come to bed. The painting would consume her. It was her escape, but it came with a price. She had broken her ankle shortly after her fourth late-term miscarriage. She had gone into labor at just 22 weeks and given birth to a stillborn baby boy. That had been almost three years ago. By that time Chris had finished the loft and moved Carrie's painting supplies in there. She had gotten out of bed way too soon, insisting she was fine, climbed up into the loft and began painting with single-minded intensity. The third day of painting, with little food and even less sleep, she had tried to climb down the ladder, slipped and fallen, breaking her left ankle. Since then, Chris kept a sharp eye on her, which caused friction between them, and insisted she regularly stop for meals and rest.

"Morning sweetheart," Chris called, "ready for some breakfast?"

"I'm not hungry." Carrie didn't look up from her sketch. Her eyes were red-rimmed and drawn tight with exhaustion. He wondered how long she had waited before slipping back out of bed and climbing up the ladder to the loft. Probably not long.

Chris tried again, "I could make you something simple. An egg or…"

Carrie flushed with anger; she was right on the edge, "Chris, leave it be."

He took a deep breath and fought the desire to argue with her. He had half a mind to go up and drag her down from the loft by force, but he couldn't bear an argument right now. Better to go talk to Liza and see what she had to say. He knew his sister-in-law would shake her head and beg Chris to try to convince Carrie to stop trying. The last miscarriage, just seven months ago, had shaken them all. She had lost a great deal of blood, collapsed, and Liza had feared for her sister like never before. Between that and Fenton's slowly succumbing to heart disease it had been an incredibly difficult year for everyone. And Liza didn't need any stress either. Carl had quietly pointed that out to Chris the other day. After all, she was in her final trimester and they were expecting the baby to come any day.

With one last look at Carrie, who sat less than ten feet from him sketching with an intensity he admired and hated at the same time, Chris left the tiny homestead and headed for the main house.

A TIME FOR WRITING

The role of a writer is not to say what we all can say, but what we are unable to say." – Anais Nin

It had already been an excellent day for trading. David felt on top of the world. He and Jess had made it official with the kids, and even shared the news of their new relationship with a trusted few: Thurman Banks, who had dropped by unexpectedly and caught them holding hands, and Sarah Turner, who had smiled and nodded her approval.

It was a moment in time when everything seemed bright, anything was possible, and there were no clouds or harsh words that could mar their happiness. Jess had reminded him that there was a trader leaving town soon and asked if David could find her some paper, "I'm running low. I'm finishing up with Sarah Turner, and then I'm hoping to speak to Mr. Stevens and write down his story." Jess had been writing down the various townspeople's stories for a while now and filled several notebooks. There was a large stack of them in one corner of her room, filled with personal stories, accounts of the invasion of Warsend, descriptions of lives before and after the war, and so much more.

Jess had earned quite a reputation around town, and residents now sought her out and volunteered their stories. She had heard heartbreak and tragedy, but also she had listened to the young and the old alike as they smiled and relayed tales of falling in love, of babies born and accounts of a world now that was harsh, simple, and, in some ways, more real than the old one. Through the people and their stories twined hope and love like threads of shining gold. She had filled countless notebooks with delicate script and was close to running out of the last battered one in the stack.

"Whatever you can find would be wonderful."

David caught the trader just in time. He had been packing up, having stayed in a small room in a decrepit building across from Sarah Turner's café for two full days. When David had asked for paper, he had rustled around in the back of a still overly full van filled with boxes overflowing with a wild medley of tools, fabric, shoes, and more. A moment later he had handed over two simple student notebooks with lined paper.

"I think I have something more here," he had said, and began digging further into the stacks of items. David marveled at the man's ability to find anything; it looked for all accounts like a hodgepodge with no rhyme or reason, but the trader always seemed to know exactly where to look. He pulled out a large tote, shifted another to the left and began pawing through a third one. "Ah yes, here it is." The trader handed David a journal encased in a soft leather case. It had obviously been handmade, was soft and supple, the pages within were thick and sturdy. It was thick as well, the paper roughly cut and of different shades of cream and pale yellow. The thick leather smelled vaguely of lemon.

"I got a whole crate full back in Tennessee a few months ago. This kid, Joseph Perdue, lives in this hole-in-a-wall town, makes Warsend look positively metropolitan, and he makes them all by hand. Traded 'em for auto parts." David felt the well-cured leather and noticed a small raised area on the back—the initials JP were embossed on the back. "He does quality work," the trader added, anxious for a sale.

Neither of them had noticed Sarah Turner's face when the name Perdue and Tiptonville had been mentioned. She had turned pale and excused herself without a word. As she slipped away, Sarah couldn't help but wonder who Joseph was. Possibly a grandchild of old Fenton Perdue? She recalled that he had a son who had moved away to New York. In a small town like Tiptonville, everyone knew everyone else. It had been years since she had been there. More than half a lifetime since she had run away in the night with her two small children and left Wes Perkins behind. For the first time in twenty years, Tiptonville suddenly felt close enough to touch. She wasn't that frightened young woman any longer. She disappeared into the café and lost herself in making preparations for the lunch crowd.

Neither the trader nor David had noticed her departure. David looked at the well-made hand-crafted journal in his hand and nodded. They began hashing out a trade. The trader was itching to return home after a month on the road. He had accepted five dozen eggs and three jars of preserves along with a bag of deer jerky in trade for the journal and the two notebooks. It was a good trade, and they had plenty of extra eggs these days with the expanded chicken house and yard and an overabundance of fruit to can into preserves. The trader had also given him three clean and empty jars in return.

David brought it back to Jess that night after visiting with Sarah Turner, who seemed quite distracted and quiet; not her usual ebullient self. He had also run a handful of errands for old Mister Banks who had been having trouble getting around lately due to swelling in his knees. The old man was having more and more difficulty getting around, and

Jess, David, and Jacob visited him often to help in whatever way they could.

As he handed over first the notebooks and then the journal, David hadn't thought much of it. Jess had asked for something to write in, and he had dutifully found it. It was paper and leather, nothing special in David's eyes, but the reaction Jess had to it made his heart stutter. Even now, three months into their new relationship, a simple touch or look in her eyes brought on such overwhelming feelings of wonder and desire. Knowing that she returned his feelings was staggering, new, and each day he wondered when he would wake up from this beautiful dream he was having.

Her fingers stroked the leather cover, and then opened the book to fan the pages within. She smiled, unconsciously, her eyes soaking up the thick, rich paper, and like David, her fingers found the embossed initials. "JP?" she asked, her eyes flashing up to him.

"Trader said it was some kid in Tennessee, who made them all by hand. A Joseph Perdue, I think."

"David, it's…it's *beautiful.*" Her crayon-blue eyes smiled up at him. "*Thank you.*" She couldn't imagine what she would write in this thing of beauty, but she knew it would have to be something special, something different.

David had been surprised at the force in which she hugged him. Later that night, after they had made love, she had slipped out of bed. "I'm going to stay up a while," she had said, kissing him.

She had selected the leather journal, slipped quietly down the hall and sat down at the kitchen table. The night was quite warm, now that it was early June, and the cicadas were thrumming noisily outside. In the far distance you could occasionally hear the low of a cow. The horse and goats inside the garage-turned-barn were silent and the stars glinted in the clear night sky.

Jess sat at the kitchen table, a small candle glimmering and expanding on the moonlight that spilled in through the window. She stared at the journal, touched the soft leather with her fingers and wondered what to do with it. Several minutes went by before she slowly opened the journal and began to write…

"There are moments when all of it is too much, too painful to remember. Yet then I look around at those I love and realize I would not be here, with these people who I love and who love me, if those awful things had not happened to me. How do you reconcile that?"

I CAN'T STAY HERE ANYMORE

"Where we love is home, home that our feet may leave, but not our hearts." – Oliver Wendell Holmes

The soft creak of the box springs woke Chris. Carrie had slipped into the bed quietly and, once she heard his breathing change, she slid close to him and kissed his ear softly. He shifted, turned toward his wife and pulled her close.

"Is the painting done?" he asked.

"Yes."

"I've missed you." She had slept each night for the past two weeks in the painting loft on a small couch. It had been a compromise early on to the all-nighters she pulled when lost in a new painting.

"I know. I missed you too." The past two weeks had been hard. There had been words exchanged, harsh ones, mainly from her. He didn't understand this need she had to finish a painting before returning to him, to her life and family.

Carrie sat up, her hair reflected in the moonlight, cascading down and brushing Chris's chest as she straddled him. He started to speak, started to object that it was too soon, but she shushed him and put a slender finger on his lips. It smelled vaguely of turpentine.

"No more arguing," she said, "Not tonight."

Her hands moved and Chris felt his body respond, just as it always did, to her touch. They made love, slowly, coming to a climax together. Afterward, they spooned, wrapping their bodies around each other, their bodies replete. They may not have children, but they had love, so much of it that it sometimes hurt. He wasn't always sure where he ended and she began. They lay there and said nothing for a long while.

"Chris?" he jerked awake at Carrie's voice, having just dozed off.

"Yeah, babe?"

"I can't stay here anymore."

"Here in this house?" he asked, confused.

"No...here on this farm...in Tiptonville."

"Wait, what are you saying, Carrie?" He feared hearing the words. Had he just gotten some crazy, twisted goodbye screw? Was she leaving him?

"I'm saying I can't stay here anymore, Chris. Not on this farm, not in this town; hell, maybe not in this state. I've got to get away from all the memories— my mom, the babies, even Gramps. I see him everywhere, you know, and I miss him so." Her body shook with emotion and he could feel her tears drip onto his arm.

"And what about me, Carrie?" he asked, terrified of her answer.

"I don't want to leave *you*," she said, sounding affronted, "I love you, Chris. And through all of this, you have loved me and stayed by my side. I don't want to lose that. You aren't tied here, you know. Come with me, we can travel the roads again and be safe. The Reformation has taken care of that."

Relief flooded through Chris. After all they had been through she still loved him and wanted him by her side.

Carrie continued, "Remember the trader who bought that box full of journals from Joseph and several of my paintings from the Trade Mart? The one who insisted on meeting me? He talked about the new government, about the new Capitol in Denver. He told me I could get good money for the paintings, that there has been a resurgence in American art in the past three years now that The Collapse is over."

Over was a bit of an overstatement. Chris had said that there were two stories going around. One proclaimed that The Collapse was over, that life was back to normal. As if by simply saying it enough, the bigwigs in D.C. could make it so. The truth was, much of the country, especially a wide swath of the central states, was *not* back to normal. The coasts had their electricity, more cell phone towers than ever before, and in no small part due to the European contingent in the East and the Chinese contingent in the West, back to normal was a relative term.

"*Sure* we're back to normal," Wes had growled, "as long as you ignore the fact that the Chinese occupy California and a huge swath of the West Coast. Christ, they own us, and they're gonna make sure they get their money's worth. And don't even get me started on the fuckin' East Coast. Goddamn sellouts."

Chris thought about all of this, about the quiet life that he and all of the Purdue family led here in Tiptonville. He rested his nose against Carrie's head, breathed in her unique scent of sage and wood smoke. He thought about Missouri and home. It did, after all, hold a huge part of his heart. Mom, Dad, Jess, his friends. His thoughts drifted west, to Colorado, and his grip tightened around Carrie.

"Yeah, baby. Let's go. We can do this; we can head west, to Colorado, or wherever you want to go."

CHAPTER TWENTY-FOUR

A Café on Main Street

"Betrayal is the only truth that sticks." – Arthur Miller

"That...*whore,*" Cooper fumed, as he stabbed into the hunk of meat he had taken off of a deer. It had been a perfect opportunity; the fool thing had just stood there in the clearing long enough for him to get a shot off. And it was a good shot at that; it had killed the creature instantly. "I'm going to kill her. Stick a knife right into that pregnant belly and..."

Armando sat a few feet away from Cooper, saying nothing, his eyes on the small amount of food on his plate. There was plenty to be had, although it

Page | 279

was a little stringy and not evenly cooked, but Cooper had only given him a small amount, commenting that the boy was useless and lucky he got anything at all. At the moment he was back on the same old subject—his cuckolding—Mama had always made sure Armando had learned plenty, despite the lack of books. And Cooper had definitely been cuckolded by his wife and her new lover.

Cooper still wasn't sure *how* she had done it, but whatever Delwen had done, it was enough to get her appointed as leader in Cooper's place when her father suffered a series of convulsions two weeks prior. And right after that she had announced she was pregnant…with that idiot Heimdall's child.

"I'll cut that little bastard out of her and shove it down her throat…"

Armando let Cooper's curses wash over him. He chewed on a hunk of venison. It was dry, tasteless, and Armando remembered with longing his mother's cooking. They were never given much, despite her being the camp doctor, but what she made with those scraps of food and the wild edibles she taught him to collect for her was a feast compared to this.

He took another bite, forced it down, and thought of her face and her words, "Eat, Armando, eat and be strong. It is fuel, and you cannot stay strong without it." How many times had she said that to him? How many times had he nodded obediently and eaten whatever was on his plate? He

Page | 280

knew too that Cooper would just as soon *not* feed him. The older man only kept him around because he was small and could fit into tight spaces. A couple of days ago that had come in handy. Cooper had ordered him to find out what lay within a small shed on the outskirts of a farm. It had been difficult, but he had managed to squeeze through between the bottom of the shed wall and the dirt floor beneath. There had been grain, some farming equipment, and several knives, including one tiny and one half buried in the dirt.

Without really thinking about it, Armando had slipped one of them into his pocket. It was a small Swiss army type, just one blade, a space for a toothpick—although the toothpick was no longer there—and a small screwdriver as well. He wondered how he could get away from Cooper. Armando was nearly nine, and he had had to be rather self-sufficient, but making ends meet in the middle of Tennessee was frightening, especially since anyone he encountered was either shooting at them or dead or dying from Cooper shooting them first. Cooper didn't seem to have any other setting—killing seemed to be his primary way of dealing with people.

"Choke on the blood…you damned whore!" Cooper was still going. Armando's thoughts turned to the knife in his pocket. How he wished he had the strength to end this terrible man's life. The tiny, dull knife certainly wouldn't do it—and he was no killer, despite his genetic inheritance. The fact that he was here, in the middle of nowhere, hungry and cold, was Cooper's doing. The boy hadn't exactly been welcome there in the neo-Nazi camp, but when Delwen turned her sights on him, declaring Armando to be Cooper's illegitimate son, the rest of the camp had been happy to see the back end of him along with this monster.

Armando missed Sully, his only real friend; she had stood silent, tears streaming down her face as he and Cooper had been thrown out of the AR camp. Cooper had been so angry, so furious at everyone, that Armando had wondered just how long it would take before Cooper turned on him. How long before he too was dead by Cooper's hand? The man might be his father, but he didn't give a damn about him insofar as he could use him to serve his own needs.

The last of the light disappeared from the horizon. The nights were dark, even more so than the Amerika Reborn camp had been. In the last two years the camp had cobbled together a small system of electric lights that ran off of a series of solar panels they had acquired during a trade or raid, Armando wasn't sure which. The light from the campfire gave off a dark red glow and Armando knew better than to add any fuel to the fire. They hid in the shadows, traveling mainly at dusk and dawn, and slept during the day.

Cooper was still ranting, although it had grown quieter, and Armando pulled his knees up, lowering his head and hoping the man didn't turn his rage onto him. The swelling from Cooper's last fit of rage was finally going down, although his cheek remained mottled in yellow and red bruises. All that Armando could think of as he slipped into a doze was that he wished his mom was still alive. Even if it meant being back at the AR camp…anything but this.

The next morning found them on the outskirts of a small town. It was early still, barely light out, and there were no signs of activity; everyone in town was still sleeping. They edged around the town, Cooper muttering quietly to himself as he scoped out the town's defenses.

"Sentries, at least one there at the end of the street. Another up in that high hide in the south. Burned vehicles with skeletons…nice touch." He rambled mainly to himself, noting the defenses, before turning his attention on Armando. "You'll go in there. Tell 'em you're an orphan, ask 'em for food. I'll watch from here and come tonight; you'll let me in so I get what I need."

He nodded, narrowed his eyes, "I've been to this shithole before. They grow some nice tail 'round here." He stared at Armando, "You do what I say, or I promise you, you'll be sorry you were ever born. I'll come at midnight." He gave the boy a rough shove toward the small town.

As Armando walked toward the town, the boy thought about the past few weeks. Three times now, Cooper had sent him in to farmhouses, isolated, alone. Three times, the boy had done what Cooper demanded. He'd convinced an old farmer he was all alone, then two men, a father and his grown son, and finally a young couple who had just lost a child to a fever. The last one, that one had been the worst. He didn't want to think about what Cooper had done to the woman.

He had hid in an outbuilding after being tasked to remove the husband's body and the bloodstains from the front porch, just in case someone came by. Afterwards he had hid in the shed several hundred feet away and tried desperately to *not* hear the woman's screams. When they had gotten back on the road several days later, well outfitted now with a rifle and plenty of ammo, Armando had thought about what Mama would have said to him.

At the camp, she had always kept him out of sight of most of the more militant ones. His skin was dark; not as dark as hers, but still darker than acceptable when surrounded by racist white men. The neo-Nazis hadn't been eager to include him in their fighting lessons, other than to use him as a punching bag. One or two of those sessions had taught him to lay low, but here, with Cooper, there was no lying low. Mama would have stopped them, threatened them by saying she wouldn't patch them up if they kept going, but Mama was dead, and he was all alone.

As he put distance between him and where Cooper was hiding, a set of high-powered binoculars in his hands watching his every move, Armando realized he had to make a decision. He thought of what his mother would have said, would have thought, if she had known that he had had a part in the deaths of five innocent people. She would have been horrified and she would have reminded him that God would judge him, most severely, for what he had done. Part of him wanted to wail and cry, to hide his head in her lap and beg her to help him. He was so very lost without her.

As the town drew near, he heard a sentry ring a bell. They had seen him. Soon he would have to tell the lie, how he had been orphaned, that he was all alone. The shame he felt at his part in the old farmer, the two men, or the young couple—it felt like a lead weight in his heart and his steps slowed.

"Reverend." Jeremy Deeds looked up from the sermon he was preparing to honor Mr. Liles and saw Joseph Perdue standing in his office. According to the town records, the ancient man had died just three days short of his 116th birthday. He had been so involved writing down notes for the sermon he hadn't even heard the teenager come in.

"Reverend, I'm sorry to bother you, but we have a situation down near the Trade Mart. Some kid just walked in on the main road."

Jeremy gave Joseph a befuddled look. Kids, and plenty of other people, had been making their way into town for years now, and for the most part things went peacefully. Either way, they had never needed him involved. "The kid is asking for a priest, so Wes sent me to get you."

"Is the boy ill?" Jeremy asked.

"Not that I can see, sir. Although he's got plenty of bruises on his face and arms. He just won't say anything past that he needs to speak with a priest and confess his sins." Joseph shrugged, "And he looks scared."

Jeremy stood up painfully. His badly damaged leg, nearly pulverized in a car crash over nine years ago, would always give him terrible pain. During the winters, when he felt every step even more keenly, the congregation had grown used to seeing him give sermons from a tall chair. It was hell getting into it, but once he did he was good for the entire service. Joseph stepped forward to offer his assistance. Jeremy had learned to accept others' help and he leaned on the young man and slowly walked to the door of the church where a small crowd was gathering, the boy at their center.

The boy was thin, painfully so, with large brown eyes and jet black hair. His skin was tanned and Jeremy could see the remains of several bruises on his face and arms. He was dressed in a ragged T-shirt and worn blue jeans that had patches; his feet were bare. The boy stared back at Jeremy, "You don't look like a priest."

"And what do priests look like?" Jeremy asked in return.

The boy shrugged his thin shoulders, "I don't

know; I never saw one. Mama said they had funny little collars and they lived in the church."

Jeremy nodded thoughtfully, "I see…well, I do have a funny little collar I wear on Sundays and I do live here in the church. My faith may be different from your Mama's, but in the end, we believe in the same thing. Will that do?"

The boy nodded solemnly, "I must confess my sins."

Jeremy nodded as if it were the most normal thing in the world.

"Come up to my office with me, and tell me what you need to say." He shooed Joseph and the others who offered to help, and slowly made his way back to the office with the boy, closing the door firmly behind him.

A few minutes later, Jeremy stuck his head out and asked for a large lunch for two to be sent up. It was nearly half an hour after that before Jeremy asked for Wes to join them in the office. An hour later, and Cooper watched through binoculars as the church bell rang and people began to gather outside.

He cursed as he packed up his binoculars and began to run north, putting as many miles between him and the small town as he could. He ran for the backwoods, where cars and horses alike would have difficulty following. He was gone long before Armando, surrounded by well-armed militia, led the townspeople to the camp he and Armando had made the evening before.

Armando stared into the distance. The stark dead trees that populated Reelfoot Lake stood in the far distance. He knew Cooper wouldn't be back, no matter what he had threatened. The priest, *no, not a priest, they called him Reverend here*, had told him he would be safe and that, no matter what he had done, God would forgive him if he only asked. Armando wasn't so sure about that last part, but he made a silent promise to his mother that he would do his best to earn that forgiveness.

The Reverend's wife had been kind as well. Heavily pregnant, and awkward with her big belly, she had still found a place for him to sleep for the night there in the sanctuary. Most of the children the makeshift orphanage had housed were now living with foster or adoptive parents. The large room was still filled with beds, but it was mostly empty. Miss Grace had explained that she knew someone very special who was looking for a child to take in.

She patted his shoulder, "You'll like Abby; she's raised two kids of her own and just has Tabitha still at home now. She's got room and I've told her all about you."

Within a few weeks, Armando had shortened his name to Andy and fit in seamlessly with the Carters. He missed his mother, more than he could even say, but for the first time in his life, he finally felt safe.

Miles to the west, Scott Cooper walked on.

CHAPTER TWENTY-FIVE

COUNT ME IN

"The best day of your life is the one on which you decide your life is your own. No apologies or excuses. No one to lean on, rely on, or blame. The gift is yours - it is an amazing journey - and you alone are responsible for the quality of it. This is the day your life really begins." – Bob Moawad

"Are you insane?" Wes barked at Chris. "Completely certifiable?"

Chris was packing a large backpack at the moment, trying to puzzle out how to fit the clips of ammo and the rest of the loose shells in one of the smaller sections.

Wes stared at the mounds of packs as well as

boxes of paints and supplies.

"You can't just waltz out of here with a bunch of …" He waved his hand at the far corner that was occupied with a maze of paintings, "A bunch of… *art*. The roads are still dangerous, the Reformation is a frigging joke, and you are both going to end up dead."

Chris ignored him. Wes was plain-spoken, and Chris had grown used to that over the years. The older man glared at him for several long moments before stalking out of the tiny house. Chris suppressed a twinge of regret. Despite their difference in age, or a host of differences, Chris had found a solid friendship with Wes. Despite his angry façade and harsh words, the man cared for others far more than he could admit, even to himself. Since the raid that had killed his fiancé and the mother of his unborn child, and even before that, years before, when his wife Sarah had left him, disappearing into the night with their young son and daughter, Wes had been unable to give voice to the part of him that was good and kind. He rarely smiled, other than a sarcastic sideways smirk, and still called Chris "soldier" far too often.

The older man hid behind his gruff exterior so that others wouldn't get close, so that he wouldn't ever be given love or acceptance only to risk losing it again. That was what Carrie had once said, and Chris knew she was right. Wes worked hard, spent long hours toiling on the Perdue farm and then heading up to see Jim Dorian, who had recently had a stroke and shortly after that fallen down his rickety old stairs, breaking his leg in the process. The simpleminded man was now in his mid-50s and had trouble understanding why his body was betraying him in such a strange manner.

Outside of the stone house he could hear Wes start his truck up and gun the engine, driving down the rough dirt road and back toward town. They were leaving tomorrow, first thing in the morning. He had hoped Wes would stay for dinner at the Perdue farm, where Carrie already was now, saying her goodbyes. She had put on weight the past few weeks, inching away from the skeletal frame and looking younger and less haunted. It was if the decision to leave had taken a weight off of her she hadn't realized existed. She had sent letters ahead to the art gallery in Denver, but there had been no response. This wasn't surprising; mail was still rather spotty and there were still some routes that took longer than others—the highly efficient system of mail delivery had been lost with the collapse of the country and they were still struggling to put it back to rights, along with a host of other creature comforts that most people took for granted decades before.

That evening at the Perdue's was not easy. Liza, expecting her fourth child, was exhausted and beside herself at the thought of her older sister moving away. The children, even little Abby, were voicing their own distress. Abby climbed onto Carrie's lap at one point, and said in her tiny baby voice, "Au Cree, no go!" Which caused tears to spring in both Liza and Carrie's eyes.

Liza's husband Carl said little. He wasn't a talkative man, but obviously he too disapproved of Chris and Carrie leaving. Chris turned to him at one point in the evening and asked, "Did Wes say if he would be by for dinner?" Carl just shook his head.

Chris thought briefly of running into town and seeing if Wes was holed up in his house or at Dorian's ramshackle trailer, and decided against it. Perhaps this was for the best. He couldn't explain it to anyone. Not Carl or Liza; not even to himself. What mattered was Carrie. If she thought leaving would make it better, then leaving is what they would do. As it was, he found himself thinking more and more of Warsend.

Mom, Dad, Jess, and Allen—they were all dead. But the town was probably still there. He found himself wondering about it; how much had it changed? Was there anyone left that he knew? He had resolved to make sure they stopped there, at least for a day, before moving on to Colorado. Just to see the old house, just to say goodbye properly this time, and take a moment to remember the happier times. He knew that Carrie wouldn't begrudge him that, even if the detour was slightly out of their way.

"Chris?" Joseph was standing there in front of

Page | 292

him.

Chris hadn't even noticed his arrival from town because he was so lost in his plans for visiting Warsend. The little kid was now grown into a rather self-assured, yet quiet teenager. He was fourteen now and had taken over Mr. Liles automotive store more than a year ago, caring for the aged old man, crafting leather-bound books out of deer hide Wes shot and then taught him how to cure. The books were then lined with paper from a printing supply company that had sat abandoned for more than a decade. The kid had weathered Fenton's death, then Mr. Liles's less than two months later, with a quiet reserve that belied his years. His blond hair was spiky and short, his haircut a parting gift from Carrie, who wielded more than just a paintbrush with quiet accuracy.

The boy had a box perched near the front door, "I brought you more of the journals. Thought you might use 'em for trade."

The journals were made from rich cream vellum he had found beneath boxes of envelopes and cheap stationery. The butter-soft deer hide was embossed with his initials. Chris picked one up and ran his hands over it.

"These are great Joe; you really have been improving, and the hide seems quite supple. No more shrinkage?"

The teen winced a bit at the memory of his first attempts at curing the hides Wes had brought him. There had been a trial and error phase, but he had quickly learned how to mend his mistakes and create quality hides. Books were his first project. Now he was starting on working leather belts.

"Yeah, I've got the hang of it now." Joseph paused, looked down at the ground, "I wish I could go with you Chris."

Chris laid a hand over the boy's shoulders, but said nothing; he knew Liza would lose it completely if both of her siblings answered the siren call of the West. He felt a sharp pain in his chest, and he couldn't help wondering how long it would be before he saw the boy again. Tiptonville had been his home for over ten years, and Joseph was the little brother he never had.

That evening they spent a restless night in the small stone house. One last night of banking the fire, checking to see if there was anything they had missed, anything that just had to be included. The van they were using had been the Carter's—Carl's mom and stepdad—but they had given it to Chris and Carrie when they first heard the news that they were leaving.

"We barely use it, and it's in good shape and you can carry the gas cans on top. It should be enough to get you all the way to Colorado," John Carter had told Chris.

They had accepted the gift gratefully, then packed the van full of paintings, items to trade, foodstuffs, and a handful of personal belongings. There was barely any room left for them in the front, and even the open space between the two front seats was piled high, every inch of space spoken for.

As the pale rays of the sun lightened the treetops, Chris scrambled some eggs and wrapped up a fair-sized bag of sandwiches for them to eat on the road. He walked outside just as Wes's truck came rumbling around the bend. The truck had a camper shell on the back, something Wes usually only put on when he was going hunting. It wasn't really hunting season, but perhaps the older man felt the need to kill something soft and furry in response to Chris and Carrie's departure.

Chris grinned at the sight of his friend. He had been sick at the thought of not saying goodbye. After all, they had no idea when they would return, if ever. "Hey there, Wes, come to see us off before you go off on a hunt?"

Wes shook his head. "I'm coming with you, you damned idiot." Typical Wes; kind and heartfelt words were not his strongest suit.

"You're what?" Carrie asked, having just emerged from the house, with the last of their belongings in her arms.

"I'm comin' with you. The two of you'd end up dead 'fore you got halfway there and then damned if Fenton would raise outta the grave and give me what for," Wes said, taking the bundle of food from Chris, who stood there in shock. "Besides," he said, "it's high time I saw more of the world 'sides sand and them damn sand-nigg…" he glanced at Carrie's stern look, "Yeah…lotsa *sand*. Figured I'd get out and see the world."

Carrie burst out, "What about Jim Dorian? He's still hobbled up with that broken leg."

Wes nodded, "Yup. Dropped him off with Reverend Deeds last night. Jim'll be right as rain in a few more weeks and then he can help out 'round the parish. 'Sides, they need some help now that little KG is in the world."

Jeremy Deeds and his wife Grace had just welcomed their second child, a little girl named Karen Grace, or KG for short, after her mama and grandma just two months ago. They already had a very boisterous little boy, Anthony, who adored Jim Dorian. "Dorian needs to be with others; ain't good for him to be livin' alone in that leaky old trailer."

The older man lifted up the back of his truck and displayed a host of items to trade or sell. "Hell, I gotta get rid of this crap, and you ain't got any more room in that van. The way I see it, you two could use the company." Wes had his trademark smirk plastered on his face. He had thought of everything, it seemed.

Chris felt Carrie's eyes on him. This was far from what she might want, but the more Chris thought about it, the more he couldn't help but like it. An extra eye, an extra gun, and, despite his gruff and taciturn ways, Wes was a good friend.

"Well, all right then. Let's get moving."

A few minutes later, they drove away from the

tiny stone house—the van in the lead and Wes in his truck behind. Within an hour they were making time down the cracked highway heading west.

CHAPTER TWENTY-SIX

REUNION

"The most important thing in life is to learn how to give out love, and to let it come in." – Morrie Schwartz

"Morning, Mom. Thanks so much for taking Hunter; I totally forgot about working at the food bank," Sarah's daughter Laura said as she gave her mother a quick kiss and hug, awkwardly balancing the sleepy toddler on one hip. "Are you sure he won't be a problem?"

Sarah smiled at her daughter. Hunter was a little hellion, and that was for sure. But he certainly came in handy at times. The last time she had babysat her grandson he had broken two plates, burned his fingers on the stove, and then finished off the day by biting Mayor Farley on the arm after the overstuffed shirt had complained about the serving size on his plate. Considering his shirt was straining its buttons, and that Sarah had already served him a helping nearly twice that of the other diners, she hadn't concerned herself much with his opinions. The plates were a bit of a problem—she was getting low on the larger dinner plates—and the little boy had cried so when his fingers were burned, but the mayor's effeminate scream that followed the toddler's bite was well worth the trouble. She would have paid good money to see the mayor leave and never darken the door of her establishment again.

"Oh, don't you worry a bit, Hunter is a sweetheart, and I just love having him here," Sarah said, her smile full of mischief. It was a Tuesday, after all, and the Mayor often came by for an early lunch. She wouldn't mind a little more biting on Hunter's part; perhaps the Mayor would catch the hint.

"We will have a great time, won't we, Hunter?" She adored both of her grandchildren. They were the spitting image of their mother, except for the red hair, which was all her son-in-law Todd's contribution.

She reached out and took Hunter from her daughter, and hugged him close; he nuzzled her shoulder and sighed sleepily. "Bah, Mama. 'Unter tay wit Gamma."

Laura laughed and gave him a kiss on the cheek, "Be good for Grandma, sweetie, and don't touch that stove!" She headed for the front door of the café, turned and called, "I'll be back by sundown, Mom; just let me know if you need me to come sooner!" Laura had already dropped Melody, her three-year-old, off with Allen and Gina Stevens, Todd's father and stepmother.

Sarah hugged her grandson close and said, "We have a busy day in front of us, don't we, sweetheart? Well, I guess we best get started."

She fed him some pancakes, his favorite, and watched him as he ate with single-minded intensity. He looked so much like his grandfather. It startled her to see him in her grandchildren's faces, especially Hunter's.

Despite the long years apart she still thought about him from time to time—more now that the grandkids had come. The 'what ifs' came frequently to mind. If she had stayed, if he had changed back to the man she had married, what would their life have been like?

Sarah wondered about Tiptonville often. No traveler would even really remember if they had stopped in a tiny town in the middle of nowhere—but she asked anyway. It was always the same answer, a shrug, a shake of the head, or, from those who had been out on the road way too long, "Those little towns just kind of blur together after a while." She had long given up asking. It had been a shock when the trader had mentioned it last month. Ever since she hadn't been able to stop thinking about it, or kicking herself for not having stopped the trader to ask a hundred questions about that "little Podunk town" he had visited.

There were customers to wait on, and Hunter had shaken off the last vestiges of sleepiness and begun running up and down the length of counter, without a care for who he might run headlong into. Sarah distracted the boy by setting him up with some dough and a cookie cutter. "Will you make me some cookies, Hunter?"

"I make cooees!" the boy crowed and got to work, cutting the dough into ragged shapes with one hand, while stuffing handfuls of dough into his mouth.

The front door bell clattered as a small group of strangers walked in. The café had been busy all morning, but now at just after ten a.m., it had fallen quiet. The noon rush would start up in an hour, and with it would come the mayor. Sarah suppressed a sigh; she had hoped for a moment's peace before having to prep for lunch. The first two to walk through the door were young and in their mid-20s.

The woman was blond with striking green eyes. She carried herself with a quiet dignity that also conveyed a sadness beyond her years. Sarah wondered what had made the girl sad, for the young man beside her was quite obviously her husband. He was tall, blond, and had beautiful crayon-blue eyes.

He looked familiar to her, but Sarah was equally certain that she had never seen him before.

Then the third person came into view and Sarah's heart stopped. Standing before her was an impossibility and she felt terror and wonder and hope all at the same time. The man stared at her for a moment, blinked, and said wonderingly, "Sarah?"

Carrie searched her memories for the details of a woman she had not even known, one who had disappeared years ago, fleeing from her husband and taking their two young children with her. No one had ever known where she had gone, but it had been the talk of the town for years. And here she was, apparently, in Warsend of all places, where Chris had insisted they stop and visit, if only to see his childhood home.

Chris had talked with Wes once about his family. Well, better to say Wes had talked *to* him, and Chris had simply listened. The older man had admitted he had returned from the Second Gulf War messed up, suffering from PTSD and mad at the world. He had taken it out on Sarah one too many times, and the last time had culminated in her disappearing with the kids. Never to be seen or heard from again. And here, apparently, is where she had ended up.

Sarah stood there in shock, "Wes?" She didn't say anything, none of them did, until Hunter, tiring of the dough, covered in the remains of it, tugged on her hand, trying with his chubby little toddler hands to open her fingers and place a lump of dough inside.

"Gamma…eat!"

Wes stared at the little boy, then back at Sarah, and then back down at the boy again. He took in the boy's features, which reminded him of Cody at that age, "Is he…?" Wes stopped and sat down heavily in the nearest chair, staring at the little boy, a look of wonder settling over his face. He had a grandson. A *grandson*.

There they all stood, wordless. Chris and Carrie didn't know what to say, and quite obviously neither did Sarah or Wes. They might have stood there until sundown if Mayor Farley hadn't chosen that time to walk in the door. He had been craving a plate of Sarah's famous biscuits and gravy all morning. It was distracting him from his duties, these visions of the creamy gravy and fluffy biscuits, and he had headed over to the café early to avoid the rush.

He preferred to be given more preferential and individual service, which seemed impossible when other diners hogged Sarah's attention. And although biscuits and gravy was a breakfast item, and he was a stickler for eating the proper three meals of the day, he would make an exception in this case. After all, he reasoned, it was technically still morning and certainly too early for lunch. That made it perfectly reasonable to order his second breakfast that day. The mayor was surprised to see people in the café at this late point in the morning, and even more surprised to see three strangers. Well, that was all right; it was a fine time to establish himself as the authority in town. He straightened himself, sucked in his gut as best as he could, and boomed out a greeting.

"Good morning, Sarah! I've come for a plate of your biscuits and gravy. Make it a double and add extra gravy to that, would you?" His voice broke through their immobility, and Chris and Carrie stared at the rotund man for a moment before slipping to a back corner and sitting down. The mayor sat in his customary seat in the center of the café.

Wes, however, didn't move. He continued to stare at Sarah and Sarah could not take her eyes off of him. She ignored the mayor.

Wes found his voice first, "Sarah, I'm, it's, *good* to see you. I've wondered, I mean, I've wondered if you were all okay. Is, I mean, are Cody and Laura, are they here too?"

Sarah relaxed, just a bit. She allowed a small smile and nod to appear. He had a right to know his children were alive, healthy, and happy.

Wes was older, visibly so. He had white sprinkled liberally through his brown hair and his face had lines where there had not been when she had last seen him. He seemed steady, not drunk, not angry, and she felt a small ray of hope. Would he forgive her for running? For taking his children?

Wes stared at his estranged wife. *Wife…*it felt so odd to think of her as that. But there had been no divorce, no day in court, just an empty house. She was older, the laugh lines had deepened, and her hair was streaked with wiry gray hairs that she had plucked out ruthlessly when they first arrived years back, and eventually given up and allowed to grow.

Her shape was thinner than he remembered, but then she had been a bit heavy after Laura was born. His cheeks burned at the memory of himself, drunk and angry at the world, pointing out her defects—her weight being one of the many ways he berated her. He looked into her eyes, warm and brown, but a little scared. Scared of him, he realized, scared of what he might do.

Wes tried to imagine what she must be feeling. Was she scared that he was still that man? That he still carried that war inside of him? He stared at her, wondering how he could explain, wishing he knew the right words to tell her how different he was, that time had healed him.

He wanted to tell her how sorry he was, how much he had missed her and the kids, that he hadn't deserved to have them, that he had nearly died when they left. He stared into those brown eyes and everything else melted away. It didn't matter how long it had been or the changes they had come through alone; he was hit by the memories of her, younger, full of laughter, heavy with child, his child, and the frenzied, tearful reunions when he would come home on leave from boot camp.

The mayor, who had at first been interested in this odd scene only because it was the chance to impress new and different people, was quickly becoming incensed at being ignored. Who was this upstart, anyway? And the two young ones, who were they? He grumbled at the thought of the militia just letting them sashay on in this way, armed to the teeth from the look of the older one, and no one to watch them.

Oh sure, sure the war was over and there was talk of a new centralized government. But that wasn't much more than a promise of taxes and some damn bureaucrat trying to wrest control away from him.

He had built himself a nice little empire here, one that he would pass on down to his son one day, if that boy didn't stop screwing up everything he touched. James had been a disappointment in many ways, the most recent being his loss of control of the town militia and some damned girl he had managed to knock up. The boy spent more time carousing about in one of the few working trucks and drinking moonshine than he did keeping the town safe.

And that damned Todd Stevens, who had re-assumed control of the militia, had the audacity to lock him up for two days after he accidentally sideswiped one of the town's cattle, breaking its leg.

Mayor Farley felt his pulse increase, beating an angry rhythm in his neck, his face flushing. Why, damned if they weren't all ignoring him! He was sitting in *his regular seat* waiting for Sarah to snap to and fix him up her delectable biscuits and gravy and she was just staring at this man like he was a ghost.

Couldn't she see he was *waiting*? It was bad enough she had that damned grandson again today. The little beast had bit him, bit *him*, and she had simply apologized and let the boy go without tanning his behind. His eyes traveled to where the little beast had been sitting, covered in flour and dough, but he had disappeared.

Wonderful, Mayor Farley thought, *she can't be bothered to do her job and now she's let the little crapper wander off. What was the world coming to?*

"Sarah Turner, have you gone deaf?" Farley said loudly, startling Chris and Carrie and earning a sharp look of displeasure from Wes. "I'm waiting for my biscuits and gravy here. And pour me a mug of that hot chicory as well; I'll take it black as usual. And make sure you add some bacon and…" the rest of what he was going to say was lost in a howl of anger and pain.

Hunter had crawled under the tables, wound his way around to the table that housed the mayor's large bulk, and bit down firmly on a fat ring-encrusted finger.

It was Wes who was able to scoop the wayward child out from under the table before the mayor got some bright idea to kick out at the child. As it was, the rotund man roared from his seat, maddened that the little beast had bit him not once, but *twice*, and without any kind of consequences.

"You hand over that little brat, right now, I'm of a mind to show him the back side of my hand," the mayor panted with fury, "but I'll settle for one good crack of my belt," and his hand went to loosen his belt. "Teach him once and for all not to bite honest, hard-working men, by God."

Sarah bristled. Honest and hard-working most definitely did not describe the mayor, and she would be damned if he was going to show her grandson any kind of violence. Instead it was Wes who quelled the red-faced mayor with a look, the little boy struggling in his arms to get another chance at biting the offensive man. Wes didn't say a thing, just stared at Mayor Farley in a manner that made it clear he would tolerate no violence toward the child.

Jonathan Farley had never been a particularly bright man. His father had quietly maneuvered him into positions of power, taught him a few tricks on how to make others look dirty while he appeared clean, and generally railroaded him into the bank president position he held for nearly two decades, until the world had been set on its ear. Through a little luck and happenstance, perhaps his daddy's spirit guiding his steps, he had managed to convince the shell-shocked remains of the town populace that he should be mayor, and he had quickly taken control of the reins of power and held on tight.

To say that Mayor Farley was used to getting his way was an understatement. But standing there facing this grim-faced stranger—who held the toddler with such ease and showed such certainty in his ways—Farley realized for the first time the adversary before him. He had no idea what the man was capable of, but he doubted it would be anything short of violence.

Suddenly, biscuits and gravy didn't sound appetizing at all. In fact, his appetite had plumb vanished. Mayor Farley turned silently on his heel and slipped out the door, intimidated enough to say nothing, and leaving Sarah gaping in silence at the effect her estranged husband had on the pompous, rotund old man.

Wes didn't bother looking at the mayor's departure. He was examining his grandson closely, damned if the kid didn't look dead-on like Cody when he was two. The only difference was the shockingly red hair the boy had—which was a mess of sharp angles and coated on the sides in flour.

The little boy stared back, his eyes warm brown pools, just like his grandmother's…*grandmother, my God, that makes me…a grandfather,* Wes turned that realization over in his head, as the boy grinned and giggled, then wiggled impatiently to be let down. He hadn't been the least afraid of this tall strange man. Wes set him gently on the ground and the boy ran on his short little chubby legs toward the back door where he knew there were toys to play with.

Chris looked a bit disconcerted; the fat man had looked familiar somehow, but he couldn't put a name on the face. This woman, Sarah, didn't look at all familiar, yet Wes had called her Sarah.

The Sarah? *Wes's long-disappeared wife Sarah?* This

was getting crazier by the moment.

Wes watched the boy disappear and then focused again on Sarah. He managed a small smile, "Turner? So you've remarried, Sarah?" Why did his chest squeeze tight at the thought of her married to another? No ring on her finger, but not everyone wore one. Their wedding rings, along with Angie's, were still there, solid, warm and heavy on the chain against his chest. He had worn his wedding band for years before finally slipping it off again and adding it to the chain.

He had thought briefly of leaving all of them there in the drawer in the house in Tiptonville. Those days were so long past, his children a snapshot of a memory. Grown or dead, they were gone forever. And Angie, along with their unborn baby, gone before they had any chance at a good life together. He had pulled the chain off of his neck, stared at it for several long minutes, and then quietly put it back on. They were a part of him, his memories of a life he hadn't deserved but wished he could make right.

Sarah shook her head, "I took my name from a highway sign, changed the kids to that too; I figured you wouldn't let us go without a fight." She was right.

He had done plenty of searching for her himself, hired a private investigator for a short time, before the world had gone to hell in a hand basket. The trail had gone cold in Texas and when word of the nuke had come, he had feared the worst. Now, thinking back on it all, he simply nodded; of course she would have done just that. He had looked under her maiden name, tracked down every boy in middle school or high school that had looked twice at her, dated her, *tried* to date her, and got nowhere. She had disappeared, slid into a world full of people, full of opportunities to remain anonymous, to remain hidden. He tried to summon anger or resentment, but it was impossible. He had hurt her, emotionally, verbally, and, finally, physically. He'd deserved nothing less.

Chris leaned close to Carrie, "Perhaps we should leave them to talk. We could walk over to the house; see if it is still there. It isn't more than twenty minutes or so from here." Carrie nodded and they slipped out. Wes and Sarah didn't even seem to notice. They were too busy staring at each other in a way that seemed peaceable enough. A few years ago, Chris wouldn't have thought it possible that Wes would be able to hold it together like that. Now? Chances were pretty good that he would be reconnecting with his long-lost family. His mind reeled at the thought. He missed Mom and Dad. He missed Jess. *Damned if it isn't a small world.* How he wished the impossible could happen for him too.

The bell on the door quietly chimed as the young couple made their exit. Sarah and Wes stood frozen, their memories, their ghosts between them, plenty of questions in their eyes. Sarah broke the silence first,

"Let me get you some coffee."

She slid behind the counter, her mind awhirl with the shock of seeing a man she had loved once upon a time. She poured the coffee with both hands to stop the shaking that had suddenly started up. He had always taken it the same way, black, one spoon of sugar. But this was chicory, not the real stuff, and she suddenly panicked; what if he didn't like it? She looked up, startled, as he closed a hand over hers. He'd moved with cat-like stealth, silently slipping behind the bar. She looked up, her heart thumping hard, wordless.

"I take two spoons now; the chicory is so doggoned bitter." He smiled. "Sometimes I even add a splash of milk as well." He paused, his expression turning sober, "I'm glad you are alive, Sarah. You and the kids. The world seemed a darker place without you in it." His hand still covered hers; it felt calloused, strong. "Can we sit a bit? And talk? I'd like to hear about Cody and Laura…and you."

Sarah nodded, her eyes filling. The man she had married, full of hope and youth and love, was standing before her. He was different, but so was she —older, wiser perhaps. She didn't see the Wes she had run from. Instead Sarah saw the Wes who had loved her.

She squeezed his hand, walked to the front of the café. She closed the curtains, turned the "Open" sign over to "Closed" and locked the door. The townspeople could go elsewhere for their lunch today; it was time she and Wes had a talk.

"Come on," she said, "let me introduce you to your grandson."

CHAPTER TWENTY-SEVEN

A GHOST RETURNS

"How do I even describe today? There was so much joy, such indescribable joy. Shock too, for both of us. I had given up hope and so had he. Standing there, face to face, was like a page out of one of my dreams. How often had those dreams haunted my nights? I hated waking up and realizing I had only dreamed it. I think tomorrow I will pinch myself, and check here in this journal, before I believe that it is really real." – Jess's Journal

Chris and Carrie walked down to the end of Main Street and turned right, heading first north and crossing over Highway 58. It wasn't much of a highway, just a two-lane road running from east to west.

"Do you think Wes and…what was her name…Sarah?…will be all right?" Carrie asked.

The look on the older man's face was one that neither of them had ever seen. It might have been twenty years or more, but the woman had run off with his kids, and no matter what had prompted her to do it, would Wes be able to forgive her for it?

"Yeah," Chris said, and he squinted in the bright sunlight; it was a hot day, "I think they'll be okay."

He stared at the remains of what had been the new Price Chopper, which had opened just a handful of years before the Collapse. The walls had collapsed in, the insides blackened with fire. He wondered when it happened. It had been cleaned out early on, after the trucks stopped showing up with food and goods. One of the first signs of the Collapse had been the breakdown in the chain of deliveries. Slowly stores found themselves out of one item, then another, until finally a cascade of outages, combined with ever-increasing blackouts and a panicked rush on the foodstuffs that remained, had caused the store to close. Chris could still see a portion of one of the handwritten signs that had been placed in the glass windows. It should have read, "store closed until further notice," but all that remained was "store clo" and the rest of the sign was long gone, as was the glass window it had hung on inside.

Now they were passing the road to nowhere—an

access road that had been planned, along with several miles of walking trails, and never finished, yet another victim of the financial troubles years before the actual Collapse. The pavement was now cracked and warped. Several trees had pushed through the tarmac and were flourishing, undeterred by their asphalt surroundings. The road was clear, and there was little traffic, either on foot or by auto. It was obvious that the town's population had been severely decimated. Prior to the collapse, there had been more than 20,000 residents in Warsend. From the looks of it, there was perhaps ten percent of that number now.

The day before, they had made their way slowly through parts of Kansas City. The highways were in tatters, all overpasses had long been destroyed, and huge swaths of the city appeared to be nothing but blackened ruins. Wes had spoken with a few others shortly outside of St. Louis and learned that Kansas City had endured several large fires over the course of a decade of hot and dry summers.

It had destroyed most of the inner city, sparing only a few homes in the historic Northeast district, and leaving the West Bottoms full of blackened and crumbling brick buildings. Most of downtown had been lost, as well as nearly all of the poorer neighborhoods where the old houses were filled with dry, brittle wood just waiting for an excuse to go up in flames.

The city had suffered greatly in the aftermath of

the Collapse. The loss of many of its inhabitants from the inner core had occurred years before the Collapse, but it was hit hard when the country descended into anarchy and war. In wide swaths throughout the state, homes were left abandoned, crime rose, and those who could, fled to the suburbs and surrounding countryside. This had all occurred years before the Collapse, but it had set the tone for what came next.

Despite the efforts of many to re-populate the city at the turn of the century and try to save some of the historic, yet crumbling, buildings, when the Collapse finally came, it hit hard and fast. The loss of utilities—clean water, dependable electricity, and finally gas main breaks—was only the beginning of Kansas City's woes. Quickly, food shortages and water-borne illnesses due to the lack of utilities began to take a horrific toll on the inhabitants who were left. The hospitals collapsed next, due to the shortage in supplies and loss of infrastructure—it was a scene that played out in city after city; one that resulted in mayhem, death, and the panicked flight of the remaining population.

Kansas City had become a ghost town filled with collapsed buildings and a general sense of empty decay. There were a few pockets of civilization— certain areas that had held out and refused to fall into ruin. Here and there, scattered through the city, people bustled about, tending large gardens in empty lots, repairing what they could of the damaged buildings closest to them, and working toward opening trade routes.

Warsend was a world of difference from the chaos and destruction they had seen when passing through the city. Chris had winced as he pointed out much of the cultural center of Kansas City, which was now abandoned, looted and destroyed; even the grand stone edifice of the Nelson-Atkins Art Museum had reflected the devastation of the Collapse and the warring troops that had fought for control of the ruins of the former United States. It had been heavily damaged during mortar fire and most of the roof in the older section had collapsed.

The highway overpass that bisected the town of Warsend into its east and west sides had been obliterated. The on and off ramps still remained, but they were closed into narrow sections, of which a normal car barely fit through, intentionally. Military vehicles, large trucks, especially a tank or Humvee, would not be able to pass through the choked-off passage ten feet high on each side of twisted rock and metal rebar. The van and truck waited for them near Main Street, but it felt good to stretch their legs, and gas was too difficult to find to waste on a little side trip.

As they walked, slowly approaching a large network of fences and walls with the obvious smell of cattle emanating from them, Chris was experiencing what could only be described as double vision. The memory of what had been a United

Rentals and Casey's gas station next to it was clear in his memory. How often had he taken a run with his dad to rent an auger or chipper? How often had he and Jess begged for a treat when stopping at the Casey's for gas? It was, however, overlaid by what now existed—blackened ruins with amorphous lumps within. His memories of his hometown were sharp; it felt as if the past twelve years had passed in a quick snap of the fingers, and Chris felt as if he was waking from a dream. He wondered why he had never come back, never tried, not once, to find out what had become of the home and the family he had lost.

In the distance, coming toward them, was a man on a horse. He wore a bandana, most likely to soak up the sweat from the heat of the sun pounding down on him. Chris stared at him, thinking he looked vaguely familiar and the man stared back, a look of shock on his face.

"Chris Aaronson?" the man asked, a tone of wonder in his voice. His hair was red, and Chris couldn't place him, but he appeared close to the same age, late 20s, early 30s at the most. He certainly knew Chris, which made Chris uneasy and embarrassed he couldn't place him.

"Yeah, I'm Chris, and I'm sorry, it's been a long journey…you are…?" he stared at the man as he dismounted.

"Todd Stevens. I was a couple of years ahead of you in school and at Scouts." The man grinned, and shook his head, "I just can't believe it's you! Where in the hell have you been, Aaronson?"

Chris's memories of a red-headed lanky teen a couple of years older than him came flooding back. They had bunked in the same tent one year when the Scouts went on their annual campout. Todd had been a cool guy, and he hadn't been a jerk to Chris and Allen; he'd shared his homemade beef jerky and shown them some tips during archery lessons.

"Man, Todd, I remember you now." He reached out and shook Todd's hand and turned to Carrie, who had been quietly watching the exchange, "This is my wife, Carrie. I've been in Tennessee for nearly twelve years now, in a small town by the name of Tiptonville. We're moving on, going on to Denver, but I had to stop and see the town before I went. See if the house is still standing." He shrugged. "Pay my respects to anyone from before…you know."

Todd had a strange look on his face. "Well, your house is still there, Chris. Still there." He looked as if he wanted to say more, but thought better of it. "Let me walk you over there." He waved at one of the other sentries, which Chris had noticed were posted every few hundred yards, watchful, with horses saddled and ready to go nearby. "Most won't remember you, and we don't allow visitors through the gate without an escort." He shrugged, "The Reformation may be in full swing on the coasts, but I guess we have got a ways to go before it stops being the Wild West 'round here." He nodded to

Carrie, "Nice to meet you, Carrie."

They walked for another block, passing a sentry along the way. It appeared that everyone was heavily armed and quite watchful. "Have trouble with raiders?" Chris asked.

"Yeah, now and then. It just makes sense to be more watchful. Word gets back to 'em, and they stop trying. Leastways, the attacks have petered off to nothing, down from a swarm of them last year. We lost two men and 20 head of cattle, including two beautiful heifers we were hoping to breed."

They passed through a set of heavy metal cattle doors. Half of the block had burned, but the houses here had been torn down, hauled away, and the empty lots filled with gardens. Every possible space was being utilized. They were quickly approaching Chris's old street.

As the small group turned onto the street, Chris's pulse quickened. He could see his childhood home, just barely; it was hiding now behind tall trees and massive blackberry bushes. Most of the houses were gone on this street, but there were fruiting bushes, fruit trees, and rows of in-ground plants in various stages of growth. From the looks of it, the land was intensively planted, every bit of it utilized to grow something. It was a riot of green growth.

Chris stopped in the middle of the road as a boy, aged eleven or twelve, popped out of a long line of corn, chasing a dark-haired girl, pelting her with what looked like overripe grape-sized tomatoes as she screamed and laughed. One hit her square in the back as she skidded to a stop in front of the group. The boy, also dark-haired, was so intent on chasing her that he nearly ran into the back of her, crashing to the ground to avoid knocking her over. Both kids stared at Chris and Carrie curiously.

Todd Stevens laughed, "You kids are sure working hard, I see." He reached a hand down, helping the boy up. Chris thought the boy looked eerily familiar. But he couldn't possibly know this boy; he would have been an infant, at most, on the day Warsend was invaded. Todd asked, "Where's your mom? Tell her I've got someone she would like to meet."

Chris stared as the boy, who looked so strangely familiar, as did the girl, they were obviously siblings, gave Chris a short, appraising stare with his crayon-blue eyes and ran off calling to his mother.

"Mom! Hey Mom! We got visitors." He disappeared around a row of trees, and several hens squawked in alarm at his passing.

"Someone's living here, then," he said, a statement and a question rolled into one.

Todd nodded, a peculiar smile forming on his face—as if there was a joke that Chris should be clued in on. Chris's heart panged a little at the thought. The memories, some of the best memories of his life, were of that house. It felt both good and painful to think that someone was living here. The house looked relatively well cared for, and the garden would have made his mother proud. How she had loved her garden and teaching her neighbors how to grow luscious fruits and vegetables out of soil once reserved for immaculate lawns and ornamental flowers.

A young man with unruly dark brown hair and patched jeans came around the corner with a wheelbarrow. He was in his early 20s, and his arms and chest were tanned dark from the sun.

"Hey, Todd, what do you know?" He asked with a friendly smile on his face, a look of curiosity at the strange man and woman in front of him.

"Hey, David, I have some folks here you'll want to meet," Todd said, nodding to Chris and Carrie. "This here is Carrie, and this is Chris…Aaronson."

David's face changed from a look of welcome to one of shock. He had been in the act of shaking hands with Carrie and froze at the mention of Chris's last name. "Aaronson?" He glanced at Todd, "Does she know?"

Chris wondered who "she" was. He began to page through his memories. Had there been a girl or woman here who knew him? For a brief moment his hope surged at the thought that possibly his mother was still alive. As quickly as the hope came, it died. Allen had been sure. Chris had wrested the memories from his friend, insisting he know in every detail. They had both died, his mom and his dad, and the children who had fallen behind and slowed them down had died with them. Allen had been certain and God knows Chris had tried to convince himself that it wasn't true, but reality was harshly indifferent to hope.

And Jess; those scumbags had told them all about how she had died, her and Erin. The dull ache of her memory thumped in his chest. Losing Jess, knowing she was gone and he had failed to protect her, that was the worst part of it. And it is what had set his feet walking far, far away from the only home he had ever known.

There was a woman approaching now. Lean, slender build, golden hair tumbling in curls over her shoulders and down her back. She was preceded by the dark-haired boy, and followed by a girl with red hair who was perhaps six, maybe older. The young woman drew near and Chris's heart stuttered to a stop. She was equally as shocked, stopping in mid-stride with a gasp, her mouth a perfectly round 'o' of disbelief.

"Oh my God…*Chris?*"

Chris blinked in shock and finally found his voice, "Jess?"

CHAPTER TWENTY-EIGHT

I'M WHAT?!

"What you need to know about the past is that no matter what has happened, it has all worked together to bring you to this very moment. And this is the moment you can choose to make everything new. Right now." – Author Unknown

There would be little sleep in the long evening that followed the reunion. There was far too much to catch up on. Far too much to share and learn about each other.

Tears, anger, sadness—and the stories. They tripped over each other's words, eager to describe the lives they had lived since that fateful stormy night so long ago. Jess mourned once again her friend Erin as she recounted the few months of freedom they both had before losing her so tragically in that abandoned farmhouse outside of Clinton.

The others, Becka, Erin, and David, along with Carrie and Todd, circled about in the background as Jess and Chris laughed, cried, and hugged and described the past dozen years. It would be hours later that a meal was set before them, eaten and barely tasted, as Chris described old Fenton and his cleaning the shotgun, or Jess spoke of Serena and adopting Becka as her own.

She did not elaborate more on Jacob's beginnings, other than to describe his birth in the ruins of Clinton, tousling his hair, and pleading silently with her eyes for Chris to not ask more details. The boy stared at Chris silently, his face and hair so reminiscent of the nightmare they both had endured. It wasn't anything the boy said or did; just the way that he looked so exactly, *exactly* like that monster…except for Jess's crayon-blue eyes.

Chris swallowed the revulsion he felt with difficulty, tried to remind himself that where the boy had come from was not who the boy was.

We are defined by the responses we make to the circumstances that surround us, not the circumstances themselves.

Although his mind reasoned this, his stomach churned at the thought of what his sister had gone through, all alone.

In the days that followed, the plan to move on to

Denver was delayed indefinitely. It was high summer and there was plenty of farm work to be done. Chris stepped up when Jess came down with a strange, intermittent flu. It would hit her especially hard in the morning, so Chris took over milking the goats, two of which were vicious beasts well known to bite when one least expected it. Carrie found herself painting murals in the old downtown where they now had a small school set up, and lunching with Sarah regularly at the café.

Chris had made a special visit on his own to visit with old Mr. Banks. He had explained what he knew of Allen's death, filling in the details that no one else had known. The old man's grandson had died a hero, protecting the information of which direction the girls had fled that stormy night a dozen years past. His silence had cost him his life and given Jess and her friend Erin the small window of time they desperately needed to escape.

The old man had listened, nodding as Chris told him what he knew, a small tear trickling down his weathered cheek. A week later he had turned over the farm to David and Jess and headed into town to register as a challenger to Mayor Farley in the upcoming election. It was an odd move for the old man, who had been happy to keep to his homestead on the outskirts of the town for years.

And so it was several weeks after arriving in Warsend that Carrie suddenly found herself between painting jobs. She walked over to the house, looking for Chris, and found Jess instead, looking miserable and ill. "I just don't understand it, this horrible flu," Jess said, her face pale with dark circles under her eyes. "Just when I think I'm over it, it comes back."

The two women were less than a year apart in age and Jess had been disappointed when she came down with the flu and wasn't able to spend more time with her new sister-in-law. She wanted to ask Carrie so many things, personal things. She suspected that her brother's wife couldn't have children. At first she had just assumed it was by choice. Then she had seen Carrie interact with little Erin, joke and laugh with Becka and Jacob, and kindly volunteer to paint a mural for the new school, which had been re-established just two years ago in the remains of an old hardware store on Main Street.

The school was only open in late fall through early spring half days, allowing for children who lived in the surrounding countryside to attend around their family's farming schedules. The school had dismissed for the summer before Chris and Carrie had arrived but the building was now being retrofitted with a small kitchen and other improvements. The mural that Carrie had painted was the crowning jewel to that.

Carrie leaned close to Jess and gave her a hug. She missed Liza and Carl and the kids. She hadn't realized how badly she missed them until she stopped long enough from painting to interact with her sister-in-law. What a miracle it was for Chris to find Jess alive here. And after so many years! She smiled at Jess, who looked beautiful even when she was sick. And then as a click of recognition slammed into her brain, she gasped and covered her mouth.

"What is it?" Jess looked confused.

"How long have you been sick with the flu, Jess?"

"I don't know." Jess shrugged, "Maybe a week or two?" As she said it out loud, a conversation from the past exploded into memory…

"How long have you been sick, Jess?" Erin's voice was clear of any sleepiness now, and she sounded frightened.

"About…ohhh!" Jess listed back toward the stream and heaved again, "Oh man, this sucks! Um…going on," she bent and retched, "about three weeks now. Ohhh!!! Why?"

"When was your last period?" Erin persisted.

Jess looked at her oddly, "I dunno, a month, maybe two."

"When exactly?"

"How the hell should I know?"

"Well, do you think it's possible that…"

Jess stared at Carrie with wide eyes, "Oh my God. Oh, oh, oh my God, I," And without saying another word she turned and retched into a nearby trash can.

Carrie had smiled and brewed some raspberry tea for Jess, searched out some dry, stale biscuits from a couple of days ago, and hugged her sister-in-law and congratulated her. Then she had locked her own pain down and given Jess some space to herself to think about the life growing inside her and form the

Page | 331

words that she would say to David and the rest of the family. It was mid-afternoon by the time she made her escape, and Carrie aimlessly walked back into town and into Sarah's café.

Sarah had been well occupied with Wes and her children and grandchildren during the past few weeks. Carrie had sensed a very kind soul in her, but had not had a chance to speak with her much. The lunch rush was long gone, and the café didn't serve dinner. Sarah had almost finished cleaning up, and Wes had gone with Chris and David on a trip into the city to trade for supplies. When Carrie appeared at the door, Sarah opened it and insisted she come in.

A few pleasantries aside, Sarah stared at Carrie sharply and said, "You have something weighing on you terribly, girl, what is it?"

That simple question had broken the dam. Carrie burst into tears. It took several long minutes before she was able to explain. She spilled about Jess being pregnant and sobbed again as she described the miscarriages and stillbirths. "We have lost so many babies, Sarah. It has been so hard, so painful. I guess…" She stopped and brushed her tears away, "I just…so many times over the years I have wondered why Chris even stuck with me."

The older woman nodded, placing a warm hand on Carrie's. "I see how much he loves you."

"He'd have to…every time, every time…I get so sad, so *angry*…" she shook her head, "I push him away."

Sarah laughed softly, "Oh Carrie, that man loves you far too much to be deterred by a little push away now and then. I'd imagine that it might actually prove an irresistible challenge." She squeezed the younger woman's hand. She stroked Carrie's hair, "It's okay to cry, to be sad, and to want what you want."

The older woman was so kind, and for the first time in what seemed like forever, Carrie simply gave in to the years of disappointment and loss and sobbed in Sarah's arms. She cried until she couldn't cry anymore. Sarah just held her, stroked her hair, and rocked her.

Carrie couldn't help thinking of her mother, and the hole her absence had created in their lives, even more so than their father's. She had been the eldest, and she had had to be strong for Liza and for their baby brother for all of those years. Learning to hide her pain from her parents' loss had provided an easy segue into hiding her pain during the stillbirths and miscarriages. After Carrie had cried herself out, Sarah had given her a cup of tea and led her to the back rooms to a comfortable couch to lie down on.

Sarah hugged her again. "There now, you are safe here. Get some rest, my dear; you have just let out a flood of sadness. And there's nothing like a little nap to set you right after that."

She closed the door quietly, leaving the younger woman in the room alone. Carrie had tried to fight it at first, telling herself she should return to the house and help get dinner started, or work out in the yard. But every part of her felt hulled out by the storm of emotions. Her eyelids slowly became heavier. She closed them, thought of the look of terror and joy on Jess's face, and smiled sadly at the thought of her husband's sister in love and expecting a child. The world spun around these children, born into a different time than she or her parents had been born. It spun around and around, babies were born, people died, and still the world kept spinning. She slipped into a deep sleep on the soft couch, barely aware of the bustle in the kitchen and restaurant outside of the door.

CHAPTER TWENTY-NINE

TRADERS AND RAIDERS

"The first evil choice or act is linked to the second; and each one to the one that follows, both by the tendency of our evil nature and by the power of habit, which holds us as by a destiny." – Tryon Edwards

In the end, the old man hadn't gone peacefully. Cooper found himself fascinated by how some people fought so hard against the inevitable, while others simply faded away. Sulwyn had once talked about some Eastern religion where there was an endless cycle of birth, death, and rebirth. The object of the game, from how Sulwyn explained it, was to get off that cycle of rebirth, somehow ascend to a higher plane of existence. He had said, "Some people are closer to that higher plane than others, so they don't fear death; they welcome it as the next step."

At the last house, the bright yellow farmhouse that sat outside of the tall fence surrounding the town's cattle herd, the mother had gone quickly. In truth, after he had killed the woman's husband, she had frozen, unable to cope. The girl had struggled. But she was young, sixteen or seventeen at the most. No matter what horrors life had dealt, she desperately wanted to live. At the end of three days there at the house, the most he dared to stay, he had moved on to the old man's house, leaving the flies and blood behind for others to find.

Cooper hadn't known any of the people he had killed to *welcome* their imminent death, but there were some who seemed to go with only a small show of resistance, while others fought tooth and nail to the bitter end. The old man had been one of the latter. Every breath he had taken was impossible, a fight against all odds, as the blood pooled around him and his breaths became shallow and far apart, ending in hitched gasps. He had stared at Cooper as if he knew him but said little. "You … it's *you*." Cooper was pretty sure he had never met the old man before, but who knew, maybe he had.

Thurman Banks had taken a long time to die. Cooper had watched it with the clinical detachment that comes from not just seeing death, but dealing it out with regularity and precision.

He had waited until the last rattling breath had come and the light had died from the old man's eyes before exiting the bedroom and shutting the door behind him. He figured that he had a day, maybe two, before the summer heat would betray what had happened here. Meanwhile, he would have a nice nap on the living room sofa and see what there was to eat.

He had tricked his way into the farmhouse, and now this old man's house, by pretending to be a trader. In reality, the items he had for sale were nothing more than the loot gathered from his previous stopovers—a trail of bodies and trauma that extended through three states now.

A few blocks away, Jess had gone to the west garden to pull weeds and collect some tomatoes that were heavy and ready for picking. She had asked Carrie not to say anything about the pregnancy. She was still struggling with the reality of it and the complicated memories her condition brought up.

There was a tiny pooch to her otherwise flat stomach, and she felt exhausted by midday, but other than that, there was nothing to indicate a child growing inside of her. Despite this, Jess knew it had to be real.

Once her shock had receded, she had found herself excited at the prospect. But there was a deep sadness, as well as guilt, as she recalled her first pregnancy. Although she reminded herself time and again that the circumstances had been drastically different, a part of her felt great guilt at not having wanted Jacob from the beginning. Those months, filled with fear and running and escape with her friend Erin, had left a mark deep within her. She had hated the child growing inside her, actively hoped it would die, and been horrified as it had grown and thrived, taking over her body, before finally finding herself in the throes of labor and delivery.

If that soldier had not thrown open the door right then, his presence reminding all of them of how close death was and how important being alive could be, would she have ever loved him? She loved Jacob now—deeply, irredeemably—even as she watched her brother's face as he struggled with the reality of his nephew's grim origins.

So, in addition to feeling happiness and excitement over this new life growing inside her, Jess also felt guilt and shame at not feeling this way about Jacob, so she said nothing, hoping she could reconcile these different feelings, and also wait until she was a little further along and sure before sharing it with everyone else.

A car horn sounded from the street outside the front of the house. The Jeep was obscured behind the rows of corn, now over five feet tall, and the fruit trees. The family emptied out of the house and grounds, converging on the front road. It was Todd Stevens and his face was pinched with exhaustion, his mouth set.

"Hey there, Jess." He nodded to Chris and David and the rest who had come from their work in the garden and inside of the house. "We have a problem."

Todd's presence at the house, along with a serious look and the word "problem" raised all of the adults' hackles. Todd had been re-established as the head of the town militia after the mayor's son had made a royal mess of it, too busy riding on his wave of new power to follow the tried and true strategies of protecting the town from raids.

Entire families had died, but the raiders had been run off over the past year, thanks to Todd's leadership. Once again, all able-bodied adults in town were required to do their part and serve on a rotating schedule for the militia. The raids had fallen off dramatically, and there hadn't been a problem in months. That, however, appeared to have changed.

"It looks like the Franklin place was raided a week ago," Todd said, looking grim. The Franklin home was north off of Kentucky, outside of the outer fence. They kept pigs and chickens on their ten-acre plot and came into town every couple of weeks to trade. "They were due in last week, and when they didn't show and Sarah let us know they were overdue for a delivery of chickens she had ordered we went up there."

Jess felt her heart thump in her chest. "Raiders?"

Todd looked over at the kids clustered around, "Yeah. Looks like they stayed a day or two." The

Franklins had two kids, both in their late teens, the daughter Mary had helped out a handful of times caring for Jacob and Becka when they were smaller. A sick dread spread through Jess's stomach.

Todd met her eyes, "They're all gone." He said it with finality, his even tone did not betray the turmoil he had felt when faced with the reality of what he had seen. He beckoned to Chris and David, "I'll need you two to help me search. We think they are still out there."

Both men were already carrying a small sidearm at their waists. Chris nodded and opened the back door, but David hesitated, staring at Jess. He didn't want to leave her, not if there was danger in the area. She caught the look, and gave him one of her own that clearly said she could take care of herself. Her hand strayed to Lady, a tiny revolver that hadn't left her side in years, not since Old Coop had given it to her as a gift all those years ago.

Thinking about him now, she wondered if the old man was still there, raising his hunting dogs and setting traps. He had been a good man, and she could still remember the last thing he had said to her, his hand on her rounded belly.

"I can't blame you girl if y'think you hate this creature inside you, but it's a blessin' and someday you'll see it that way."

Old Coop had been right; Jacob was one of the best parts of her life, and she wished she could tell the old man that.

"Go," she said to David, "I'll be fine and we have Jacob here as well."

David had spent the past few summers teaching Jacob archery, how to handle a small or large firearm, and tracking techniques. Todd Stevens had taught Jacob and others hand-to-hand combat as well once he resumed control of the militia.

David smiled at her, kissed her, and then he jumped into the Jeep as well. "See you soon."

It was nearly dark when they returned, both men grim-faced. Jess had extended the offer of dinner to Todd, but he had politely refused, his eyes haunted, saying only that his wife and kids were waiting.

"Anything?" Jess asked.

"No tracks past the creek." David said, his lips set, "It looks like only one guy, but we aren't 100% sure. Todd thinks he might have headed north, but I'm not convinced. I think we need to keep a sharp eye out, keep everyone close."

Chris nodded, "Me, too."

Dinner was a muted affair and Chris looked tense and on edge. Danger was lurking, far too close to home for anyone's comfort.

CHAPTER THIRTY

THE TRUTH OF THE MATTER

"Are you willing to believe that love is the strongest thing in the world - stronger than hate, stronger than evil, stronger than death?" – Henry Van Dyke

Chris was angry, uncharacteristically so. Perhaps it was the fear of raiders in the area. The Franklin family, not more than a mile away, all dead —it brought back all too familiar memories. Dead, staring eyes, the violation of the women, and the stench of death. Would he ever escape this endless cycle of death? Would he ever be able to *un*see the terrible sights he had been witness to?

The boy hadn't said or done much of anything,

just made a joke, and Chris had strode off into the house, unable to think, to speak, past the blinding hatred he felt rising up inside of him. What had Jess been thinking? Keeping a reminder like that near her all of these years. Jacob was a carbon copy of the man, except for his crayon-blue eyes, of what had come to be the main character in his worst nightmares. He fought for control. Carrie didn't understand, Jess didn't, none of them did.

God, how many times had he dreamed of Jess, dead by that monster's hand? Finding her alive, realizing that he had his sister back, that she had been here for years, rebuilding her life even as the ghosts from their previous life haunted her. How could she stand to look at that boy? How could she force those words, "I love you," out of her mouth?

He heard a soft tread behind him and Jess's hand reached out and squeezed his shoulder. "He didn't mean to make you angry, Chris. He's just a boy."

"He's rude," Chris ground the words out, "A real smartass."

Even saying the words, he knew they weren't true. He knew his emotions were colored by the past, by what was long gone. He had tried so hard to close off this anger, to recognize that the boy wasn't to blame, but it was all too much. The way the kid's lips had twisted, almost in a snarl, reminded him of blood and death and darkness, months of it, and the years of grief that had followed. How could he look at that boy and see anything else but that?

Page | 344

Jess couldn't understand where all of this anger was coming from. Chris had never been like this; he'd been kind and patient. Why did her brother hold such animosity towards Jacob? Above all she wanted peace. They were all family, all together now, for the first time in years, underneath one roof, an impossible and beautiful thing. Why was he being this way?

"Chris," Jess fought to keep her tone even, "please understand."

"Understand what, sis? That that raping bastard is his father? That damned Lieutenant Scott Cooper destroyed your life? That Jacob was born because an evil man, who raped and murdered countless women, put his seed into you?"

Jess stood in shock, "You…know?"

Chris practically snarled, "How could I *not* know? Looking at him is like seeing that bastard's face over and over and over again. It makes me sick, seeing what he did to you, knowing what you went through."

Her tongue felt heavy, unwieldy, and she couldn't form the words to explain that Jacob was nothing like Scott Cooper, that he was good, that she loved him more than she had ever loved anything else, more than life itself.

"Chris, you don't know what it's like. Jacob is my *son*. I love him. He's not like that…that monster. He isn't."

Her brother stared at her, his mouth turned

down at the edges, "For Christ' sake, Jess, how could you stand to keep him? After what happened to you? Knowing who his father was…hell, *still* is for all we know. We never caught him. How can you stand to look at him knowing *what* Jacob is?"

There was a small sound behind them, a soft scuff of shoes on the worn floorboards, and Chris and Jess turned to see Jacob, his eyes round, full of anguish and betrayal.

Jess gasped in horror; the very thing she had dreaded happening had occurred. She had told no one, not even Sarah Turner. David hadn't even known who it was, although he had sussed out the overall idea of it all long ago.

"Jacob! Oh baby, no, no, no! Listen to me, I…"

The boy was already backpedaling out the door.

"You told me my dad had died. You said he…" overwhelmed by the sheer horror of his origins, he turned and fled, quickly disappearing into the dark night.

Jess screamed after him, "Please Jacob, please wait! I can explain!" She turned back to Chris, her face chalk-white, "How could you, Chris? How could you? He's my *son*. It doesn't matter who his father is. It doesn't matter, because he's my son and I *love* him. That's all we have ever needed…love… oh, how could you possibly understand?"

And she ran then, shoving past him, running blindly into the night.

Chris took a step to the doorway to follow her,

to try and help, as Carrie arrived. She had heard everything. She reached out a hand, firmly grasping his arm. Her face was hard, tight with anger.

"Let them go, Chris, you've done enough, don't you think?"

"Carrie, I…I didn't mean for him to hear," he said, taken aback by her fury.

Seeing her face made him realize how his dislike of the boy must look to the others. They couldn't understand, they didn't see him like that, they didn't see Scott Cooper sneering out at him through that face. What Carrie and the others saw was his unreasonable disgust and contempt for his sister's only biological child, a boy who had done nothing to him. Jacob didn't deserve this.

Chris watched her go, a sickness rising up inside him. What had he done?

COLLISION

"Life is a series of collisions with the future; it is not the sum of what we have been, but what we yearn to be." – Jose Ortega y Gasset

Jacob suddenly remembered being five and hiding from his mom.

"Come and find me!" he had called while huddled under the blankets.

He had heard his mother's steps on the floor, she stood for a moment by the bed and then reached out and patted him, her voice had a playful lilt as she said, "Ah, there you are, kiddo!"

"How do you always know where to find me?"

Jacob had demanded.

Jess had smiled and had hugged him and said, "I just do." Her smile faltered for a moment, her eyes far away, caught in a dark memory, "I'll always find you. I'll always come for you. You can depend on that."

How many times through the years had she told him that? Not just when he was playing hide and seek, but when he had gotten separated from her at the town picnic a year later, or when he had wandered off in the woods when they had been hunting for morels? She had always found him. And when she did, she would wrap her arms around him, kiss the top of his head, and say the same thing, "I'll always find you, Jacob, how could I not?"

His head was aching painfully. The man had hit him hard on the head, stunning him, and then dragged him inside of the dark house. Jacob felt tears coursing down his cheeks.

He closed his eyes, repeating silently, over and over, *"Please come find me, Mom. Please."*

His father was a rapist. A murderer. Someone his Uncle Chris obviously hated and probably his mom too. He had run away into the night, his eyes burning and his stomach heaving. He had run, without direction, without purpose, everything he had understood about his life turned upside down, even as he heard his mom's voice in the distance calling his name. He ran, fast, and before too long her calls faded into the distance. How could she have lied to him like that?

Jacob felt as if something dark and unclean had occupied his body. He had asked a handful of times about his dad. Mom had always looked so sad, so haunted, that he had backed off and accepted the short, unsatisfactory answers she had given.

"Your father, he, lots of people died, Jacob. Lots of people died."

He had figured that she must have loved his father a lot, and that it hurt to talk about him, so he had stopped. But now, to realize that his father probably hadn't died, wasn't someone his mom had loved, and worse, was a rapist, seemed overwhelming. His footsteps slowed, his heart pounding in his chest, and he looked around for the first time.

The moon was out, and its bright sliver of light added enough illumination for him to see where he was. Over the rise, the herd of cattle gave off little noise, their nightly routine barely affected by the boy so nearby. To his right, Jacob saw Mr. Banks's house. A dim light glowed from one window. And Jacob, not knowing who to turn to, approached the house to see if old Mr. Banks was still awake. The old man was like a grandfather to him. Since Chris and Carrie had come, the normal routine of having him for dinner each Sunday had fallen by the wayside.

And if there was anything that could be done about the strange and disturbing situation at hand,

Mr. Banks would be the person to know what to do. Jacob crossed the yard, realizing for the first time that he had run off without shoes as his feet encountered a mostly dry cow pie.

When he knocked on front door, there was no response. It wasn't that late, but Jacob wondered if the old man was all right. He hadn't been feeling well last month…and Mr. Banks was getting up there in years; what if he had slipped and fallen and was lying on the floor of his bathroom? What if he had suffered a heart attack?

These questions and concerns emboldened Jacob to try the front door. It was locked.

He knocked, called out to the old man, "Mr. Banks? It's Jacob…I…uh…Mr. Banks, are you all right? Can I come in?"

Jacob missed Mr. Banks. He wasn't much of a talker, and he would retreat into silence when there were more than a handful of people in the room. Like most of the residents of Warsend, he had seen great loss.

In the outbreak of war, he had lost his wife, along with his only son and grandson. His grandson Allen had died before Jacob was born, but since Chris had returned he had heard more details about him, and his death.

Jacob stopped in his tracks. Chris had said that Lieutenant Cooper had killed Allen. And just a few minutes ago he had said his name again.

"That damned Lieutenant Scott Cooper destroyed your

life! Jacob was born because an evil man, who raped and murdered countless women, put his seed into you…looking at him is like seeing that bastard's face over and over again."

He could hear those words repeating in his head.

Cooper was his father. And he had murdered Mr. Banks's grandson Allen. Perhaps, upon hearing the news, Mr. Banks wouldn't want anything to do with him. Jacob faltered, uncertain, fearful. He was about to turn away when he heard a creak on the floorboards inside. Jacob turned back toward the door in time to see it quickly open and a man who was definitely *not* Mr. Banks step into the doorway. Everything moved too suddenly. Jacob was still trying to puzzle out who this man was when the man's right hand lashed out and clocked him hard on the side of the head. Jacob slumped to the ground.

Scott Cooper stared at the unconscious boy at his feet and contemplated whether or not he should kill him now. The boy was dark-haired, thin but wiry, and looked to be around twelve or thirteen. He wouldn't pose a problem to Cooper, and he might actually come in handy.

He looked out into the night filled with dim moonlight. No one else in sight. The kid might have some information. He might know if that family out on Kentucky Road had been found yet. He probably also knew about militia watch schedules. He was old enough to participate, by the looks of him. And it was time that Cooper was moving on.

Cooper reached down and grabbed the boy's arms and dragged him inside.

THE RECKONING

"Life moves on, whether we act as cowards or heroes. Life has no other discipline to impose, if we would but realize it, than to accept life unquestioningly. Everything we shut our eyes to, everything we run away from, everything we deny, denigrate or despise, serves to defeat us in the end. What seems nasty, painful, evil, can become a source of beauty, joy, and strength, if faced with an open mind. Every moment is a golden one for him who has the vision to recognize it as such."
– Henry Miller

The roads were empty and Jess couldn't hear anything but the distant lowing of the town's cattle. They had been moved to one of the eastern paddocks the day before. Jacob could be anywhere. The night sky was free of clouds, allowing the sliver of moon to light it well. Well enough that Jess didn't need a lantern to see, although she occasionally stumbled on debris.

Her heart ached in her chest at the memory of her son's face. He had looked so bereft, so betrayed and horrified. She had never wanted that for him, never wanted him to know the darkness that had helped make him. She had tried so hard to forget.

Jess's hand strayed to her stomach, to the small bump of the unborn child was already pushing its way out, making itself known. She hadn't told David yet. In fact, no one knew except for her and Carrie, and she knew her sister-in-law was waiting for her to say something, for her and David to announce the news.

Jess couldn't help but make comparisons. Her first pregnancy had been filled with such horror, such disgust; she winced at the memory of wanting her unborn child dead. The condition had been forced on her, and she had hated every moment of it, as her body was taken over by another's, distended, changed, slowed down, and exhausted. She had been frightened, terrified the soldiers would find her again and kill her or, worse, take her back there.

This pregnancy was different, and how often had she reminded herself of that? And yet, the memories she had of being pregnant with Jacob gnawed at her

—filling her with guilt and sadness. She felt she was somehow betraying him if she allowed herself to be happy with this child, one created in love and passion instead of fear and pain.

She was startled out of her thoughts by the sound of footsteps behind her. She whirled around, "Jacob?"

The gloom resolved into a taller shape, "No, it's me." It was David, he reached out and hugged her to him. "I'm so sorry he had to find out like this." Jess let him hold her for a moment, took a small measure of comfort from his embrace.

"You knew?"

"I didn't know his name. But I knew something terrible had happened to you. That was obvious." He kissed the top of her head, "You are one of the bravest people I know. Jacob is lucky to have you and he is a great kid. Chris just needs time to see that."

"I don't really want to talk about Chris right now." She could feel the anger building inside her. How could he judge her? How could he judge Jacob? He hadn't been there when Jacob was born, when her friend Erin had died, or Madge, or…she knew that David was right, that Chris needed time, but her son had deserved better than to find out like this.

"I know you don't. Carrie made sure he stayed there at the house and didn't come after you." He hugged her, "Come on, let's find our son."

"*Our* son?"

David put his face close to hers, "Yeah…*our* son."

David could just barely make out her smile in the dim light of the moon.

"Okay. Jacob first and then, then I need to tell you something." She looked around at the empty street. To the east were a couple of homes and families to the west was Mr. Banks's property—Jacob could be at either, and she wasn't sure who to target first.

"What do you want to tell me?" His arms were still around her and he leaned in to kiss her neck.

"*After*," Jess insisted, wiggling away, "you take the Stevens's and Devonly's houses to the east. I'll check in on Mr. Banks."

"Okay," Dave said, and released her, his hand lingering on her arm, "I'll meet you back at the house in half an hour. Just in case he heads back in that direction."

He turned away and walked toward the two nearest occupied homes. Jess watched him go for a moment before turning and heading toward Mr. Banks's small home two streets over. She nearly fell twice, thanks to the cracked concrete and various sticks and rubbish strewn over the roadway after the creek flooded last month during a heavy rain.

It wasn't long before she was knocking on the door of the darkened house. It was probably past ten at night by now. And Jess felt rude for knocking on the door and possibly waking the old man. Mr.

Banks had been feeling under the weather, a late summer cold, and she had been so busy with having Chris back in her life that his inclusion in their day-to-day lives had fallen off dramatically in the past few weeks.

There was a muted sound coming from inside. Jess stopped knocking and leaned close to the door, trying to tell if the old man was coming toward the door.

"Mr. Banks?" she called softly, "It's Jess. I'm sorry to bother you, but has Jacob come by here tonight?"

There was no answer, but there was another sound coming from within the house, a thumping of some kind, a muffled yell.

Jess felt a small panic. Had the old man fallen? Was he hurt and unable to come to the door on his own? She tried the doorknob and knocked louder, calling to him, "Mr. Banks? Are you okay?"

More thumps came from inside and she turned the doorknob in her hand. It was unlocked. She gave the door a shove, and half fell through it when it opened suddenly. The living room was dark. Mr. Banks had to be in his bedroom or the bathroom, and probably hurt if he wasn't answering. She stepped inside the house, her eyes struggling to adjust to the gloom. She never noticed the tall man step out from behind the open door and reach out for her until it was too late.

The blow he delivered stunned her. She had had

a nanosecond to react. A soft creak of the floorboard and a rush of air as he closed the distance between them had been her only warning. She spun through the air, fell to the floor, the air whooshing from her lungs with the abrupt contact with the floor and Cooper on top of her in a tangle of limbs.

His breath was rank and she couldn't see much detail. This was *not* Mr. Banks, or Jacob, or any other of the town residents. Her jaw ached and she could taste coppery blood where her teeth and tongue had connected in his initial blow. And now, as they wrestled on the floor, the memories of those first few days in Tent Five came flooding back. Jess felt her breath coming in hitched gasps, terror over just who this man was and what may have happened to Mr. Banks flooding through her, adding to her panicked punches. In the other room she could hear the thumps clearly now, the sounds of someone trying to break free of his bonds. Her attacker's hands closed on her throat, narrowing her world, edging it in blackness. She tried to reach his eyes, to tear them from their sockets. She kicked with her legs, hoping desperately to connect with some part of her attacker that would be made of soft, vulnerable flesh. He blocked every move, pinning her beneath him. The blackness closed in and Jess's arms and legs felt heavy, impossible to move. She tugged at his hands weakly, scraping him with her fingernails before succumbing to the all-encompassing dark.

Consciousness returned slowly. Air moved over her. Jess struggled to remember where she was. A small lantern now lit the room and she pulled at the bindings around her wrists. Some cord tied them tightly together above her head. It was immovable and it cut painfully into the flesh of her wrists.

"I know you." Her attacker's voice sounded mildly amused. She felt his hand on her leg, felt his knife cut through her pants, slicing the fabric from her body. "You are the whore who got away."

Jess felt a scream bubble up in her throat. He had gagged her though, and all that could be heard was a guttural whine as she struggled to free herself.

"I was on top of the world before that," he continued, now running his knife up her other pant leg. Her shirt was already gone and she shivered in fear. "Right after you and those others took off, things really went to shit." He reached out and grabbed her right breast, squeezing it painfully in his hand, "But I'm thinking that you and I are going to have some fun now. I'd take the gag off, but I really can't risk it this close to others. That family on Kentucky sure was a lot of fun. And I must say I even enjoyed slicing on the old man."

He cut the last of her clothing off and settled himself on top of her; Jess felt the tears slide down her face. His voice was soft, almost conversational, and she wanted to scream, to buck him off, to stop him, but all of the horror, the memories of those months of hell, they had made her limbs rigid and unresponsive. In her mind she was screaming.

He sighed in her ear, "I really, really wish I could hear you scream. I think it would make me feel better." His mouth was at her ear and she shuddered in fear, "And the time I would spend with you, let it last for a few days, maybe even a week; it is a shame that I can't. In fact, I'm pretty sure I'm out of time already. But life isn't any fun if you don't take a few risks. Don't you agree?"

The cold blade of his knife slid along her side, before viciously slicing into the muscle of her upper arm, her right arm. Hot agony flooded her and she did scream then, although the gag blocked most of it. She felt him reach down, fumble with the waist of his jeans and her limbs were energized with a new panic. Her mind screamed in terror, the thought of him raping her now, all of these years later, violating her body after she had spent so many years trying to forget, terrified of ever having any man come near her. She thought of the baby inside her. He would kill her, and her child. David's child.

The fear lent her body more energy than she thought possible. She bucked against him, kicking, pulling at the bindings at her wrists with such violence that her skin was torn and began to bleed.

He laughed with delight, "Now that's the whore I remember!" She could feel him becoming even more excited, struggling to push her legs apart, eager to take her violently. His hands once more closed on her throat. She wondered, as her vision began to narrow, if he even particularly cared if she was alive or dead when he got around to raping her.

The thumps from the other room had stopped, and as she struggled against Cooper, as the will to fight slowly left her body, she looked up and saw why. Jacob had managed to break loose. He stood above them both with a baseball bat in hand. She blacked out again as she watched the bat come crashing down on Cooper's head.

"Mom? Mom? Mom!" Jacob's voice sounded very far away. Jess coughed and tried to roll to her side. Her bones felt like mush. Jacob's hands were on her, helping her to turn on her side. She felt his absence keenly for the few seconds it took for him to run to the other room and find a blanket to lay over her.

"Jacob?" her voice sounded as if it were full of gravel. Her throat ached. She coughed again.

"I'm here, Mom. I'm here." His hand draped the blanket over her, covering her exposed skin, his work-chapped hands busy trying to loosen the bindings on her wrists.

"Where is he?" she managed to croak. She struggled to sit up.

"He's here. I think I killed him." Jacob looked over at Cooper's limp figure. "He isn't moving."

"Good." With her son's help she sat up. The boy nestled his head against her and she crumbled, dissolving into tears. "I love you, Jacob. I've always loved you. I'm so sorry I didn't tell you about him sooner. I just didn't know *how* to. I never wanted you to think less of yourself, to think you were anything like him. Because you aren't. You are good, you are kind, you are *my* son. You are nothing like him."

Jacob clutched at her, staring at the prone form of the man on the floor. Jess winced as his hand tightened on the stab wound on her arm.

"Is it *him*, Mom? Is he the one?"

It was hard to force the word out, "Yes."

"He killed Mr. Banks."

Jess felt a stab of deep pain. The old man had been so kind to them. He hadn't deserved that kind of an end. How many times had they sat together? Eaten meals side by side, planted trees, harvested crops, and more. He had been like a grandfather to them. He had held baby Jacob in his arms. After all of these years, he had been family. She had imagined him passing someday, but in a non-specific sentimental sort of way, surrounded by those who cared for him as much as if they shared blood with him. The thought of him dead, at the hands of that monster on the floor, was too terrible to comprehend.

She looked around the dimly lit room. How long had he been here? How long had Mr. Banks been dead or dying in this house and they hadn't even known? She clutched her son to her and felt a deep cold inside and out, despite the lingering summer heat. She reached out with her left hand and took ahold of the knife lying on the ground near Cooper's body. Her right arm was bleeding freely, but she barely noticed.

"We need to get out of here, Jacob."

She levered herself up painfully. Her head was pounding, and the side of her face that Cooper had struck felt like raw meat. One of her teeth felt loose and the coppery taste of blood was still on her tongue.

"We need to make sure he's de…"

Her words fell away as she turned and saw Cooper rise up, blood running in a thick rivulet of gore down the side of his scarred face, and absolute murder in his eyes. He reached for her throat.

CHAPTER THIRTY-THREE

HOPE AND LOSS

"Life is not measured by the number of breaths we take, but by the moments that take our breath away." – Hilary Cooper

David stood at the gravesite clutching Tina's hand. She had returned from Kansas City with Penelope and Kip when she had heard the news. She was fourteen now, and she had grown nearly as tall as her brother. She stood quietly by his side, her long fingers clutching a bouquet of flowers.

The masses of people gathered around the gravesite were a testament to the mark left on so many. In their loss, and everyone had lost so many in the past ten years, the grief had not lessened at the passing of someone so intrinsically a part of the community.

Nearby, another grave had been dug, but no one paid any attention to it or cared. It had already had a body lowered into it, been filled, but there was no marker. It wouldn't take long, perhaps a few years at most, for the wound in the soil to become grass. And then no one, not a single person, would remember that he was buried there. And that was for the best.

On David's left side stood Tina, and on his right was Jess. Her arm was heavily bandaged, and her neck bore livid bruises, the sharp outlines of fingers now smudged in red and purple. Her left eye was black and her cheek still swollen. Despite her appearance, Jess felt stronger than she had ever thought possible.

That night, as Scott Cooper's hands had closed around her throat, she had held his knife tightly in her hands. The nightmares, filled with darkness and fear and hands groping her, touching her body, using her—those nightmares had resolved into one clear and focused thought.

This man before her had to die. Despite his strong grip on her already bruised throat, despite the screams of her son as he struggled to stop the man he shared a genetic heritage with, she had kept that one thought firmly in mind. She hadn't panicked.

The knife had slid in…softer, easier than she had

expected. Scott Cooper had looked…surprised…and rather shocked. She remembered to use a sideways motion, a quick slice to the left, and to the right, severing arteries, intestines, spilling waste inside the abdomen, ensuring a horrible, elongated, and certain death.

As if in slow motion, his hands had fallen away. His body angled backwards…slowly…as if time had reduced itself to a crawl, especially for them, in this moment. She fell with him.

Together, Jess and Cooper connected with the floor, Cooper's knife between them, slamming into the carpet, the knife finding his spine beneath. This close to him, she could feel his heartbeat, strong at first, but slowing as his life drained away. Cooper's face wore surprise, a look of mild alarm, and he stared as Jess slowly pulled away, Jacob frantically searching her for wounds, asking if she was hurt. His voice was muted compared to the dull roaring in her ears.

All she could do was stare into Cooper's eyes— locked in that moment. She would not look away until it was over. There was so much blood. It was black in the weak moonlight, warm and wet, bathing them both in a pool of it.

It wasn't her blood though; at least, not the majority of it. She let Jacob wrap the blanket around her once again, never breaking eye contact with the man on the floor. Jess stared at the monster from her dreams…bleeding out…his body disjointed and slack, a puzzled look on his face. There was a pounding at the door and Jess could hear David, her brother, and others. The door crashed open and people poured inside—militia members, her brother and David, everyone heavily armed.

The moment though, stood suspended. Like a mosquito in amber, a fish frozen in ice. She stared into Cooper's eyes, ignoring the sounds around her, the shouts of the others as they moved into the house and found the old man's body. She ignored David asking her if she was all right.

Nothing else mattered in that moment. Cooper stared back at her, his eyes slowly glazing over. She stood there, unmoving, unresponsive, until she saw the life leave him. *The eyes are the windows to the soul.* She had heard that once. She waited, until the lights turned off for the very last time.

Only then had she allowed David and the others to lead her away.

Now, standing at Thurman Banks's graveside, she felt a strange sort of bittersweet peace. The old man had been Cooper's last victim. And he was mourned. Not just by her little family, but by most of the town. There were people all around her, and their low murmurs saturated the air, reminding Jess that even in death, life goes on. The pastor had given a short speech and now it was her turn, as the town historian. She stepped forward, out of David's protective embrace, unfolded a piece of paper and began to speak.

"I shared many moments with Mr. Banks over the years. The first two years after we returned he made sure we stayed fed, he shared his harvests with us, the meat and eggs from his chickens, and his knowledge. He was the grandfather I never had." She paused, and felt the emotion swell up inside her, "Last year, he asked me if I could write down his story, and I of course told him that I would. And here it is…

Thurman Banks was born on a hot September day in 1946…"

Hours later, after the grave had been filled and the tears had been dried, the dark beauty of the late summer night stole over them. The cicadas hummed noisily, their rhythm rising and falling in a cadence known only to them. The house was full, but everyone inside was preternaturally quiet. Jess felt as if everyone was hovering around her, nervous and watchful. Jacob and David had maintained a regular, almost obsessive presence around her, barely leaving her side at all in the past two days. She could feel them watching her now as she pecked at her food, not really seeing it, the vision of Cooper's death replaying in her mind.

David's hand on hers, "Jess? Are you okay?"

She returned to the kitchen, looked around and saw all those who she loved. David, Jacob, Becka, and Erin, along with Tina, Penelope and her husband Kip, Chris and Carrie. There was concern written on many of their faces, held quietly in their eyes as they stared back at her.

Jess felt her mouth tug and re-shape, lips curving into a huge grin, "Yeah," she said simply, "I'm okay. I really am." She took David's hand in hers, "We are going to have a baby."

The room erupted with surprise and excitement.

Outside, the cicadas sang.

LIFE IS PRECIOUS

"I finally understand it. The meaning of life. Life is love and hate, pain and bliss, gain and loss, life and death. And in between, among the cracks of all that we have endured, life is precious." – Jess's Journal

The room was full. David was on one side of Jess, Carrie and Erin on the other. Tina stood at the foot of the bed with Dr. Farley and was speaking in low tones to the doctor about the healing properties of a certain native plant as they finished putting the room in order.

The baby lay nestled in David's arms, her blue eyes wide open and staring at the world, a look of bewildered amazement on her tiny face. David stared at her intently, surprised when he had discovered his cheeks were wet with tears. He gazed at his newborn daughter, shocked at how tiny she was, and how perfect.

Twin wails began piercing the room as Chris bustled in, a tiny bundle in each arm. As usual, they were wailing in symphony, one after the other. "I held them as long as I could," he said to his wife, "but they definitely want their mama." Carrie's thin face lit up, and the circles beneath her eyes were testament to the lack of sleep she had been receiving as of late.

"I think they just wanted to meet their new baby cousin," Carrie said, as Michael and Julie instantly quieted in her arms.

Her heart surged with happiness. Her pregnancy had coincided with Jess's, but Carrie had been terrified to hope, even once her belly had pushed out to an enormous size and Dr. Farley had told her he thought she might be pregnant with twins. Her labor had been quick, and the babies had been tiny, not quite five pounds each, but perfect. There hadn't been a whisper of complications and both were thriving, despite being born nearly a month early. That had been nearly two weeks ago.

How many times had she despaired of ever having a child? Of being able to hold her own flesh and blood in her arms? And yet, after all of the years of pain and misery, of miscarriage and stillbirth, she held two perfect and beautiful babies in her arms. How she wished Gramps could have seen them.

Joseph, newly arrived from Tennessee, stood uncertainly in the doorway. He had come out with traders and a stack of hand-bound journals to sell, somewhat rudderless since Mr. Liles had passed away last summer. Tall and handsome, he had locked eyes with Tina and suddenly a short visit had turned into a semi-permanent stay. He had stayed in the city, welcomed instantly into the large, brick Victorian that housed Penelope and her husband Kip, along with a small health clinic and dorms for the interns. There they had stayed until two months ago, when Chris had asked for Joseph's help cleaning up Mr. Banks's home.

There were new families moving into the area, but Mr. Banks had willed it to Jess and David, and they had in turn given it to Carrie and Chris. It didn't feel right letting it sit vacant, despite what had happened there, and the homes were close to each other, allowing the siblings, along with their families, to be within walking distance of each other.

Chris and Jacob's relationship had smoothed out in the months following the deaths of Cooper and old Mr. Banks. Seeing how much the boy had tried to protect his mother from the psychopath's attack had brought home to him how different Jacob was from his father, and how much of Jess's goodness he held within him.

Jess smiled at Chris's brother-in-law. "Would you

like to hold her?" she asked.

Joseph nodded, and David handed the newborn gently to the teenager. Joseph was well familiar with babies, from Liza's to the recent birth of Carrie's twins, and now this one.

Her tiny eyes opened briefly and he smiled at the flash of blue, "What is her name?" he asked, staring transfixed at the newest member of his extended family.

"Hope." Jess was surprised as she uttered the name aloud.

She and David had stayed up late so many nights, working through names, trying different combinations. Nothing had seemed to stick and eventually they had agreed that they would just have to wait and see who their baby was—boy or girl.

"We will know when we see the baby," she had told David. "We will just know, I will know, in that moment."

And that moment had arrived.

For all that they had been through. For all that they had endured and lost and for the friends and family gained along the way.

For the nation they had seen crumble and the new world that they had built with their hands, sweat, blood, and tears.

Hope.

The rays of the sun peeked through the window. The warmth crawled along the floor and lit up a newborn baby and the family she belonged with.

It was a brave new world, and a beautiful life had just begun.

AUTHOR NOTE

Thanks for reading!

- Please take a moment and post a review of this book on Amazon and/or (preferably AND) Goodreads. Put simply, reviews indicate that someone has a) read the book and b) thought enough of it (either way) to post a review of it. Your opinion does matter.
- Read for free by signing up for my monthly newsletter here at: http://eepurl.com/bwbQAH (*Note: I will NEVER share this list with any other person or company*). My monthly newsletter provides:
  - A free short story (*exclusive for subscribers*)
  - A summary of all of my blog posts
  - Special book giveaways and 99 cent promotions
  - Updates on upcoming classes and my current writing projects

And, just for you, here is the first chapter of *Gliese 581: The Departure*

GLIESE 581: THE DEPARTURE
CHAPTER ONE

CODE RED

"Always listen to experts. They'll tell you what can't be done and why. Then do it." – Robert Heinlein

Date: 01.27.2104
Calypso Colony Ship

Somehow he had to save them. Daniel's hair was matted on the left side of his forehead, still actively dripping blood from a gash near the top of his head. Each breath was a challenge. It felt as if he were underwater, sharp knives with each gasp in and thick bubbles on the way out. He tried to breathe shallowly; it hurt less when he did that. One of his ribs felt cracked, possibly broken and he tried to think clearly as dizziness and pain fought for his attention. Attention that was desperately needed elsewhere.

"I never should have left them." His fingers moved feverishly over the damaged keyboard and his vision blurred. The blood dripped into his eyes and a fresh wave of dizziness washed over him.

Oxygen levels must be low.

A dull red light flashed through the Cryo Deck, accompanied by the thick, oily smell of melted plastic from the handful of Cryo pods a few rows over. His mind, desperate to compartmentalize, to avoid the full panic he found rising inside, lingered on the memory of Janine's skin beneath his. The memory of Toby's small hand on his cheek, his brother Luke and his easy smile hung there beside him, real enough to touch. The years had passed easier for him – not knowing, barely realizing the truth until it was years gone. Were they all ash and bone now?

Each Cryo pod was equipped with a shrieking alarm. They were designed to emit a series of escalating warning sounds from a simple "Hey, something seems out of place" warning beep to a "The pod is failing and the subject will *die,*" shriek that energized each nerve in a Cryo Tech's body to do something *now.*

But Daniel wasn't a Cryo Tech, Deeks, Daniel's poker buddy and best friend on Calypso was. And

Deeks was dead, along with his assistant, Evers. Their lifeless bodies had been shoved into storage lockers at the far end of the Cryo Deck. And the doors leading to the rest of the ship, where there were others far more capable and knowledgeable than a Comm Tech could ever be were shut, the opening mechanism fried. Daniel was trapped and alone.

He could hear them, working at the doors, doing whatever they could to get through, the banging only adding to the cacophony provided by shrieking alarms.

All of the doors on Calypso were thick, reinforced steel, with rods of titanium woven through for maximum security. Space travel was an uncertain thing, and all areas of the ship had double and triple protections to stop any hull breaches as well as prevent against the unlikely event of a ship-wide contagion. However, the blast doors were something new, yet another layer of protection that ensured that anyone remaining on the Cryo Deck had the best chance of survival.

It was ironic that this added security precaution might be their undoing.

The people in these pods were integral to the mission. Without them, those currently not in Cryo would have a hell of a time and that was just the realistic side of his brain talking. God damn it, *Sam* was in one of these things.

The screen on the console in front of him

scrolled the same message...

**OVERRIDE PASSWORD FAILURE
PERSONNEL RECOGNITION FAILURE
SYSTEM FAILURE - CODE RED
SYSTEM RESET ON ALL CRYO PODS
IN 14:39 MINUTES**

Daniel pounded the keyboard in frustration. The man on the floor to the right of his foot moved slightly and moaned. Like Daniel, he was bleeding heavily from several wounds – one on his head, where Daniel had slammed it against a pillar during the fight. Daniel gave the man a hard kick.

"You sonofabitch! What the hell were you thinking? Why would you do this? WHY?"

Daniel's left arm hung uselessly at his side. His left foot slipped sideways and he realized there was a sizable puddle of blood on the deck, accumulating over the long moment he had fought with the half-melted keyboard. The hole in his shoulder screamed red hot agony at him every time he moved, but the arm itself just hung there, whatever muscles it needed to move rendered useless by the knife still buried in it. It hurt, bad, and Daniel debated pulling it out.

"Not low oxygen levels, no. It's got to be from the blood loss, onset of shock."

He said it, mainly to himself, a part of him distanced from what was happening, the words sounding as if they were issuing from someone else.

"Yeah, blood loss. It affects higher brain function and reasoning skills."

His voice was barely registering over the endless shrieking of the alarms. Had his lips moved? Had he actually spoken out loud? Another wave of dizziness washed over him.

Behind him, the hammering at the doors had taken on a different tone. Sharper, higher grinding sounds, instead of the dull pounding. What was it? Some sort of saw? Daniel felt a flicker of hope. Perhaps they could break through in time, do something he couldn't.

But did he really have time to wait for the others to break through? Should he wait for the captain and the others to get here, so he didn't screw something up further? He wiped the fresh blood from his brow; droplets fell to the view screen below, almost obscuring the countdown. The message continued to scroll...

OVERRIDE PASSWORD FAILURE
PERSONNEL RECOGNITION FAILURE
SYSTEM FAILURE - CODE RED
SYSTEM RESET ON ALL CRYO PODS
IN 14:18 MINUTES

The door behind him looked untouched, despite the application of the saw or whatever they were using on the other side. It could be hours and from the looks of it, none of the people in the Cryo Pods had hours. How the hell had this madman done it? And why?

Daniel struggled to clear his mind, muddled and confused from the fight, filled with memories of the past. He had to stop this countdown before it was too late.

Interested in reading more? You can find this book (and so much more) by visiting my author website: www.christineshuck.com

ACKNOWLEDGMENTS

Dave, for all that you do and all that you are. I look forward to the decades to come.

To Dori, Kate and Rachel—three special teachers who allowed me to fly.

For P.E., you are both the inspiration in all that I do.

To B.B., I still dream of what could have been.

Kerrie, for chocolate chip scones, proofreading, Yapping Mommy playdates, and a long list of other blessings.

For the members of The Mental Militia. You know who you are. Keep building those gulches!

To Victoria and John Friend, and their amazing herbal knowledge. I'll come pick elderberries with you any ole day!

To Roger Renner, for your knowledge of firearms and a host of other survival skills.

To my many friends who read my books and keep me motivated to write more. You know who you are.

And lastly to Briall. What a beautiful future your life could have held. I treasure the memories of the hours we spent together. I miss you, child, and I always will.

About the Author

Christine is an author, occasional artist, unreliable gardener, real estate entrepreneur, mother and foster mom. She lives in an 1899 Victorian in Kansas City, Missouri.

Learn more about Christine's books, her busy life, and much, much more by visiting www.christineshuck.com.

All Published Works

Christine writes cross-genre and her books can be found in e-book and in paperback through most book distributors.

Non-Fiction:
Get Organized, Stay Organized
The War on Drugs: An Old Wives Tale

Fiction Series:
War's End
The Storm
A Brave New World
Tales of the Collapse

Gliese 581g
G581: The Departure
G581: Mars
G581: Earth

Chronicles of Liv Rowan
Fate's Highway a.k.a. Schicksal Turnpike

Benton Security Services
Hired Gun
Smoke and Steel

Children of Ruin
Winter's Child

www.ingramcontent.com/pod-product-compliance
Lightning Source LLC
Chambersburg PA
CBHW070642310726
48982CB00001B/381